EVAN & ELLE IN HEAVEN & HELL

A LONG DISTANCE SOCIAL MEDIA AFTERLIFE LOVE STORY

CHRIS RODELL

COPYRIGHT

EVAN & ELLE IN HEAVEN & HELL
 A Long Distance Social Media Afterlife Love Story

Copyright © 2022 by Chris Rodell

All rights reserved. No part of this book may be used or reproduced by any means, graphic, electronic, or mechanical, including photocopying, recording, taping or by any information storage retrieval system without the written in triplicate permission of Chris Rodell except in the case of brief quotations embodied in critical articles and reviews.

 Cover image conceived and developed by graphic designer Robyn John.
 Edited by Bill Hudgins.

Author's note: This is a satiric novel based solely on the author's imagination. The views expressed in this work are unique to the author and do not necessarily reflect the views of any of the indifferent big shots toiling on behalf of the publishing industry. Any resemblance to persons living or dead is purely intentional.

ALSO BY CHRIS RODELL

Fiction

The Last Baby Boomer

The Story of the Ultimate Ghoul Pool (2017)

Nonfiction

Undaunted Optimist

Essays on Life, Laughter & Cheerful Perseverance (2020)

Growing Up in the REAL Mr. Rogers' Neighborhood

Life Lessons from the Heart of Latrobe, PA (2019)

Arnold Palmer: Homespun Stories of The King (2018)

Use All The Crayons! The Colorful to Simple Human Happiness
(2012, Deluxe edition, 2017)

Chris's books can be purchased on-line at www.ChrisRodell.com.

1

EVAN & ELLE IN HEAVEN & HELL

It was, to the stone-hearted cynics, an open-and-shut case of the good girl falling for the bad boy. She'd been tempted, they'd said, by the forbidden fruit. Took a walk on the wild side. Gone rogue.

As far as bad boys go, Evan Lee had been to them one of the very worst. For just one dark day. He was handsome, generous, and he had the self-deprecating sense of humor a charismatic person uses when he or she wants to deflect attention. It was a defense mechanism that he could not deploy the day he became the most hated man in America. It was on that day that he killed 37 men and women, including a busload of nuns.

Oh, and he killed a cat.

The cat was not included in any of the final tallies because, though many people were upset about the cat, it was still just a cat.

Elle Lavator paid them no mind. She knew it was true love, even as she'd freely admit calling theirs a match made in Heaven was logistically impossible. That was the foundational fact upon which the critics anchored their arguments. She just didn't care.

Her critics, she'd say, could all go straight to Hell —

"Just as long as they take me with them!"

Even as a boy, Evan had the warm, knowing smile of a man who got all the jokes. Call him a bad boy and he'd deny it — contending he was a good boy who'd had one tragically bad day, one that made headlines around the world. It was a day even forgiving folk found difficult to forgive. But at its heart it was a love story and all the romantics were real suckers for love. And as love stories go, theirs was, all would admit, a real doozy.

Elle loved Evan and Evan loved Elle. A greater case of opposites attracting in all human history there'd never been.

She was angelic. Forever youthful, she was well-mannered and deferential about the feelings of others. She was a good listener and people instinctively knew they could confide in her. She was curious about everyone she met and had a nifty knack for putting all at ease. She was open-minded and forgiving of flaws. She saw the good in everyone, even seeing the good in the bad.

Evan? He'd become, well, one hell of a guy.

They met and fell in love the old-fashioned way: He'd bamboozled her with a bouquet of artfully crafted introductory lies. He said he was a good kid who came from a good family. He'd had a good job, was a good provider, had good taste, and was good, good, good for goodness sake.

He'd cunningly hacked her social media accounts so they simultaneously sent out Elle-signed notes saying she'd fallen on hard times and needed money sent to a secret offshore bank account. They were so persuasively forlorn her friends responded with a generous outpouring of casseroles, noodle salads and beaucoup wines of precocious vintage.

Evan forgot to take into account that in Elle's realm money was meaningless.

But they'd reacted as best they could. They dropped everything they were doing to help out a cherished friend. Their festive response to his attempt to defraud intrigued him. Who was this beloved girl who could inspire such soulful merriment?

Despite knowing it would lead to harsh community disapproval if anyone found out, he sent her a Facebook friend request. She confirmed it knowing, too, the disapproval on her end would be just as damning. Well, it would be darning. None of Elle's friends ever swore.

The virtual appeal was instant.

She'd never experienced anything like it in her 24 brief years, a mortal portion that had been festooned with laughter, love and crocheted mementos of everlasting glee. Neither had he. Evan told Elle things he'd never told anyone. He was vulnerable to her typed teasing and when she asked if he was a bad boy, he had to admit, yes, he was a bad boy. Boy, had he been bad.

"How bad?" she asked.

He paused for what in other places, other times, would have seemed like an eternity, his fidgety fingers poised above the decrepit, old keyboard. Did he dare? "Pretty bad," he admitted.

"You can tell me," she said, and Evan instinctively knew he could. And, really, what the hell did he have to lose? A lot, he fleetingly thought, but he figured if he couldn't unburden himself to Elle right then, when could he?

"I did some things I'm ashamed of. Some of the worst things you could imagine. Promise me you won't unfriend me. I've never had anyone in my life I could trust the way I trust you. Our chats make all the difference in my days, and

I'm afraid you'll cut me off when what I really want is for our relationship to flower."

She thought his use of the word flower was fragrantly botanical. She typed, "I promise!" She vowed to honor her pledge while steeling herself for grim revelation. She was so steeped in innocence, she thought by "rough crowd" he meant people who TYPED IN ALL CAPS. But she didn't allow herself to think the worst. Now, she was all in.

"Tell me everything," she typed.

Evan drew a deep breath, exhaled and typed his stark, momentous confession. "I killed my Mom and I killed my Dad," he typed, pausing before adding, "Oh, and I killed Mom's cat."

He deliberately framed it in the harshest possible light, figuring if she didn't instantly unfriend him, he might have a chance. Elle felt the breath whoosh from her chest, but felt spiritually bound to honor her vow. She responded with one word: "Explain."

Evan's mother had been the light of his life. She'd been his nurturer, his cheerleader and most ardent public defender, much more ardent than all the court-ordered public defenders hired by the state of Ohio.

"So, when she began to succumb to early onset Alzheimer's right after she turned 50, it just broke my heart. I was truly devastated. She sensed it coming and made me swear before things ever got really bad I'd help her die with dignity. That meant assisted suicide. I got in touch with the Hemlock Society and started a playbook."

He followed their applications with conscientious rigor and even did some deathly freelancing.

"I took her on a Caribbean cruise — just the two of us. And we spent a week in New Orleans and then Vegas. We put the whole shebang on her credit card hoping we could use her death as an excuse to avoid having to pay it, you know? Like some kind of hillbilly Make-A-Wish," Evan typed. "I wanted her to go out in style. She'd seen her best friend die of prolonged Alzheimer's and swore it wasn't for her. She knew what was coming, and she didn't flinch. She had determined assisted suicide was a moral option."

He conveyed to Elle all the wonderful times and laughs he and Mom had shared, and how — yippee! — she'd won $225,000 on Black 19 at the Luxor. The windfall delighted her. Evan said she knew he'd always struggled for money and to hit that jackpot on her way out really meant the world to her. It had all been so dreamlike that Evan, like his mother a connoisseur of dark humor, felt certain it would all end badly.

Boy, did it.

"It was December 20, the day after her 54th birthday. I was 35. I filled her bedroom with scented candles. Lavender. She always loved lavender. In the background, Stevie Nicks was softly playing. Mom adored Stevie. We shared one last bottle of wine, an Opus One '96, a fine cabernet blend. And with tears in my eyes, I began to read the 23rd Psalm. I held her hand and softly told her how much I was going to miss her and how one day we'd meet again in Heaven. Then I gave her the pills and hooked her arm up to the IV. I had tears dropping out my eyes in syncopation with the drip of the potassium chloride designed to stop her heart's beat.

"That's when I heard my old man kick down the kitchen door."

Rusty Lee'd been estranged from them both, but had heard about the loot, and it had brought him running.

"I hear him storming through the house and I just pour

the whole bottle of pills down Mom's throat, pinch her nose and spill the rest of the wine down her gullet. She made me swear I'd finish the job no matter what. So I did what I had to do. Well, Mom just starts fighting back. She's scratching at my arms and just fighting for dear life like it was all some big mistake. It was too late for that. So, I shove a pillow over her face and just start pressing down with all my might."

His words on the screen were a blur to Elle as she tried to comprehend the mounting mayhem.

"Well, then Rusty comes barging into the room, waving a gun and screaming. I thought the bastard was going to kill us both. I forget about Mom for just a second and push the mean old son of a bitch with all my might. He trips over Copy and starts stumbling backwards down the hall."

Elle collected herself enough to seek clarification. "Who's Copy?" she typed.

"Copy was Mom's cat!" He resumed, "Well, Rusty backpedals and trips over the Copycat. The frightened cat jumps up on a table, and his tail hits a lit wick and starts to sizzle. Copy lets out this otherworldly scream and darts behind the drapes, which instantly go up in flames. Now, the whole room just ignites."

He said he gave his supine, motionless Mom a quick peck on the cheek and sprinted out the room and down the hall, never pausing to confirm if she was dead or alive. So much for death with dignity, he remembered thinking.

"I'll never know if it was the fall that killed Rusty or if he'd had a heart attack. It could have been the eventual explosion. We'll never know. All I know is he had high blood pressure and a ticker that was tuned to tank. Either way, he looked deader than Hell to me."

He said the one thing he looked back on with real regret

was stepping over Rusty's lifeless body and prying the Smith & Wesson from his cold — lukewarm, really — dead fingers. Just like it said to do on the NRA bumper stickers Rusty had on his old pickup truck.

"And because I wasn't thinking clearly and had by then drunk a lot of Mom's wine and had popped a fistful of spare Xanax when she wasn't looking, I stopped and blew out the pilot lights on the gas stove as I ran through the kitchen."

He was about a quarter of a mile away when he heard the house — *kerPOWWW!!* — blow to smithereens. He'd been a regular drinker at The Canteen, a cowboy juke joint outside of town and pulled in to have some nerve-settling belts. He tucked the still-smoking peacemaker in his pants.

"It was just my bad luck that Billy Leonard was tending bar that day. We had a history that went way back to high school. He was just back from a stretch in the state pen for domestic violence. Everyone knew Billy was packing — and, man, that's a clear parole violation. Not that it justifies what I did to Billy. He had a bad temper and nursed a high school grudge against me for stealing his prom date. Her name was Brandi Conroy — and she didn't even put out!"

"Anyway, Billy sees me and turns the satellite radio to the hip-hop station 'cause he knows I can't stand rap. I sweet-as-can-be ask him to turn to Outlaw Country and MoJo Nixon. He sneers and says he'll get to it. I order a shot of Wild Turkey and tell Billy to leave the bottle. He snorts real rude-like and walks away. I pour one shot then another. Outside we hear the sirens go screaming past."

Evan was typing like his fingers were about to fly off at the knuckles.

"By now I'm good and drunk and sensing my day's about to get a whole lot more complicated, and I've had just about enough of Billy. So I pull out Rusty's gun and — Boom! — I blast a hole clean through the stereo.

"I should have figured what would happen next. Billy goes for his gun, and I know he's going to shoot to kill, all because of that stupid Brandi Conroy. I wanted to just wing him, but because I was drunk my aim was way, way off. Instead of his arm, I blast him right between the eyes. Can you believe my luck that day? It was purely self-defense. Still, I should never have shot the stereo. I should have handled the situation with more maturity."

Elle nearly typed a sarcastic comment, but didn't want to interrupt the story flow. She was very considerate.

"I take the bottle with me, already way too drunk to drive, and head out to Highway 101 and just crank up the Ray Wylie Hubbard. By then I didn't even know where I was going or why. I just thought I'd head up into the mountains, get good and drunk, and try and sleep it off like maybe it was all a bad dream.

"Well, I'm all over the road and this busload of nuns returning from the casino is coming straight for me because, well, I was so drunk I wound up in the wrong lane. The driver tries to avoid a collision and careens over the guardrail and rolls 70 feet down a cliff before landing upside down in the Hocking River. What a busload of nuns was doing coming back from a casino on a Monday afternoon, I'll never know. There were 33 of them plus the driver, but he was really old. It just wasn't my day. Theirs either, of course, but that kind of goes without saying."

The full report stole Elle's breath. It was just so much to comprehend. "How many died that day?"

"There were 37 if you don't count the Copycat."

"Gee," she typed in brittle exasperation, "did you just happen to kill anyone else?"

"Just one more guy. But by then there wasn't a soul left on Earth who gave a damn about that sorry bastard."

"And who was he?"

"Uh, that was me. And that's how I wound up here in Hell."

2

LYBERTY ERDETH

Lyberty Erdeth took one last sip on her Caramel Brûlée Latte from the Starbucks just down the block and folded up her *New York Times* to the daily crossword puzzle. It would be her happy distraction clear to quitting time. She booted up her laptop and used the small black Bose stereo remote to decrease the volume so the Broadway show tunes wouldn't disturb the conversation.

She had a love for all music, but nothing stirred her soul the way Broadway show tunes did. She dreamed of one day starring in one of the great Broadway musicals — "West Side Story," "Music Man," or her favorite, "Singin' in the Rain" — but there was plenty of time for that. After all, she'd only been in Heaven for 162 years, so there was no need to rush.

She looked up at the grandfather clock her grandfather had built special for her in 1907 and said a quick prayer of euphoric thanks as she watched the second-hand sweep toward 9 a.m.

It was another day in eternity, and she was ready to go to work.

Well, she didn't really consider it work. Born in 1840 into a family of Dadeville, Alabama, slaves, hers had been a harsh, brief life spent picking cotton under the scorching sun and the whip's bitter sting. Now, *that* was work. Cruelty, deprivation and hardship were all she knew her whole life until she died at the age of 20 while giving birth to her owner John Lee Pettimore IV's son. So, given those extenuating circumstances, she got to bypass all the tests and paperwork and zoomed straight to Heaven. Her sunshine and soul were instantly restored and she was made whole. She remembered seeing herself in the full-length mirror and being overcome by the ethereal beauty she'd never once imagined was hers.

Just like that, the worst day of her life had become the first best day of her afterlife. Like all new arrivals, she was greeted in Heaven by her ancestral loved ones and, a bunch of cheerful moochers just looking out for any free fun. It was a party with champagne and cake. The champagne was Cristal, the cake angel food. Of course, all the cakes in Heaven were angel food. But that's nitpicking because everything the angels eat in Heaven is angel food.

In contrast and by the way, John Lee Pettimore IV lived a long and prosperous mortal life. He was highly regarded by his peers, revered for his keen business sense, his military zeal and the way he ensured strict domestic discipline among his family and those who worked his fields during times of extreme national tumult. When he died in 1867, then-Alabama Gov. Andrew B. Moore ordered state flags flown at half-staff and his body lay in state at the Alabama capital building. Every honor The Yellowhammer State could bestow upon a prominent white man like Pettimore was bequeathed upon his corporeal remains.

This was all happening while his ever-loving soul shot straight to Hell.

Lyberty didn't have to work — no one in Heaven did — but most found work stimulating. She enjoyed helping people. That's what she did as office manager in the HR Department. It had initially been the AR, but everyone felt Angel Relations seemed a bit stuffy. And anyways the majority of new arrivals just naturally gravitated to referring to it as Human Relations, just like they did when they'd been when they were toiling on behalf of the godless Earth corporations intent on squeezing every penny of profit for the already affluent while sucking the souls from their forlorn mortal employees.

Her human counterparts dealt with HR issues much more pressing than post-humans did in Heaven. Earth issues included pay disputes, parking concerns, injustice, sexual harassment, supervisor hostility, job-related stress, threats of gun violence, stabbings, bombings, stranglings, dismemberments and, as always, gripes about running low on Quilted Northern Ultra Plush in the ladies' lavatory.

Most of the complaints Lyberty heard involved what on Earth were considered petty nuisances: A neighbor's dog barked too much in the middle of the night, the dry cleaner was using too much starch, people were talking too loudly during the movies and the crooked cable companies were charging too much for channels nobody wanted.

With the exception of complaints about cable service, Lyberty could usually arbitrate mutually satisfactory conclusions to each of these disputes. Everyone would have to compromise. Give and take. Even Steven. It worked that way for all but the crooks who ran the cable companies.

Nobody could get the cable companies to provide satisfactory service. Sure, it was Heaven, but even in Heaven some things were still impossible.

The temperatures were pleasant, the sunsets gorgeous, nonsensical hatreds non-existent and the joys abounding. People endured aggravations with a cheerfulness all had found impossible to maintain on Earth. Sure, there was still traffic, but there was no road rage. Eternity had a way of smoothing out so many of life's aggravations. No one was ever in a hurry. No one was ever in a panic. People were more polite, more considerate, more understanding.

It was Heaven.

That's why Lyberty was startled when Pat Finder, 15, came breathlessly bursting through the door just as the clock struck nine.

"I've got, like, huge news!" she said. "You're not gonna believe it, I swear! It'll, like, blow your mind!"

Perpetually perky, Pat was Lyberty's brand new scout. She'd died in her sleep of carbon monoxide poisoning the year before after her elderly grandfather had nodded off in the family garage with the car running and the tank full. His carelessness had killed Pat, her parents and himself. He was 84. Dead eight months, PapPap had already earned heavenly renown for being an elite bocce ball player, which was great because he'd played so poorly on Earth he often had to cheat to remain competitive — and bocce cheating was no heavenly disqualifyer.

Many people who died young became fact-finder scouts for HR chiefs like Lyberty. The job gave the kids an opportunity to mingle with all ages and ask all their inquisitive questions about life and afterlife without appearing too pushy. Lyberty, too, liked it when people coincidentally took jobs that matched their names. It's why she enjoyed getting postal correspondence from a girl named Maley, buying her bookshelves from a carpenter named Wood, and waving to a friendly barber named Comey.

Pat had quickly become one of Lyberty's favorite scouts. She was vibrant, bubbly and impatient to learn everything. She had curly red hair, an athletic physique and a lightning laugh that flashed across her freckled face the instant she found anything surprisingly funny. She behaved like people on Earth behaved if their blood were carbonated. She was effervescent. Sure, it'd been a pity she'd died so young, but she'd really embraced Heaven and Heaven had embraced her right back.

"Calm down, Pat," Lyberty said. "You have to remember you're not in 9th grade anymore. You've heard the phrase, 'You have all the time in the world?' Forget it. That's finite. It no longer applies. Here, you have all the time — all the time. You're not going to miss recess if you take your time telling your story. This is Heaven. We're nothing but recess. And please take that gum out of your mouth."

Pat took the gum out of her mouth and stuck it behind her ear. She took a deep breath and settled into one of the two leather chairs on the opposite side of Lyberty's desk, her legs folded up beneath her.

"Okay," she said. "I rushed over here because I heard some really juicy gossip. Like, super juicy."

Expecting to be underwhelmed, Lyberty settled back in her chair and said, "Well?"

"Elle Lavator has a wicked crush on a guy," she said, her eyes wide with expectant reaction. "It's wicked, I tell ya. And I mean wicked." She was disappointed when her teaser revelation didn't cause all the hairs on Lyberty's head to simultaneously launch off her scalp.

"Now, Finder, that shouldn't come as any surprise. It's

only natural. Elle is beloved. Why, just last month I saw a Buzzfeed poll that ranked her as the fifth most popular woman in all of Heaven. She came in behind Joan of Arc, Sacagawea and the two Marys."

Pat looked confused. "The two Marys?"

"Yes," Lyberty explained, "Mary Magdalene and Mary Tyler Moore."

"Oh, yeah," she said, even as she registered some mental disagreement with the list. She thought Sacagawea and Joan of Arc were kind of overrated, although the old martyr had helped improve her backhand during a jiffy tennis lesson. And she had to admit, it was hard to top either of the two Marys. Everyone loved the two Marys.

But Pat really, really loved Elle. She was her No. 1 in every category. She was the sweetest, the prettiest, the funniest, the kindest, the warmest — the zestiest, the bestiest, the -estiest of 'em all. Lyberty could tell she was feeling a little deflated that she hadn't been bowled over by her revelation. She was, after all, a tender child. She didn't want to stunt her enthusiasms so she gently stoked the conversation.

"It's okay, child," she said. "Really, I'm surprised she hasn't become smitten before. Who's the lucky fellow? Caesar? Copernicus? Elvis?" she said naming some of the popular bachelors.

Glumly, Pat Finder shook her head. "Nah," she said. "It's none of those guys. He's nobody famous. You've never heard of him, I'm sure. He's not even from around here."

Now, it was Lyberty's turn to be confused. "Not from around here? What does that mean? You mean he's still on Earth?"

"Nope. He's from a little farther south."

"Mississippi? Nicaragua? Patagonia?"

"No, south of the whole world."

"What could be south of Earth?"

"It's some guy from Hell. He's one of the condemned."

Pat's mood brightened considerably when it looked like all the hairs on Lyberty's head were about to simultaneously launch off her scalp.

THERE WAS nothing in any of the protocols about such a situation. None of the manuals mentioned it. It was entirely without precedent. No one from Heaven had ever consorted with a soul from Hell. There had been no illicit fraternization. It just wasn't done. Everyone knew that. Or at least they used to.

Then came Facebook and the cascade of ever-more stylish smartphones. Together they exerted their insatiable pull. It was a trickle at first, so minimal few even noticed. Facebook wasn't invented until 2004, and its first devotees were youthful with long lives ahead of them. But by October 2012, it had a billion users, most of them accessing it on handheld devices. And by then its devotees were of all ages and all demographics. Even Granny was posting updates about her bingo winnings. It had become like a high school yearbook that was updated in real time, but with food porn and cat videos.

No one even noticed the first Facebook users in Heaven. They were quiet, less euphoric than other new arrivals. Everyone at first mistakenly thought Earthlings were becoming more devout or maybe less enamored of the NFL. Many men and women prior to and through the 2000s arrived in Heaven and did a sort of end zone dance to demonstrate their euphoria at having proverbially taken their soul "to the house." Excessive celebrations had at one time been penalized in the NFL. Not in Heaven.

But that all began to fade with the first Facebook generations. They were more muted, more subdued. Their heads were bowed in what appeared to be reverence. They'd often stop in their tracks and raise their right arms in a stifled sort of salute.

"They're taking what are known as selfies," explained Kirby Richards, an astute observer of humanity and something of an angel anthropologist. "Selfies are pictures you take of yourself with a smart phone extended in front of your face. You then post the picture to Facebook to prove you were there. People would do this at iconic places like the Eiffel Tower, Easter Island, and while drunk at the White Castle on Friday night. Telling social media what you were doing all the time has become an intrinsic part of the human experience."

But, it was pointed out, they didn't possess smartphones or Facebook in Heaven.

"Then for some people it's obviously become something of a reflex. Pure muscle memory. They simply can't help themselves."

Soon, everyone's idea of heaven became less heavenly without their smartphones. People became anxious. Restless. The smartphone had become a dominant part of their Earth lives. It depressed them that they couldn't make it a dominant part of their afterlives. Heaven ought to modernize, they petitioned.

Yes, even Heaven has suggestion boxes, and the suggestion boxes in Heaven are always full.

What, it was decided, could it hurt? And Steve Jobs was more than happy to develop and manufacture a snappy smartphone for Heaven, one that would give "cloud computing" a more literal meaning, so much of Heaven being clouds and all. Jobs, in fact, tackled the assignment with sufficient gusto that he soon began issuing updates with slightly different graphics and primary colors every six months. And everyone felt compelled to obtain the newer one before they'd even mastered the old. To Jobs, it was Heaven. And just like Earth.

Soon, everyone was using his or her smartphones to take selfies with Cleopatra, Benjamin Franklin and even camera-shy Greta Garbo. Sure, she *vanted* to be alone, but in Heaven she didn't *vant* to appear rude.

And Garbo had plenty of time. Everyone did. It was one for all eternity and eternity for all. Philosopher Henry David Thoreau wondered on Earth if it was possible to kill time without injuring eternity. Not in Heaven, it wasn't. In Heaven, you could kill time without even leaving a mark. The snooze alarms in Heaven had settings measured in centuries.

Facebook in Heaven also led to a dramatic decrease in requests for Earth hauntings. A typical haunting was complicated and involved a lot of paperwork. But social media nearly eliminated the need for ghostly gas lighting. Checking up on an old girlfriend, teacher or boss was a routine hack. The only people who applied for actual hauntings were those souls who were really bitter about either an ex or maybe some had some descendants who'd gotten greedy over the wills. But those were very few. In Heaven, most people were happy to let bygones be bygones.

No one dared make contact with any of the Hellions. It was just understood. No matter how forgiving the angels were, everyone knew forgiveness wasn't any of their business.

But there was no doubting the impact social media and

smartphones had on Heaven. Some thought it was progress. But not the old-timers. The old-timers thought it was a big mistake.

Because in the eyes of many, Heaven was already heavenly enough. It was carousels, cotton candy, movies where nobody talked or texted. It was reading Dr. Seuss to babies at bedtime. Sometimes it was having Dr. Seuss himself over to do the reading. It was long, soulful walks with the crunch of autumn leaves at your feet. It was all hammocks and happy hours. Yes, all dogs went to Heaven, but so did all the unicorns and Yetis — and neither of them ever accidentally crapped on your lawn. This was good because in Heaven most everyone went everywhere barefoot.

There were rainbows without rain, streams stocked with trophy trout, ice cream that satisfied without the calories. Things like love handles and male pattern baldness were purely optional and mostly surfaced as part of elaborate Halloween costumes. Racism and injustice were non-existent, as were hunger, want, belligerence, pettiness, haste and simple chronic halitosis. No one felt pain. Every soul felt respected, confident and useful.

But Heaven was not static. It had once been an Eden-like splendor, sylvan and green as the Berkshires before gasoline. But as more and more worthy were welcomed throughout the millennia, Heaven became more refined. Fashions changed. At one time on Earth, running water was considered a luxury, but the whole arc of human history is bent on transforming every single luxury into a necessity. TVs with rabbit ear antennas were once considered a show-off appliance. But soon people mocked the contraptions as woeful. By the year 2025, every new arrival was accustomed to 60-inch flat screens with HD and theater surround sound. If they were going to be spending a good bit of eternity binge-watching "Seinfeld" reruns, by God, it had better be on a deluxe home entertainment system.

So Heaven progressed, almost always for the better. Even after the advent of the smartphones, Heaven was to always remain a holy realm of love, joy, tranquility and utter peacefulness — as long as all the phones were set to vibrate.

Heaven was, indeed, Heaven. It's just that Heaven was subject to evolutions that would have surprised Charles Darwin. And the old timers began to notice a shift. A once-assured social fabric began to fray. Conversations became distracted. Fewer families ate meals together. Newspaper circulation began to decline. Volunteer fire department memberships dwindled. Fewer people bowled.

The old-timers blamed the smartphones. They said — and they were only half-joking — that the introduction of the first smartphone was when Heaven went straight to Hell. What did they know? Being in Heaven still meant existential euphoria, everyone agreed. The old-timers were just a bunch of technophobes. Cavemen, really. The observers weren't being impolite when they called those who disliked technological advances "cavemen." In Heaven, all the cavemen were really cavemen.

3

PAT, LYBERTY & PAIGE TURNER

Lyberty took a moment to compose herself. The thought that anyone in Heaven was consorting with anyone in Hell shook her soul — and she was all soul. The thought that it could be anyone as truly angelic as Elle Lavator was flabbergasting.

"You're telling me," Lyberty asked Pat, "they're actually communicating? They respond to each other's thoughts? They converse?"

Pat nodded. She'd pulled the gum from behind her ear and had resumed her chew. Lyberty hadn't noticed. Her mind raced. The implications were too great. Lyberty was a problem-solver, someone who confronts each challenge with logic and bedrock wisdom. Was taking the word of a precocious 15-year-old logical? After all, Pat Finder had only been in Heaven for less than a year. A naif. A newbie.

"How do you know this, Finder?"

"Saw it with my own eyes."

"She could have been messaging anyone."

"No," Pat said, "it was a guy from H-E double toothpicks. I'm sure."

Lyberty asked if Elle'd shown her.

"No. I picked up her phone. We'd been white-water rafting and had left our stuff there on the banks of the New River."

Lyberty was aware of the New River. On Earth, it was in West Virginia, a state whose motto — "Almost Heaven" — was taken from the 1971 John Denver song, "Take Me Home, Country Roads." West Virginia tourism boosters were chagrined upon arrival when they realized, in fact, they'd actually undersold the state and its outdoorsy charms. Parts of the scenic state were, indeed, Heaven.

"Finder, you weren't snooping, were you?"

"Not really. Nah. I went to get it for her while she was changing, and it happened to flip on to her Facebook messenger while I was holding it. Honest. And I saw the message from that Hell guy."

Lyberty suspected her precocious young charge was fibbing, but knew she couldn't prove it. It was possible Elle'd left her phone on and Pat just happened to spy a private message. It wasn't like Elle would have secured it with a password. No one in Heaven did. In Heaven — thank God — there were no longer any passwords.

"What did the message say?"

Finder, her jaw working at full nervous chomp, said, "Just boyfriend/girlfriend stuff: 'I can't stop thinking about you. Thoughts of you are what get me through this Hell. What'd you have for lunch?' It was all very chummy. Guy's name is Evan Lee."

She still wasn't convinced. It could have been some sort of role play. Role playing in Heaven was a popular pastime. It wasn't until Finder described Lee's profile picture that she realized the biggest HR problem in the history of Heaven had fallen right into her lap.

"Nice looking guy, dimples, the kind of smile Mrs. Amos, my old 3rd grade teacher, described as devilish, and curly brown hair. Wanna see?"

She should have known the spritely girl would have pilfered a picture. Normally, she would have lectured her on invasion of privacy issues and proper respect, but this was too momentous for etiquette lessons. She reached out her hand and Pat presented her phone.

It wasn't the picture of Evan Lee that drew her scrutiny, although she noted Mrs. Amos was correct: He was devilishly handsome. No, it was the leering disheveled face over his right shoulder that convinced her the alarm was authentic.

It was Ted Kaczynski. He'd been convicted of using the U.S. Postal Service to distribute bombs that from 1978 through 1995 killed three and maimed 23 others and resulted in after the most expensive investigation in FBI history. He was sentenced to life in prison in 1998. He died in 2020, but no one noticed because, geez, it'd been such a busy news year.

His soul immediately went to Hell for his violent crimes and for foisting his boring manifesto on the public, and because of the work's mis- and overuse of hyphens.

Kaczynski had only been in Hell for mere days when angelic intelligence agencies noticed his bearded visage popping up in the backgrounds of picture intercepts. Famously reclusive while on Earth, Kaczynski had in Hell become the oddest kind of publicity-seeker.

The Unabomber had become a photobomber.

Lyberty had work to do. And she'd have to rely on a guileless innocent like Pat Finder for help and discretion. That meant she'd need to find an experienced cynic, a wily veteran steeped in the nuances of afterlife emotions, a man of cunning and insight.

Lyberty told Pat Finder all this and the kid asked if he was some kind of spy, maybe a foreign agent, a spook. An afterlife James Bond.

"Sorry, no, he's a bartender. His name is Paige Turner. We need to go see him right away. He'll be at the Carnegie Library."

Lyberty asked her secretary to cancel all her appointments for the next two years and tell the three dozen petitioners waiting patiently on the sidewalk they'd have to come back in a couple years or so. No one complained. There was plenty of other stuff to do in Heaven, and with eternity and all, there was plenty of time to kill.

PAIGE TURNER WASN'T JUST any bartender. He was renown for being one of the most well-read men in Heaven and for possessing a keen understanding of human nature even among souls who were no longer necessarily considered human. On Earth, Turner'd been a bartender, expert at slaking thirsts. But he was also invigorated with a thirst of his own, one on Earth he'd never managed to quench.

So it was in Heaven that Paige Turner became a voracious reader. He luxuriated in the written word. It's why the bartender naturally become a Carnegie librarian shortly after his 1892 arrival. In Heaven, all the librarians were revered for their contributions to the enlightenment, elevation and mental well-being of the common good. Librarians in Heaven were like clergy on earth and spending time in the library was like spending time in church. It was essential to achieving spiritual peace.

They'd briefly tried church in Heaven, but church in Heaven never took off. Church in heaven just seemed sort of redundant. Organizers realized the whole goal of church was to get people to be good so they can get to Heaven. But in Heaven everyone was already good enough and it was already Heaven. There was no real point, so there was no real church.

But there were libraries galore. Grand, soaring structures like cathedrals of holy worship if only those cathedrals were all indexed with the Dewey Decimal System. Each library had tens of millions of books — actual books — from everyone who'd ever written anything. Even all the self-published vanity crap no one on Earth ever bothered to read. And there were shelves and shelves of classics by the likes of Twain, Steinbeck, Woolf, Shakespeare, Austen and Dostoyevski. Particularly fun for avid fans, each library featured near-daily readings of classics by the likes of Twain, Steinbeck, Woolf, Shakespeare, Austen and Dostoyevski in person.

The libraries all had elegant salons and forums for vigorous debate about philosophical matters. They had lecture halls, cafeterias, art galleries, places for conversation and quiet study. As they were open 24/7, there were even nap rooms.

But Turner's was the only one of them had an honest-to-goodness pub.

It was The Lyin' Sleepin' Dog.

Only in Heaven could The Dog's bartender simultaneously be the Carnegie's librarian. The duality led to convivial social mingling and perpetual exasperation for Turner who was forever laboring to get readers to drink more and drinkers to read more. Robust, garrulous and relentlessly cheerful, Turner was the perfect advocate for the idle afterlife.

A proud East Ender, Turner'd been killed by a beer wagon mule outside The Dog in 1892 when the first car in London backfired and startled the beast. Turner was rolling a keg down the sidewalk and got kicked right between the eyes with such force it snapped his neck. He was dead before he hit the ground.

His first thought upon waking up dead was, "Blimey, I'm gonna miss tonight's dart championship ... But I'll have a great death story to tell for the rest of me afterlife!"

Death stories like the one Paige told were great icebreakers in heaven. Introductory Earth small talk inevitably included, "So, where you from?" In Heaven, everyone knew roughly where everyone was from — Earth, duh — so it was acceptable to say, "So, how'd you die?"

Everyone appreciated a story like Turner's. In fact, many souls in Heaven were chagrined they'd lived such safe lives dedicated to fitness and the grim extension of their miserable mortalities. Darwin Award winners — hapless hillbillies, mostly — who expired doing things like launching themselves propelled by backyard rockets or fell from barn roofs to their deaths while flapping beer case-cardboard wings got invited to all the cool parties.

Turner was pleased to see Lyberty walk into The Dog with her young friend. Lyberty spent lots of her free time either in his bar or with his books. Turner knew she liked to read (Tolkien, Rowling, etc.), liked to drink (pinot and the occasional tequila), and she was the rare refined woman, a true jokester, who could both tell and enjoy a good dirty joke.

When he saw her approaching the bar, he instinctively blurted out in his distinctive Cockney, "Say, 'Lyb, did you 'ear the one about the Irishman, the Jew, the Jap, and the pregnant chimney sweep?"

She shot him a look and rolled her eyes to Pat. "Not now, Paige," she said. "This is Miss Pat Finder. She got here back in November. Accidental carbon monoxide poisoning."

"Oh, welcome, Pat," he said as his face lit up her with his gap-toothed grin. "I came this close" — he pinched his thumb and forefinger on his left hand — "to corrupting yer innocence. Lyberty, you shoulda told me you were bringin' a wee sprout. Me, I got mule-booted in me brain way back inna 1892. No long-term defects. That is if you overlook my mortal demise. Okee-do. State your business."

Lyberty glanced around the bar. It was still two hours prior to the Friday Happy Hour and already crowding the bar she saw Patrick Shannon, Wendy Goldstein, Aiko Amuro and maybe a half-dozen other nationalities guzzling in cheerful communion. Had there been a llama and a pregnant chimney sweep at the bar, Lyberty would have wondered if she was confusing Turner's joke opener with that day's bar attendees.

"Not here," she said. "We need privacy."

"Then me office it is," he said. "Ladies, follow me. Aziz, please watch the bar for me, eh?"

Aziz Ahl was The Dog's assistant manager and Turner's best friend since August 27, 1883. That's when his blessed soul ascended into Heaven just beyond the smoke and ashes of the Dutch East Indies island that was once Krakatoa. Despite the cataclysmic circumstances, his death story was surprisingly mundane. He never saw it coming and was killed near-instantly in his fishing boat when a Volkswagen-sized chunk of molten lava landed right in his lap. He liked to joke that he might have survived, but he liked to fish with his fly down.

Turner began to hum "Those Were The Days, My Friend," to him the greatest pub song ever recorded, and still humming led them behind the bar and through a door to a spacious oak-paneled office that smelled like it had been marinating in fine cigars for more than a century, which it had. There was a leather couch, an antique replica desk, a humidor and an aquarium populated with exotic Angel fish that would never die.

And because the room was connected to the largest and most-respected library in Heaven, the never-married Turner had all he thought he would ever need. In Heaven, you got to do, within sacred reason, whatever you wanted for as long as you wanted. Turner chose to be a librarian who ran a splendid little pub on the side. He motioned Finder and Lyberty to sit on the couch while he took the leather chair behind the desk and put his feet up and halted his hum.

"Now," he said, " 'ow can 'elp you?"

And Pat Finder began to tell Turner the story of Evan and Elle.

4

EVAN IN HELL

The fluorescent cell lights came buzzing on as they always did at 5:30 a.m., just a moment before the goddamned music began blaring from loud, scratchy speakers. You could never tell exactly what it would be, but you could be assured it was something awful and infectious, a veritable STD for the ears.

It isn't mentioned in the Bible or preached from the pulpits, but Hell has a soundtrack. The day before it had been "Muskrat Love," by Captain & Tennille. The day before that "Baby" by Justin Bieber, and the day before that "Achy Breaky Heart" by Billy Ray Cyrus. Then there were the all the Christmas ditties. "Grandma Got Run Over By a Reindeer," "Dominick the Italian Donkey," and the Madonna version of "Santa Baby."

Bad songs he could deal with. Most of the time. After all, he was in Hell partly from the consequences of what happened when the late Billy Leonard had the foolhardy audacity to change the radio station from Mojo Nixon & Outlaw Country to hip-hop.

What was so irritating about Hell wasn't just bad songs, but that it was one bad song per day. The same bad song. All day. From 5:30 a.m. to 11:30 p.m. That meant the condemned would hear Paul Anka's 2 minute, 30 second, 1974 soft rock hit "Having My Baby," 469 consecutive times. So everyday in Hell started out with the cold realization that the whole day was sure to be Hell.

What was today's torture?

It was "Goodness Gracious Me," an obscure, faintly racist 1960 novelty ditty sung by comic actor Peter Sellers and luscious Italian bombshell Sophia Loren. Simultaneously cloying and titillating, it has Sellers lampooning an Indian physician examining Loren, who is both in her prime and in her bed for the lascivious house call.

> *Sellers: From New Delhi to Darjeeling*
> *I have done my share of healing,*
> *And I've never yet been beaten or outboxed,*
> *I remember that with one jab*
> *Of my needle in the Punjab*
> *How I cleared up beriberi*
> *And the dreaded dysentery,*
> *But your complaint has got me really foxed.*
>
> *Loren: Oh doctor, touch my fingers.*
> *Sellers: Well, goodness gracious me.*
> *Loren: You may be very clever*
> *But however, can't you see,*
> *My heart beats much too much*
> *At a certain tender touch,*
> *It goes boom boody-boom boody-boom boody-boom*
> *Boody-boom boody-boom boody-boom-boom-boom,*

Sellers: I like it!
Loren: Boom boody-boom boody-boom boody-boom
Sellers: Well, goodness gracious me.

THE SONG WAS SO PUTRID, Evan thought he'd surely one day meet its composer and do something to really ruin his day — a real sporting challenge in Hell. That's how much he hated the song. Little did he know, the "Goodness Gracious Me" composer had evaded Hell two years later with a breathtaking and enduring musical contribution that had all the angels singing hosannahs, not to mention singing, "Let it Be," "In My Life," and "Hey Jude." Yes, it was Beatles producer George Martin who conceived and produced "Goodness Gracious Me."

It was a lesson that, with all things in life, redemption is forever possible.

Of course, the soundtrack wasn't the worst thing about Hell. Not by far. It's well-known fact that all dogs go to heaven, but it's also factual that nearly all the soulless rats, roaches and snakes go straight to Hell, too.

And Hell smelled. Real bad. Sure, there were smells of overripe garbage, overflowing toilets, and stink bugs that dared you to crush them to liberate their stinky souls. There were decaying flesh, spoiled meats, roadkill, rotten eggs, old gym socks, old toilet brushes and a thousand farts from a sinful symphony of real assholes.

Of course, the music and the stinks weren't the worst things about Hell and its cruel banalities. Not by far. And neither was the housing situation, although that really got to Evan. One of the major factors of life in Hell was that everyone got a really bad roommate — and not in like the he-always-leaves-the-sink-full-and-doesn't-pay-his-share-of-the-cable-bill bad. We're talking bad as in Adolph Hitler.

Evan had spent some time in the stinking rec yard with a guy who was rooming with Hitler, and all the guy did was complain. He complained so much Evan never even had a chance to complain about his awful roommate.

Evan's roommate was a bully. A loudmouth. A racist. A homophobe and a Red Sox fan. He cheated at poker. He snored. He borrowed stuff and never gave it back. He taunted. He was negative. He sang along with all the terrible songs as if he actually enjoyed them. He made stupid wagers and never paid off when they went poof. He boasted about sex with women he'd obviously never met.

Evan's hellish cellmate was there for child abuse. Satan loved his child abusers because he knew nothing perpetuated Earth evil like the mistreatment of tiny innocents. So Evan, himself a victim of child abuse, despised him. He hated the reedy sound of endless yapping, the way he never cared even a bit about his appearance, and how he was always reminding Evan how they were doomed to spend all eternity together as cellmates in Hell.

And what he maybe hated worst of all knowing that he'd wake up every morning at precisely 5:30 a.m. to see that same hated face pop out over the side of the top bunk and cheerfully whisper, "Say, 'Good morning,' asshole! Say, 'Good morning, asshole!' Say, 'Good morning,' asshole!'"

And he'd say those same four words over and over and over until Evan responded in the one and only way the cellmate deemed acceptable. He had to say it exactly the same way each and every morning or he'd resume. And each and every time, Evan nearly choked on the words.

"Good morning, Daddy." Evan's cellmate was his very own father.

Goodness gracious me.

5

PAIGE, LYBERTY & PAT

Turner stroked his chin thoughtfully as he began to mentally digest Finder's story. He had a roguish two-day stubble, which he enjoyed for facial texture. There was no need to shave in Heaven and men could select their beard and hair length each morning as if they were choosing that day's shirt. Same for women and their hair. Best part? No one ever needed to trim their finger or toe nails ever again. It was considered a grooming godsend.

"So, Lyberty, lemme get this straight," Turner said. "Evan's in 'ell and Elle's in 'eaven. They've fallen madly in luv thanks to this stupid Facebook crap and you'll figuratively speaking move 'eaven and Earth to keep 'em apart. Is 'at it? Blimey."

Pat Finder stared at him. His accent reminded her of the singing she remembered hearing on her dad's old Kinks records. Or maybe it was 'erman's 'ermits. Lyberty sensed her confusion and spoke up.

"Paige," she said, "could you just dial down the Cockney a bit. For Pat's sake, let's please keep it English."

He glanced back and forth at Pat Finder and Lyberty, shook off brief tingle of hurt feelings and said, "I'll try me best, but it ain't like I can switch it on and off at the request of some whimsical Colonist."

Oh, yes, he could, and Lyberty knew it. But he loved the musical lilt of his own tongue and he wasn't about to abandon it just because Lyberty felt inconvenienced. He sensed Pat, as most children did, found the Cockney accent beguiling.

"Well then, how we going to 'andle this?" he said, his accent already beginning to modify. "What can I do for you?"

"First of all," Lyberty said, "we need comprehensive dossiers on both Evan Lee and Elle Lavator. We need to know all the intimate details of their lives on Earth, how they spent their time, if they ever met, if they had any common contacts and the circumstances of their deaths, and, of course, their eternal afterlife designations. And we need a threat assessment on this Evan.

"I fear this is going to get out, and we need to be prepared if it does. We're dealing with a situation that has the potential to upend the whole order of Heaven and Hell. Because if one or the other succeeds in making any kind of social bond — if there's any crack in the emotional or metaphysical borders — we could lose all this. Everything. We can't have our kind mixing with theirs."

Turner, indeed, understood and began proving Lyberty's wisdom in coming to him first.

"Well, Pat Finder and I could go right now to the library's genealogical research department and start going through the files. We 'ave records on each of the roughly 108.6 billion men and women who've set foot on Earth in its entire history. Some of the records are so old they're mere facsimiles of cave drawings. We can copy the records we need and build case files on both Evan and Elle."

He sat back in his chair and folded his hands into the curly black hair that behaved like it was having a Mardi Gras on his head. He was always up for a caper. And being a lifelong bachelor, he had no one to go home to. Maybe he was just too picky, but he wondered if he'd ever find true love in Heaven.

His dream girl? Breakfast waitress, one that always perky when they oughtn't to be. He just loved their energy, their perspective, and the sassy way they brought sunshine to pre-dawn settings.

Yes, he thought distractedly, someday I'm going to meet a breakfast waitress and we're gonna spend eternity together. He dreamed he'd one day find his true love, but in Heaven it seemed it might take forever.

He came back to focus when he heard young Finder shoot down his idea of painstaking research.

"Yeah, we could go to all that trouble, or we could just save a whole lot of time and just Google their obituaries."

Lyberty grinned at Turner's deflated reaction.

"Young lady," he said, "one of the great joys of eternity is there's no bloody hurry. We can savor the research. Be detectives ... Like ol' Sherlock Holmes! It'll be more thorough and more satisfyin'."

"I want to do it my way," Finder said. "We may have eternity, but we don't have all day."

Lyberty grinned in agreement with Finder. Indeed, she felt an unfamiliar sense of urgency, one she never felt even when angels were really upset over being unfairly charged for shoddy cable service.

"You know she's right, Paige. We should use the technology available to us to stay ahead of this. Let's Google up the obits and get started. Pat, you start with Elle. Paige and I will take the dude with the dreamy eyes."

Turner looked utterly defeated. He'd been railing against the corrosive effects of the internet in Heaven and now, boom, here it was chasing some of the fun out of his investigations.

"Oh, and one more thing," he said. "I need to swear each of you to utter secrecy. No matter what we find, we can't let anyone know of our investigation. This is potentially explosive stuff. We must keep a tight lid on it. No leaks. None! Do I have your word?"

Lyberty said, "Absolutely. I agree this is a very grave matter with consequences none of us can foresee. You have my word."

"Mine, too," Finder said. "Not a peep from me."

"Then we're all in agreement. Not a word to anyone outside this room."

Agreed, each said.

Within 10 minutes, Paige had — *"Psst!"* — summoned Aziz over and with a "Wait 'til you get a load of this ..." preface spilled the whole story. And because it was a secret too juicy to hoard, Aziz told Joan Rivers who told Jim Nabors who told Johnny Carson just to get the ball really rolling.

Lyberty texted Walter Winchell, the 1930's syndicated columnist credited with introducing entertainment to journalism. Within hours he was posting breathless teases that asked listeners if they could name "the good girl who's going bad — and I mean really bad!"

Pat Finder one-upped them both. She casually mentioned it to her neighbor during otherwise innocuous small talk. The neighbor? Johannes Gutenberg, the 14th century German inventor of the first moveable type printing press. He thought the story was just what he was looking for to stick it to those prissy internet advocates who said print was dead.

A fire had begun to crackle. Not a hellfire. Not yet.

6

EVAN ON EARTH

Evan Lee was born September 25, 1983, to Russell "Rusty" and Lola Beck Lee in Nelsonville, Ohio. Lola for minimum wage cheerfully did every icky job they all asked to help do to keep the local animal shelter shipshape. Rusty scrambled around town trying to secure clean pee so he could hurdle the minimum safety drug test requirements for working in the local cardboard box factory.

They'd met in high school and together lost their sweet virginity on prom night in the back of his canary yellow Camaro IROC-Z. Two years later when she told him, hon, guess what, you're going to be a daddy, he beat her so badly he went to jail and she to the emergency room.

Behave, the judge told Rusty.

I will, Rusty promised the judge.

The same two men were to have roughly the exact same conversation four times over the next 10 years. All the case workers were adamant that growing up amidst such violence was going to be harmful to Evan's development.

She'd need to get him away from him or who knows what kind of man he'd grow up to be? Lola finally divorced Rusty when she saw a look in Evan's eye that she knew her darling little angel was going to kill his father if he touched her again. He was 12.

Mom was mellow; dad, menace.

Rusty was clenched fists, shouted profanities, slammed doors and half-empty beer bottles heaved at the hearth. A childhood that should have been about bedtime stories, playing catch, fishing and working on cars in the garage with the old man became one of unrelenting tumult — at least while dad was home.

Because with mom, there was in her arms a sanctuary soothing as the womb. She protected him as best she could. She nurtured him. She made him laugh. She built him up when his fears knocked him down. She shared with him her love of books and libraries. She'd let him tag along with her to the animal shelter where all the tiny heartbeats strengthened his. She'd splurge on ice cream treats for him and, when she didn't have the dough to afford ice cream, she'd lavish him with the kind of affection that would fortify his soul.

With mom, it was Heaven.

With dad, well, it wasn't.

He later concluded his scrapes with the law had come from an exaggerated sense of right and wrong. He believed he could justify the crimes for which he'd been convicted. Stole a car when he was 14 (needed a ride); was busted for selling dope at 17 (needed money for prom); The assault conviction? Why, he was just acting like any gentleman would.

That cost him nearly two years. He'd said from the

witness stand he saw the accused grab the victim — she was the bully's fiancee — by the throat and shove her to the ground in the parking lot. He did 20 months for that when the judge said you can't take the law into your own hands.

But it's okay, said Evan, finding it impossible to resist being a smartass, for a bully to take a woman by the throat? The judge added another six months before banging the gavel.

He was never much bothered by jail time because he always believed there wasn't a jail on Earth that could hold him.

Watching prison movies always struck him as vocational. He couldn't get enough of "Cool Hand Luke," "Escape from Alcatraz," "Midnight Express," "Papillion," "The Green Mile," and the peerless, "Shawshank Redemption." In fact, he twice ended up busting out of jail — snuck out in the back of a garbage truck after his cellmate distracted the guards with a magic trick — and made it as far as Nashville.

Besides escape, he became adept at community service. Every time he'd get busted he'd get leniency from the courts because he by then had a portfolio of worthy accomplishments under his belt. The judges liked him because he was direct, he was charming and he was competent. And, yeah, the dude was white.

What was there not to like?

Paige and Lyberty were huddled around the computer screen trying to sort it all out, while Finder was nearby learning all she could about Elle's life on Earth.

"You can't say he's a bad guy," Paige said. "Heaven is chock-full of forgiven men and women who've dealt a bit of weed and rumbled in bars. And for 'eaven's sake, the guy he beat up for shoving the girl. How could seeing that not reminded him of his dear Mum?"

Lyberty agreed. Most men and women came to Heaven a mingled mix of good and bad. Few had spotless records. But all were forgiven; all sins, all shame vanquished. Forever and ever, amen. But still ... There had to be some point to life's decisions.

"It's impossible to overlook this December 20 business," she said. "First of all, he killed his dear Mum."

"She asked him to! He's just bein' a good son!"

"Then he killed his father!"

"Bastard had it comin'!"

"Then he killed the bartender!"

"Can't defend that one. He deserved to be winged, not whacked. But he said he was aimin' to wound him!"

"Then his homicidal negligence led to the deaths of those 33 nuns — Nuns! —and that cranky old bus driver!"

"I'm not saying there ain't some gray areas," he said with a sheepish shrug.

"And don't forget the poor cat," Lyberty reminded.

"Aye, poor little fuzzy!" he wailed in genuine pity. The cat's death got to him. Turner loved cats nearly as much as he loved breakfast waitresses.

"And then," she said, "he went and played God. Killed himself! And you know what a sin that is."

He did. Suicide was a big no-no. Lyberty looked at her friend. He was one of the most entertaining people she'd ever known, on earth or in Heaven. Always ready for lively conversation, joyful banter and a sumptuous three-hour lunch. What, she wanted to know, is there about this guy that has you so defending him, a man responsible for the extinction of 37 souls and a cat in two hours?

"The kid had one really, really bad day. And look how he started out. Poor bloke never had a chance."

"C'mon, there must be something more to it."

"There is," he said, and a twinkle began sparking his brown eyes. "He's in love! Love! Love! And love can conquer all!"

7

ELLE ALIVE

Lyberty was glad they hadn't asked Scout to do the research on Evan's life. It might have saddened her. It took a while for new arrivals to appreciate how it all worked out. If you were good and faithful on Earth, you made it to Heaven and were bestowed with an understanding that it all — all the earthly suffering, the pain and hatred — was meant to be. At least that's what everyone supposed. In fact, no one ever truly understood why being human meant being subjected to so much abundant human misery. Why couldn't Earth be more like Heaven? Why was there famine? Why was there bigotry? Why was there loneliness?

Of course, no one dwelt on it too much. Because in the grand scheme of things, a human life was microscopically brief. And, hey, as long as it wasn't happening in Heaven, who the hell cared?

"So, Pat," Lyberty said, "what did you learn about Elle?"

Two days before Pat'd died, a school psychologist had determined that Finder had Attention Deficit Hyperactivity Disorder. She would require medications and intensive focus therapy or else spend her adolescence at risk of falling behind. He was going to compile a report to send to her parents the day he heard she died, so he instead spent the magnificent fall afternoon playing golf. Shot an 86, his best round of the year.

Finder was always a bit wired, and people were fine with that. In Heaven, there were no pharmaceuticals. Eternity had a way of smoothing over every behavioral tic.

She delivered her report on Elle with the cheerful buoyancy of a TV game show host.

"Well, let's say she was an angel way before she became an angel! She was popular with the cool kids and kind to all the rest. She played the church organ every Sunday! Once, she nursed a sick pigeon back to health. And she always over-tipped all the people who waited on her! And, oh, yeah, she —"

"Pat, slow down!" Lyberty said, as Paige nodded approvingly. "Just start at the beginning."

She was born June 22, 2001, in Madison, Wisconsin. Her father was a carpenter, her mother a waitress at a local steakhouse. They never had a lot of money, she said, but they raised her with abundant love, appreciation and a joyful curiosity about everyone she met.

"Oh, and her dad was white, her mom black," she said. "So Elle's bi-racial!"

"And what," Lyberty asked, "does that have to do with anything?"

"She said she'd never forget the night her Mom came home from work crying because some rednecks at the restaurant were mean to her," Pat said. "She began reading all she could about the life of Martin Luther King Jr. The quote from her high school yearbook was from MLK: 'I believe that unarmed truth and unconditional love will have the final word in reality. That is why right, temporarily defeated, is stronger than evil triumphant.' She was like an MLK disciple."

"How'd she die, Pat?" Turner asked.

"School shooting," she said. "She grew up to become a second-grade teacher. A gunman walked in to her school and started blasting. Killed the receptionist, the principal, a custodian and four kids. Elle saw it happen and jumped on his back and held him 'til security got there. He got off one last shot before he died. Got her right in the temple. Dead before she hit the ground. Police said she died a hero. Said she saved the lives of dozens of kids. They re-named the elementary school after her."

"Can we talk to either of her parents?" he asked.

"Not yet. They're both still alive. Sort of. Losing Elle nearly killed 'em. She was their whole life. Just loved her to death. Looks like they'll never get over it."

Lyberty asked if she'd ever married.

She had not. There'd been boyfriends. In high school, she dated both the team quarterback and a burnout kid from shop class. Same in college at the hometown University of Wisconsin. She dated boys who went on to become doctors, mechanics, musicians, roofers, librarians, construction foremen, a wrestling coach and one kid who became a Hollywood hair stylist.

"Everyone loved Elle and Elle loved everyone," Finder said.

She told stories about how she volunteered to spend chat time with lonely seniors at the local center, and about how she oversaw the watering and care of the civic garden at the "Welcome To Madison!" town sign. She was active in church, delivered for Meals on Wheels, and was a card-carrying volunteer member supporting Habitat for Humanity, the Salvation Army, Angel Arms, Sierra Club, and she served as a volunteer weekend docent at the Madison Museum of Fine Art.

"And here's a picture from the front page of the Wisconsin State Journal of her stopping traffic on downtown so a mother duck and her eight babies could safely make it across McCaffery Drive to Lake Wingra," Scout said. "And the story says she came back later that day and constructed a ramp so the ducks could get over a stretch of gravel she feared would be too hard on their tender little duck feet."

Paige let out a slow respectful whistle. "When it comes to helping humanity, she makes some of the actual saints I've met seem like pikers. Imagine how she'd have helped the world had she lived to be 30? 50? 75? Imagine the kids she'd have raised. A girl like that could've maybe changed the world."

"And now," Lyberty said, "she's trying to change the afterworld."

Lyberty and Paige wondered what could lead her to breech such a taboo as sacrosanct as the one between mingling Heaven and Hell.

"I think it's a combination of things," Finder said. "She's got a really good heart and, geez, this Evan guy's got a dynamite smile."

"Stranger things have happened," Turner said.

"Just never here before," Lyberty replied. "I'm talking ever."

Both Lyberty and Turner fell silent as they began contemplating what they should do next. Together, they'd been in Heaven for more than 300 years and this was the first time either'd felt a sense of restless urgency, that they were nearing a precipice.

Pat had other things on her mind. "When do we get Jesus and God involved?" She was excited. She was sure she'd get a little face time with The Father and The Son, something she'd dreamed of since starting Sunday school. "I mean, isn't this the kind of thing the Big Guys should be handling?"

Their concentration interrupted, both Lyberty and Turner took a moment to reorient their thoughts to what to them was a question they never bothered to consider. They paused to look one another in the eye.

Then they busted out laughing.

8

ELLE IN HEAVEN

Elle rose that morning, as she did every morning, at 6:30 a.m. to George Harrison playing the intro to the Beatles "Here Comes The Sun." It was a perfectly cheerful way to start every day in Heaven, and a reminder that on that day George had promised to teach her how to play the sitar. She kept her phone on a nightstand next to her bed and beside a picture of her and her Mom and Dad. Taken when she was 6, she thought back then her world couldn't get any more perfect.

She really missed them.

She threw on some work-out clothes and bounded down the stairs of her loft above the Natural Food Emporium where her friend, Doug Root, the building's owner, worked selling things like organic squash and other superfoods that on Earth were edible to only the fanatically fit. She got on her bike and began pedaling the 5.7 miles to her favorite gym.

She didn't need to exercise. In Heaven, no one did. All personal appearance factors — weight, age, hair fullness/color, etc — could be determined each morning. It was like deciding what you were going to wear. Now, there was even an app for it.

She was 24 and she liked being 24. Maybe one day she'd want to try being older, but like most people, she remained the age she was when she gained her heavenly admission. It just felt right. There were popular theme parks that allowed for elaborate role play where you could be any age or anyone you wanted for as long as you chose.

But Elle was content being Elle. She worked out because she believed the better she took care of herself the better she could take care of others. And that's just what she did. It's what she'd always done.

She spent her days teaching pre-schoolers how to read, urbanites how to garden, and former drunks how to waltz. She gave piano lessons to one-armed soldiers, scrapbooking tips to retired steel workers and wine appreciation to suds suckers. Every day was a festival of refinement.

Today, Elle was looking forward to teaching the cavemen and cavewomen how to play Jenga. Admitting early humans to Heaven had been controversial. Their very existence went against so much Christian theology. But it wasn't their fault they'd been born before they had a chance to be saved. They had souls, albeit primitive ones, but souls, indeed. So one day it was decided, sure, come on in. And a caveman in Heaven was very low-maintenance. Give any caveman four walls, a ceiling and basic cable and, boom, they're in caveman heaven. They were very simple folk.

So Elle devoted much of her afterlife to helping others. She kept so busy, too, in part because it distracted her from thinking about Evan, and waiting for his next illicit communications. She suspected she wasn't the only one. Evan would never have found her profile had not one of the Russian hackers left his terminal unattended. Evan told her some newly arrived Russian hackers were working round-the-clock to take a stab at making Heaven less holier-than-thou, to more or less bring it down to Earth. To destabilize it.

It had certainly destabilized her. All her life, she'd been truly good. She didn't want to be sinful. It wasn't until after she'd died she'd begun to feel a yearning to experience things like getting good and drunk, and having some raunchy sex that might or might not lead to the conception of a child. She wanted to feel love and heartbreak and hangover.

It's wasn't that Elle wanted to be bad.

She just wanted to be human.

Once you died and went to Heaven, that was pretty much impossible. It's what she was thinking about that morning when she stopped in at The Has Beans coffee shop for her morning java. It was one of her favorite parts of the day. She enjoyed checking her Facebook to see if Evan had sent her any day-brightening notes. On this pleasant, sunny day the place was packed. She managed to find a two-seater in the back and plunked her stuff down on the side nearest the wall.

Evan could go weeks without computer access, she knew, and then dispatch a flurry of notes that were alternately funny, charming, literate, wise and sexy. He always knew exactly what to say.

When she told him she felt foolish dreaming of their togetherness, he responded, "True dreamers fly kites with no strings attached."

She told him she was looking to do something different for her monthly art appreciation club, something offbeat. He replied, "Tell them you've opened a new art gallery. Invite them to a big room with nothing on the walls and be greeted by 40 guys who say nothing but, 'Hi! I'm Art!'"

Part of her attraction was rooted in her bedrock belief that all sins should be forgiven. It had been her experience that those most difficult to love were always the ones who needed love most.

She'd never met anyone like him on Earth. He was a hell of a catch.

That was the problem.

Today, nothing.

She wished she had someone with whom she could confide. It'd been two years since his introductory confession and she'd never told a soul. She felt like Juliet from "Romeo and Juliet"; like Maria from "West Side Story"; like Miss Piggy in "Muppets: Most Wanted." She hadn't set out to fall in love. She was just trying to be understanding, to bridge a divide, to mend a fence, to do what just came naturally. There was so much she wanted to share.

Alas, was there no one with whom she could share her innermost thoughts?

"Is this seat taken?" It was a sweet-smiling woman in her mid-50s. She had an armload of books and smelled vaguely of lavender.

"Please, sit down," she said, smiling. "I'm Elle. I just found this place. It's wonderful. Great staff and you always meet someone fun. You just missed Rodney Dangerfield."

"Oh, he's hilarious," she said. She began stirring her coffee, paused and looked up. "I've heard about you, Elle. Aren't you the hero teacher from that school shooting?"

"Oh, I've never felt very heroic. I did what I could. It was one of those terrible days, but everyone here made me feel so welcome. They say everything happens for a reason, but no one's ever been able to tell me a sensible reason for a day like that."

She absentmindedly sipped her coffee.

"You know," she said, "I met the shooter right here in Has Beans about a month after we both got here. Came right up and introduced himself. Nice guy. He was so, so sorry. Really remorseful. He just felt terrible. Poor kid came from a broken home. His dad beat him. Mom was on drugs. He never had a chance. Just breaks your heart."

"Tell me about it," the blonde stranger sighed. "So much of our lives on Earth were so hard. You wonder how anyone ever makes it through a single day."

Elle, her empathetic sixth sense alert as ever, said, "Sounds like you knew some tough times."

"Oh, boy, did I," she said.

"Did he kill you?"

"No. He did beat the hell out of me. My son, too, I'm ashamed to admit. That sweet kid deserved so much better. I should have done more to protect him. I stayed with my husband for way too many years and for way too many beatings. I eventually left him, but he never left us. It sounds terrible, but my own son — the one I loved and who loved me more than anyone else — was the one who killed me. But that's another story."

She kind of chuckled, bemused at the homicidal irony.

"Oh, geez, Elle. Where are my manners? I'm Lola. Pleased to meetcha!"

9

EVAN IN HELL

"Say, 'Good morning, asshole!'"

"Good morning, Daddy."

And right there was when the daily fights commenced. Evan would start by telling Rusty what an awful father he'd been, what a maggot of a husband he was, and how he was such a lousy human being he deserved to be in Hell for all eternity. He'd recount in vivid detail all the beatings and horrors, the times Rusty came home drunk and locked the boy in the bedroom closet while he beat his beloved mother with his belt, her screams searing his soul. He remembered tears so hot he thought they'd groove grief gutters down his cheeks. He told him he was in Hell because he was a miserable failure as a father, as a husband as a human being in general.

"And you're here because you killed me!" Rusty would say before laughing maniacally.

The fact grated on Evan, for sure. He never once had thought of himself as a "bad" guy deserving of Hell. He instead had thought of himself as a non-conformist libertarian with zero tolerance for bullies and injustice. He thought his capital crimes — three murders and 34 vehicular homicides — all came with extenuating circumstances. His mother asked to die, his father deserved to die and Billy Leonard had it coming. He was just a total asshole.

The 33 nuns and the bus driver, well, that was just colossally bad luck. But any Earth jury would have certainly frowned on the heavenly tally. It was the same in Heaven. Accident or not, they couldn't overlook the quality of the victims. Killing a nun, even one with a gambling addiction, crossed a bright line. Killing 33 of them was going a tad too far. An example must be made. The bus driver, Steven Richards, was just a garden-variety jackass. He cheated on his wife, used the company credit card for personal expenses, and had been getting away with driving buzzed for years.

But he never killed no nun. Not even one nun. Or nun one.

Evan spent a lot of his rack time wondering if he'd be where he was if the bus he'd run off the road had been full of, say, 33 convicts. Or politicians. Or maybe dentists.

Would they send you to Hell for having a role in killing 32 NFL owners and the league commissioner?

And Evan lost points for killing himself, too. But it had been a difficult day, and he'd really had quite enough. Putting his old man's gun in his mouth and pulling the trigger seemed at the time the only sensible option. He regretted it every single day.

It provided plenty of fodder over which to philosophize and that's exactly what he did for hours on end with one of Hell's few truly worldly philosophers. The real thing. Pure Original Gangster.

His name was Judas Iscariot.

Hell had scores of fallen clergy, mostly men who'd used

their position to dupe the faithful into giving them money, drugs, property or blowjobs. They'd used their relationship with Jesus Christ to further mortal ambitions or satisfy their carnal lusts. Judas was the only one who'd used his relationship with Jesus Christ to fulfill the prophecy that led to the murder of Jesus Christ. He was one of the worst villains in human history. Evan found him so fascinating and didn't mind that Judas was also one of those guys who always asked and answered his own questions.

"Do I regret my infamous role in killing The Prince of Peace? Sure, I do," he'd told Evan in the cafeteria one day over flavorless Salisbury Steak. All the worst chefs prepared the meals in Hell.

"Do I feel like I deserve to spend all eternity in Hell? I do not," he said. Judas was a big man with a deep voice so resonant Evan hoped he'd one day hear him sing, "Old Man River," which at the moment would have been preferable to "Billy Don't Be a Hero," a cloying 1974 anti-war song by Paper Lace. Judas had dark curly hair, chiseled features, and a physical and seasoned stature that commanded respect.

"I believe I'm deserving of redemption. I was a really swell apostle for all those years — and that should count for something. But all anyone remembers is the betrayal, the goddamned 30 pieces of silver. Blah, blah, blah."

He told Evan his eternal circumstances sometimes led him to feel a kinship with baseball hit king Pete Rose, who'd been banished from the Hall of Fame for betting on baseball.

Judas had once been Satan's drinking buddy, but as he began to more and more exercise his free will more and more, to assert himself and to question Satan's reign, he fell out of favor, and Satan sent him to Time Out. Hell's Time

Out was a place where all the worst torments of Hell awaited. Way worse than "Billy Don't Be a Hero."

It's not mentioned in any of life's Biblical guidebooks, but even Hell has a Hell.

Judas told Evan the last man he remembered getting dragged off into Time Out was John Wilkes Booth. Satan, he'd said, had gotten fed up hearing the assassin whine that the critics of his one-man plays were all boors and cretins, which was wholly accurate. Not only were the people in Hell pure evil, many of them were just run-of-the-mill morons, even if they were dead right. It's one reason why Judas talked in ways that made it seem like he was always talking to himself. Articulators in Hell were rarer than snowballs.

"Do I wish," Judas asked rhetorically aloud, "that the collective IQ in Hell were higher than 75? Indeed, I do. You can go 100 years without an intelligent conversation. The poverty of wit either dulls or sharpens the intellect. I like to think in my 2,000 years here I've become more thoughtful, more considerate."

Evan looked across the cafeteria and noticed his grinning father was giving him the finger. Both fingers. And he was bobbing them up and down.

Such an asshole.

"I've tried to better myself," Judas said, "to be worthy of my human life back before my impetuous — and as I like to point out, my *pre-ordained* — betrayal turned me into history's greatest scapegoat."

It always surprised Evan that Judas carried himself with so much Zen-like dignity. Evan had known him for two years and never once seen him lose his cool. And losing your cool in Hell was not uncommon. Sure, it wasn't the proverbial Lake of Fire, but it was still Hell.

Judas had right away taken an interest in Evan, often seeking out his company for conversations that tickled his intellect. Plus, Judas just liked knowing what was going on. He'd often relate his intel with Satan, but bristled when The Lord of Darkness called him "my spy."

"I spy for no one," he said. "I'm just doin' what comes naturally."

Part of that was gabbing with Evan. He asked Evan if he'd had a relationship with Jesus. He had not.

"Man, I was just concerned with one life at a time," Evan said. "I just tried to get by not hurting anyone who wasn't hurting anyone else. I spent my days laughing and joking. Most days I spent my life just happy being human. Even despite all my troubles and anger issues, I felt life could be such a gift.

"Kind of ironic then, I guess, I spent my last two hours on Earth ending so much of it. Yeah, I wish I'd had Jesus in my life, but fate figured different. I wasn't raised with Christ in my life. It was my misfortune that the most dominant personality in my life is that guy doing an obscene puppet show with his middle fingers."

Judas looked up and three tables away he saw Rusty doing middle finger pantomime. He glanced back at Evan and felt an alien emotion. He felt pity. Most of the men and all of the women in Hell, he felt had it coming. But Evan seemed worthy of divine forgiveness. After all, wasn't all human nature divined by God?

"Can I relate? Of course, I can. Think about me. I was once BFFs with Jesus Christ. People think of Jesus and automatically think, 'Savior,' like that kind of holy designation summed Him all up. But, man, Jesus was just a great guy before He'd ever even saved a single soul. I remember spending days fishing with him, just the two of us. All we did was laugh. The man could sure tell a joke. God, I still miss him."

Evan let the frail reverie play out a while. When Judas returned to the present, Evan asked a question he'd been dying to ask.

"Say, anyone ever bust out of this joint?"

"Has anyone ever busted out of Hell?" Judas reiterated, his voice lowering to a confidential hush. "You'll want to be careful asking questions like that. People caught talking escape get thrown into Time Out. Some never come back. But it has been done. Once. "

Then Judas told Evan the story of Arthur Thou.

It was later that day that Judas persuaded Evan to start a blog about how to persevere through Hell.

"People will pay you for it, and there will be advertisers," Judas said. "It'll turn into a real money maker."

Neither eventuality came true, of course. It was, after all, just one more godforsaken blog and nobody in their right mind would ever pay shit for one of those.

But it allowed Judas to get in Evan's head, and that was Judas's whole point.

10

TURNER AT HIS HEAVENLY PUB

Asking Paige Turner to choose between his library and his pub was like asking a mother to choose between her children. Growing up formal education was, for him, an impossible dream. There were no books. No teachers. No cerebral instruction. There was only his fellow man, and to Turner each person was a master's class full of insights for him to absorb. London in the 19th Century was full of colorful and witty blokes for whom the everyday world was a magnificent canvas upon which they could paint. There were chimney sweeps, colliers, masons, quarrymen, and —best of all — sailors, men who'd seen the world. And Turner was alert with observation. His class circumstances meant he'd be denied book-learning, but nothing could prevent him from being street-schooled.

His father had died in a London cholera epidemic in 1865 (they'd since become BFFs), which left him at age 14 the proprietor of a small East End family market. Upon taking charge, the first thing he did was eliminate the shelves and their stocks of egg, flour, and cracker and replace them with a bar carved from an old plank from a discarded oak trunk.

It took a full six weeks to completely transform from pantry to pub. It could have been done in half that time had he and Mick Townsend, his carpenter, not agreed to cease working every time Mick's mutt, Sparky, surrendered to whimsical canine fatigue and plopped down to nap right in the middle of the daily construction.

"Let sleepin' dogs lie," Mick would say, "and I'll take a pint while 'e's on the snooze."

The work took so long the pub was known as The Lyin' Sleepin' Dog before it ever even opened. The people, the work and the bubbly conversation made The Dog the place Turner most wanted to spend all his time. A close second was The London Library. He remembers being awed when a worldly sailor told him what he most looked forward to upon returning from overseas wasn't resuming church attendance with his mum and dad, going to a bawdy house, or spending pub time with his mates.

What he most dreamed of, he said, was spending long afternoons at The London Library.

"It's free," he said. "They have books on any subject and you can just sit there and revel in your reading. You can read Swift, Shakespeare, Chaucer — just the other day, I was there and met ol' Charlie Dickens 'isself."

Turner felt an ache so poignant it practically shed tears. He yearned to be educated, to learn, to read. He vowed right then he'd one day open a pub right next door to a great library so he could have the very best of both worlds. He was sure it would be his idea of Heaven. It was. There was just no way it could happen in London.

True heaven can only truly happen in Heaven.

Hence, Turner was distressed when he told Aziz he'd be in charge for the foreseeable future. He reveled in lively bar conversation and knew this Evan and Elle business meant he'd miss out on so much. He could be having all the fun in the world, but it would agitate him if he suspected anyone somewhere else was having even a bit of fun without him.

He best loved the nights when they speculated over what was in all the suggestion boxes, if anyone read the suggestions and if anyone would ever act on the most popular ones. All The Dog patrons were adamant that the No. 1 suggestion on how to improve Heaven involved letting people in Heaven have consensual sex. Everyone missed sex. They thought about all the time. Dreamed of it. Yearned for it. But many said sex in Heaven would make the afterlife too messy. There'd be just too much jealousy, possessiveness, vindictiveness and petty retribution. Heaven would become Hell.

Still, many argued all that was a small price to pay for the chance to splash around in love's cuddle puddle. And it seemed natural because almost everyone in Heaven was single.

Sure, you could stay married to your Earth spouse, but you couldn't cheat. Couldn't divorce. And you had to stay married forever and ever. Amen. Being married on earth for 50 years was a golden achievement. But 50 years in eternity was barely a tick or two. Until death us do part was one thing where death was certainty. It was different where all death was vanquished.

No one counseled newcomers on staying married. It was just so old-fashioned. As Earth-like as the cavemen.

Most of the relations were purely Platonic, including Plato's, which was significant because it was assumed that, any time he flirted with a woman, he could get away with it by saying it was at heart a Platonic act.

How could it be anything but?

Plato liked to hang out at The Dog because he, Socrates

and Aristotle, also regulars, considered Paige Turner a peer. And Turner's opinion carried a great deal of weight. He was just so well read and always had the perfect quote ready to settle every argument.

And Paige had instant recall of every witty observation he'd ever overheard in the bar. "Remember, it was Socrates who said, 'By all means marry. If you get a good wife, you'll become happy. If you get a bad one, you'll become a philosopher.'"

"And Socrates says, 'Please pass me the pretzels,'" said Socrates.

But the philosophical topic that most engaged Paige and Aziz was eternity. It was endlessly fascinating. Earth lifespans were so fleeting, minuscule, really. And Heaven had only been really cranking for 2,000 years since Jesus held his first open house. In Earth terms, it was almost too monumental to consider. But in eternity terms? Two thousand years were nothing, a really small drop in a really big bucket. So were 4,000 years. So were 10,000. A million. A billion. A trillion. No number was big enough to bully eternity.

"Socrates says, 'You think you can tell time,'" Socrates said. "'Time tells you!' And, geez, who the heck is hogging the pretzels?"

Out of profound respect for the man, Aziz got off his stool and went behind the bar and got the old philosopher a bowl of pretzels.

"Thank you!" Socrates said. Even when he wasn't profound, he was at least polite.

On Earth, Aziz knew, he'd been a very common man. In Heaven, he could become a great one. Not overnight certainly. But one day.

These things took time.

11

ELLE & LOLA AT THE HAS BEANS COFFEE SHOP

People knew Elle. People loved Elle. People watched Elle. Thus, when Elle spit a misty mouthful of warm coffee toward the table to her right, conversation stopped and every head at Has Beans turned. She wiped her mouth with her forearm and locked eyes with her friendly tablemate. "Your name is Lola and you say your son killed you?"

"That's right," Lola said, smiling, but unsure.

"Is his name Evan?"

"It is," Lola said, suddenly alive with excitement. "Did you know my son?"

The Lord worked in mysterious ways, Elle thought. On Earth as it is in Heaven, too. She glanced around the room and began to feign nonchalance while her soul felt electrified.

"I think I knew a guy who knew a guy, that sort of thing," Elle said. "I'll have to tell you about it later. It's funny, really. I'm sure you'll get a kick out of it."

Lola felt a little rattled by Elle's sudden change. She couldn't bear hearing any harsh news about her boy. "I hope so," she said. "I'm in a support group for parents of children in Hell. It helps a little, but my heart still aches for him. I loved him so much. There's nothing I wouldn't do for him. Would trade places with him in a minute if I could."

Elle asked if she had any plans that day.

"No," Lola said, at once flattered and apprehensive by all the sudden interest. "I was just planning on heading home to feed my cat and then over to the library. What do you have in mind?"

"Let's go for a walk. I'd like to get to know you better."

"Okay. Around here?"

"No, let's make it special," Elle said. "Are you a beach person or a would you rather stroll the mountains?"

Lola told her neither. In fact, on her walks she enjoyed seeing iconic cities from around the world. She mentioned she'd walked in Central Park, Rio, London and Budapest. She was looking forward to spending her early years of eternity becoming acquainted with the great metropolises from throughout history.

"Ever been to San Francisco?" Elle asked.

She had not.

"Why don't we meet there? We can do the Golden Gate Bridge. It's lovely this time of year."

"Sounds great, Elle. See you there at let's say noon." Lola began to gather her things.

"Perfect. That'll give me time to go tend to my stuff, and you can go home and feed your Copycat."

Lola came to a halt. "How do you know my cat's name is Copy?"

"I didn't." Elle's eyes did that shifty thing human eyes involuntarily do when they're busted in a lie. "I didn't say Copy."

"Uh, yes, you did. I heard you. Clearly. You said, 'and you can go home, and feed your Copycat.'"

She couldn't backtrack so she tried to bury her original lie with another even less artful one. "I said crappy. What I said was you can go home and feed your crappy cat. I don't like cats. It's rude of me, I know, but I refer to all cats as crappy cats," Elle burbled. "It's not nice, I know, but it's just a habit. My mom had like 15 cats, and they were always crapping all over the place. I just hate cats."

A snoopy patron live-Facebooked the whole conversation, and it was soon a minor scandal among social media observers who'd thought Elle was perfect and incapable of saying anything mean even when the object of her derision was a crappy Copycat.

∼

Elle called George Harrison and told him, sorry, mate, she'd be unable to attend that week's sitar lesson. Could they reschedule? Sure thing, he said. "I'll be jamming later this evening with Carl Perkins and Jerry Lee Lewis. Stop by if you can. There's a rumor Elvis is going to sing."

She told him she'd try.

"And what's this," he said, "I hear 'bout you saying all cats are crappy?"

"Oh, that's Fake News. Don't believe everything you read on Facebook," she said. "That's being blown way out of proportion. I'm finding myself a bit under a microscope here. People pay attention to every single thing I say or do. You have no idea what it's like."

"Sounds to me like 1962 through '70," he said. "Don't let it go to your head, kid."

"I won't," she said with a giggle.

"Oh, and, Elle, promise me you'll never hint you're even bigger than Jesus."

"I promise!"

They said goodbye.

∼

THERE IS on Earth a big orange bridge at the spot where everyone says to look for the Golden Gate. Opened in 1937, The Golden Gate Bridge is one of the world's most iconic landmarks. There is an $8 toll to cross the bridge in a motor vehicle; $7 if the motorist is taking advantage of FasTrak technology. The steel suspension bridge, until 1964 the longest of its kind in the world, links San Francisco and Sausalito via six lanes of U.S. Route 101. Crossing the 1.7-mile bridge on foot is a bucket list phenomenon for millions of pedestrians each year.

And it's been a kick-the-bucket phenomenon for more than 1,500 depressed and suicidal humans who've felt they simple couldn't go on another day. These men, women, boys and girls, ignore 24 liberally stationed Crisis Counseling signs that emphatically urge:

> ***There is Hope***
> ***Make the Call***
> ***The Consequences of***
> ***Jumping From This Bridge***
> ***Are Fatal***
> ***And Tragic***

The blue signs with white lettering contrast sharply with the Sherwin Williams shade known as International Orange that gives the bridge its distinctive color. Look carefully in the background of pictures of people getting engaged and otherwise celebrating life, and you're bound to see one of the blue signs and, perhaps, a depressed man or woman who is contemplating disobeying it.

Experts have calculated jumpers fall 245 feet straight down for 4 seconds before hitting the water at 75 mph. The impact instantly kills all but 5 percent of the jumpers. Those who survive the splat usually drown or die from hypothermia in the 60-degree waters of the San Francisco Bay.

Only 2 percent of all jumpers survive. With near unanimity, survivors have told crisis counselors their first thought immediately after hurtling into space is along the lines of, "My God. I'm so, so sorry. What have I done?"

The Golden Gate Bridge in Heaven has no tolls and no vehicles. It's never cold, it never rains and the roadbed is see-through. Pedestrians and cyclists provide the only traffic so it's never crowded and, thus, there's zero chance of road rage. Every once in a while, a stilt-walking juggler will bump into an awestruck ambler, but it's always chill. No one gets pissed.

There's no strife, no sadness, or dismay. There's no apprehension, agitation, melancholy, low self-esteem, or bad hair days. And on The Golden Gate Bridge in Heaven, there are no suicide counseling signs. Why would there be? There's no unhappiness. It's simply Heaven, and on days like the one Lola met Elle there it was Heaven with a really spectacular view.

Carefree travel was one of the great perks of Heaven. Unlike on Earth, a trans-continental trip to San Francisco didn't require scouring websites for dodgy deals or fine-print coupons. It didn't require securing a favor-swapping friend to come over twice a day to take the dog out. You didn't have to fight rush-hour traffic to make your flight. You didn't need to wait in the TSA lines, remove your shoes, shed your belt, open your laptop, subject yourself to the indignity of intimate pat- downs.

You didn't need to wait for your row to be called, glumly stand in line only to engage in carry-on combat to get your bag into the overhead or fight your way clear back to seat 23B.

In Heaven, if you chose to travel, all you needed to do was decide in your mind where and when you wanted to go and simply blink your eyes. Souls pack light. Heaven was Heaven. But, folks being folks, the suggestion boxes still had plenty of notes from people bitching about how there ought to be frequent flier miles.

Lola was on the Presidio side when Elle got there. She'd been there for an hour, just enjoying the sights and making happy chat with the old man selling Italian ices. They each bought one — Elle's was root beer; Lola, Tutti-Fruiti — tipped the kindly gent a five and climbed the steps to the Golden Gate proper.

After about two minutes of perfunctory small talk about how wonderful everything in Heaven always is, Elle cut right to the chase.

"I've fallen in love with your son," she said. "I know he's in Hell, I know he killed a bunch of people, and I know it's wrong. And, yeah, I know he killed you and your cat — and I'm so, so sorry I called Copy crappy — but I can't help myself. I've never felt the way I feel about Evan about anyone else in my entire life. He's all I think about."

Lola was simultaneously stunned and quietly delighted. She'd disdained all of Evan's girlfriends, figuring none of them were good enough for her boy. But Elle was a real angel, and a popular angel at that. She regarded her son as a people person, a real man's man, but Elle, well, she was an angel's angel.

She told Lola of the day her friends and scores of admiring strangers began out-of-the-blue reaching out to her after Evan's fraudulent post that Elle needed money. Most suspected it was the ruse it turned out to be, but responded anyway. Phishing scams in Heaven, while exceedingly rare, weren't unheard of and, it being Heaven and full of kindly innocents, people responded the best they could. Elle remembered being inundated with sincere good wishes and noodle casseroles.

"Then I got a note from Evan," she said. "He apologized and said it had all been part of a scam and that he was, in fact, in Hell." Elle knew she was supposed to be repulsed. She was supposed to shun, to ostracize, rebuff or isolate. At the very least report him to the Heavenly equivalent of the mortal Mark Zuckerberg. She did none of those things.

Instead, she reached out, letting her native need to nurture prevail. She allowed herself to be drawn in. Evan told her he was lonely and just needed a friend. He told her, yes, he deserved to be in Hell — but that didn't mean he was a bad dude. He had no one to blame but himself, he said, a contention that made Lola reflexively roll her eyes. There was plenty of blame to go around. Most of it was on his father, sure, but some of it, she felt, belonged on her. And, yeah, Lola couldn't understand what that busload of nuns was doing coming back from a casino on a Monday afternoon either.

What? Were all the Ohio orphans suddenly unburdened by the need for further religious instruction?

"I was really attracted to his honesty," Elle said. "Other than the initial whopper, he never once tried to deceive me about either his past or his intentions. When I asked what had made him so honest, he said, 'The more we acknowledge our own perceived flaws the more slight become our actual flaws.' It seemed so profound. I began to sense his being sent to Hell may have been a mistake. I mean, couldn't he have been forgiven?"

It was all very surreal, otherwordly, to Lola. What she wanted to know was more down to Earth. "Did he say anything about forgiving me?"

Elle was taken aback. "Oh, Lola," she said. "There's nothing to forgive. You meant the world to him. Without your love, he'd have been lost. Those who feel pain feel alive. Those who feel nothing become nothing."

"I can't help but thinking if I hadn't asked him to kill me, none of those other people would have died. Maybe I should have toughed it out. I wanted to spare him from having to care for me, but my actions led directly to my boy, the one I loved more than life itself, being cast into Hell."

Elle said, "I asked him about that, if he's sorry it wasn't handled differently. He said, 'Families are God's way of proving we can't help even the ones we love the very most.'"

"He said that? I swear, I don't know where that boy got his smarts."

Elle recalled telling Evan how often petty jealousies on Earth had led to shattered friendships. "Then he said, 'The pessimist bemoans all the traitors who've thrown him under the bus. The optimist thinks one day he'll make a really swell bus mechanic.' He was just so cheerful."

But her favorite, she said, was one that most touched her soul and in her eyes elevated his. "I asked if he could live his life all over again, what would he do? He right away said, 'I'd enjoy being human, and I'd enjoy human beings.' To me, that is life itself."

She wanted to tell Lola about Evan's misfortune in cellmate assignment, but she didn't want to ruin her mood. Lola was beaming at hearing stories of how her boy had really made something out of himself. Even if it was in Hell. She asked if she'd ever seen a picture of him.

"I did," Elle said. "And that's what really did it. I took one look and felt my insides turn to warm butter. That sideways grin, that curly brown hair, and that devil-may-care look about him. I know how wrong it is on so many levels, but I fell in lust with him before I fell in love with him. He's just so damned hot."

Neither of them allowed the irony of describing a guy in Hell as "hot" to intrude on their individual reveries, both deep for vastly different reasons. Lola loved Evan, her wayward son, as only a mother could. She'd forgive his sins and exalt his virtues.

With Elle, it felt oddly animal. She'd died a sexual virgin, but her existential innocence crashed other human borders. She loved him. She wanted to save him. She wanted to be his bride. She wanted what no other woman in the afterlife had ever sought. She ached. Satan was the one with demonic antlers, but Elle was the one who felt truly horny.

Lola believed she understood and to a degree, she did. But to a much larger degree, she never could. She couldn't appreciate a mortal fear that a primal yearning could go unsatisfied for eternity. She couldn't understand the depths of Elle's feelings as her new friend stared intently over the railing and down 245 feet into the 60-degree waters of San Francisco Bay.

12

REALM OF THE ROAMERS

Arthur Thou IV recollected often of the days, years, before his self-redemption. Before he blazed his own trail in the realm where silent conformity was the rule. That was back when he devoted most of his intelligence to trying NOT to think.

He'd tell himself over and over to NOT think about sex, NOT think about food, NOT think about conversation and to NOT maybe think what existence would be like if maybe he had a companion dog or even a mostly inanimate pet turtle. So, he tried not to think at all. It was just one foot in front of the other, over and over again. It's all it would ever be. One foot in front of the other. No pausing to refresh. No contemplation. No reflection. No thought.

Left. Right. Left. Right. Left. Right. On and on and on, an eternal march through timeless tedium.

While others were destined to go on like that forever, he was not.

Rather than not think, Thou began to do just the opposite. He began to think the ever-lovin' crap out of everything.

It was in his bones. He began to apply his free-range mind to all the big topics.

What is the meaning of life? Are all sins forgivable? And, yeah, if fans of the Grateful Dead are called Deadheads, what did that make those who revered the book "Moby-Dick."

And that was mostly what he'd been doing since he'd busted out of Hell in 1976. He couldn't believe it'd worked. He was free. The torments of Hell were no more. He felt soulful relief. Liberated. Thus, it was all very surprising when he'd soon begun feeling homesick. Because he'd escaped not to Earth or certainly Heaven. It wasn't even purgatory. No, he'd escaped to the vast and somnambulant Realm of the Roamers.

For a man who'd spent so many years amidst the plodding Roamer masses, it was still fair to declare Art Thou dashing. Like on Earth, he still cared about his appearance. He'd snatched swatches of cloth from other Roamers to piece together a big floppy red hat that looked like something that would have looked right at home in one of Dr. Seuss's books.

On Earth, he'd been defiantly non-conformist. In the Roamer realm, he was one among, gee, maybe billions?

Thou spent his Earth-time as an amoral party animal. Handsome with a surfer's lean build and charismatic enough to get away with stuff, he'd raised plenty of Hell long before he'd become a resident.

He'd been raised to believe everyone was either good or bad and went accordingly to Heaven or Hell. He'd loved life, but felt no spiritual pressure to be conventionally "good." He didn't fear Hell on the grounds that he'd have more friends there.

To him, the biggest sin wasn't to live badly, but to live not at all. And that's the mindset that got him dispatched to Hell in the first place. Despite his best intentions, he still thought of it often.

It was 1967. The Summer of Love. It was the Beatles, The Stones, The Who and The Kinks. Women were taking birth control pills and setting fire to their bras. Everyone he knew was getting high, getting laid and growing their hair long. Martin Luther King Jr. and Bobby Kennedy were preaching peace, equality and freedom. It was glorious time to be alive. And it was then he began killing people for failing to realize it.

To him, the homicides were justifiable. He saw no sin in murdering men and women who didn't appreciate life. He objected, sure, to the crew-cut meatheads who believed the Vietnam War, Jim Crow and white male dominance were swell ideas, but at least they'd engaged in cognitive thought.

His mortal beef was with the people who'd sleepwalked through their entire lives, those who chose to live in the gray. They didn't read. They didn't exalt. They didn't cheer, rage, aspire or create. They shed not a tear when Lassie saved the little boy who'd fallen down the well. For them he felt nothing but contempt. Arthur figured 40 percent of the people were good or borderline decent; 40 percent were mostly bad; and the remaining 20 percent were neither one or the other and thus didn't deserve to live. Killing eight of them, as he did from 1967 though '68, did nothing to change those rough percentages. It did land him in Hell in 1969 after he'd overdosed on LSD and chased a hallucinatory psychedelic butterfly with giant boobs straight off a fifth-floor party roof.

The murders were never solved. And the big-breasted butterfly, if it exists, remains at large. At very large. The LSD was of a potent dosage.

The irony was that he escaped Hell, where he'd been sent for killing people for whom life had no appeal, only to wind up immersed in the very people for whom he held such homicidal contempt.

These were the Roamers. Neither saved nor damned, they were more like the souls of the no-one-gives-a-damn. Not good enough for Heaven, but too mundane for Hell, they were eternity's clerical errors. They'd shuffled though life on autopilot, resistant to all Earth's charms and indifferent to its entertaining vices. They never noted a sunset, paused to appreciate the charms of an autumn afternoon or revel in the cheers of a saloon league softball championship. Instead, they merely limped through life, indifferent to all the wonders and woes that make even a brief life such a sweet morsel.

He figured there must be billions of them, empty vessels who did nothing to add to Earth's palette and now in this twilight afterlife did nothing but add gridlock to an endless commute that went from nowhere destined to no place special.

He'd long since realized the folly of his crime.

You just can't kill what never lived.

And it was during this revelation that he'd begun to contemplate an alien emotion. He began to contemplate compassion. He'd begun fledgling efforts to animate Roamers who seemed to have the flicker of a candle stuck in their pumpkins. This thinking coincided with when he began experiencing feelings of remorse. Who was he to play God? And couldn't the Roamers be saved?

If so, it would have to be up to him. As far as he knew, he was the only one capable of speech or initiative. The rest all behaved like insects in the ant farm, mindlessly treading over the same beaten ground over and over again and again.

He felt if he could just speak directly to them he'd break through and begin to effect some change.

If he could reach even one and jostle him — or her — into consciousness, he was sure he could resume meaningful conversation and that could make all the difference in the afterworld.

Because what he craved most was companionship.

All in all, it made him miss what he'd had. He was truly homesick.

Homesick for Hell. Plus, he had some scores to settle.

Thus, he was totally unprepared the day he felt a tap on his shoulder and turned around in time to see a pouty pair of lips lunging for his. Caught completely off guard, he did what any man — but no real Roamer — would do.

He kissed back.

It was a long, probing kiss, very soulful. But how could it be anything but?

When they finally came up for air and it was time for proper introductions, she said her name was Bea Long and she wanted to know if Thou felt like kissing. Or as she put it, "Kissin'!"

He said he did and they resumed their intimacy.

A really good kiss between a couple who share a romantic spark can be every bit as meaningful as intercourse. Neither Bea nor Art had kissed in ages so both felt a bit let down when they came to the conclusion that there was no spark. After an awkward moment, they both realized the kisses, so long dreamed of, did not detonate because what they were most eager to do with the other was talk.

Later, they would joke about how they met and acknowledge that the kisses had been pathetic. Bea, who'd grow to revere Thou said, looking back, it was almost like The Lone Ranger kissing Tonto.

"Or," he said, "The Lone Ranger kissing Silver!" It was true, she had a bit of a horse-face, but that wasn't what would make her such a valuable companion to Thou.

The gal had soul.

That she'd been designated as a Roamer was something Thou vowed to spend eternity trying to correct. He figured it might take just that long. Because, really, who cared?

She was of no consequence. She mattered to no one. It may, indeed, have been a clerical error, but so what? The heavenly batting average if you'd round-up was close to 1000.

That's pretty good.

13

EVAN CONTEMPLATES

In Hell, Evan was something he hadn't been since he was a 15-year-old sophomore in Miss Cherry's biology class: He was a virgin. He remembered what a rush he'd been in back then to shed his virginity. He'd been having erections since he was 13, was an enthusiastic masturbator, but felt a randy ambition to have his boner put to purpose. He mentioned this in Miss Virginia Cherry's 2nd period biology class. He held nothing back. It sent ripples of titillation through the class, most of whom had been raised on stork stories.

The voluptuous 24-year-old strawberry blonde was his biology teacher and a recent primary education graduate from Ohio University. She was shocked by his graphic admission and admonished Evan that her biology class was no place for such personal revelations. She was so upset she ordered him to see her after class where all his detailed sex talk and roguish young charm got the better of her and — hallelujah! — she began really putting his boner to work. For starters, she gave him a blow job and an A on the midterm.

It was truly wonderful watershed moment he'd never forget. Heck, he would have settled for a D.

The next day Evan, a chronic truant, began attending class with much more zeal, even woodshop with Mr. Branch where he knew he had zero chance of getting laid. He belatedly became a quality student, curious and supple-minded about all subjects, but especially biology.

And he never told a soul about Miss Cherry and their long, secret summer.

He later realized what she'd done was statutory rape, a felony punishable by up to 12 years in federal prison. Corruption of a minor was certainly enough to warrant an express ticket to Hell.

He was hoping that wouldn't eventually happen to the woman he called Miss Ginny. Sure, he'd love to see her again, but he didn't feel like she deserved to catch Hell for what she'd done. It wasn't as if she'd dispatched a busload of gambling nuns. And if he saw her again, she might want to ring the bell one more time, and he'd have to gently, politely refuse.

He wasn't going to have sex with Miss Ginny or anyone else in Hell. And not for lack of opportunity.

Unlike Heaven, which was prim and chaste as an old widow's tears, everyone in Hell was always getting it on. Who could resist? Folks had sex even though they knew it would lead to petty jealousies, recriminations, mistrust, suspicions, betrayals, cold indifference, and crimes of passion. And in Hell, it was all multiplied. Love triangles became love dodecagons — something not one of the 12 sticky participants even knew existed.

Not having sex wasn't easy for Evan. Sex since his sophomore year in high school had always been an enriching component of his life. He'd had it as often as he could with any woman who'd let him. Faithfulness? It was never his thing.

Missing sex was a real problem for him. He'd spend most of his waking hours remembering joyful Earth romps with nurses, secretaries, lawyers, judges, parole officers and once or twice with their married daughters. The sin of it all made it even more splendid.

He dreamed of the times he'd enjoyed having sex in cars, truck beds, grain elevators, graveyards, coatrooms and kitchens, on tractors, mechanical bulls, in tree houses, sand boxes, and once on a tire swing. He'd had so much sex with such a beguiling array of willing women, it became hallmarked as it earned the lone compliment he'd ever received from his loathsome cellmate.

"I'll say this for you boy," Rusty said, "you sure did all right in the ol' poontang department." He said this as he was practicing card tricks. He'd been a terrible father, husband and human being in general, and now he'd become the roommate from Hell, though given the circumstances that was sort of redundant. But Evan sure admired his dexterity with a deck of cards.

"Which makes it all the more peculiar as to why since you been here you ain't once taken the time to-. What the hell's a-matter with you?"

He began a honking laugh as he made the ace of spades disappear deep in the deck. His deftness with cards was the only thing Evan found appealing about him. He could mesmerize even veteran poker players with his nimble skills. He wished his father would teach him some tricks, but he'd never dream of flattering him by asking.

He certainly couldn't tell him about Elle, their illicit connection or how his son who'd bedded nearly 100 women, wouldn't have sex for the most quaint and old-fashioned of reasons.

He would have honk-laughed his head off. But the truth was the man who'd once been a love machine, a real Romeo, had promised to stay pure.

Evan was saving himself for Elle.

∼

EVAN'D THOUGHT for sure it was fake news when he heard Russian computer experts had hacked Heaven. Hell had had crude smartphones about 10 years before Heaven. But they wouldn't hold their charge, they were expensive, the apps all confused and dropped calls — Can you hear me now? — were the rule. If there was an unnecessary device sure to annoy and agitate, Hell had it first.

Evan was aware of a communal eagerness to give Heaven a heaping dose of Hell, but no one had ever successfully penetrated its robust defenses, which were more formidable than the proverbial Pearly Gates. It just wasn't done. Social media began to change all that. People were innately interested in staying connected. The proliferation of smartphones on both sides of the great afterlife divide gave everyone a psychic sort of porthole into the lives of those on the other side.

Heavenly gatekeepers put up firewalls — Hellfire Walls — to prevent communication which everyone understood was strictly forbidden. But former boyfriends and old girlfriends couldn't resist the lure of checking up on old loves to gauge how happy or miserable they'd become without them. Smartphone social media gave everyone a way to scratch the insatiable itch to learn about the lives of everyone from their old lives. It was startling because everyone knew you couldn't just walk into Heaven and start raising Hell. And lowering Heaven was a metaphysical impossibility.

The disparity always tantalized the philosopher in Evan. On Earth, he'd raised plenty of hell, but had never once been invited by clergy or parole officer to lower Heaven. He figured he'd been raising hell since about 6th grade when he first began giving his teachers a devil of a time.

Evan wondered if Heaven was sparsely populated. He'd been to places the travel brochures described as "Heaven on Earth," but they soon become so swamped with tourists that trying to get anywhere near there was pure hell.

He remembered reading an idiomatic dictionary listing 90 entries relating to Hell, three times more than ones describing Heaven.

There were musical ones: Hell's bells. There were meteorological ones: 'til Hell freezes over, come Hell or high water, it'll be a cold day in Hell, and a snowball's chance in Hell. There were directional ones: we can go to or through Hell either in a bucket or a hand basket. Behave sordidly and you'll be Hell on Wheels. He'd heard plenty of people ask what/who/why/where/how the hell. It's questionable enough to have Evan at least wondering WTF? It all made for one hellacious metaphor.

He liked the phrase "Bat Out of Hell," but was confused by its spiritual implications. He'd been taught Hell was where evil nun-killing souls like his went for all eternity. He understood the rationale, but why was it bats had license to come and go as they pleased? Either, way, he'd never seen a single bat coming or going. Just evil people. They kept coming in all the time. The line never seemed to end.

He'd been friends with a prosperous pig farmer who

frequently claimed to be in hog heaven. He was very proud, but to Evan it stunk to high heaven.

He'd dated a lovely woman named Betsy. "Heavens to Betsy," he called her back when their attractions were still a feisty, crackling thing. She was the woman he was most convinced he'd one day see in Hell. She had one hell of a temper. She'd whacked him over the head with a ceramic ashtray after busting him in bed with the limberly efficient UPS lady.

His mother had recognized this early on. "Evan," she'd said, "you'll never be happy 'til you go through one bad divorce. You need to get your heart good and broke to fix your mind on who's right for you. Sometimes you have go through a little Hell before you find your Heaven."

She'd been at least half-right.

Meeting Elle online had been purely accidental. One of the Russian hackers showed him how to access her Facebook account. Just for fun he scammed her account and posted that she was despondent and just wanted to see if anyone still cared. The response was monumental. Heaven had never seen such an outpouring of love. By noon that day, the post had received more than 20 million likes.

She'd been golfing that day with Arnold Palmer and was unaware of the hack. Anyone could golf with Palmer in Heaven, but he forbade his partners from checking their phones until they got to the parking lot. Elle was tickled to see a fake news story about her had gotten such sentimental traction. She wasn't mad or vengeful. She was charmed. Charmed that so many people cared and that someone — it had to be a Hellion — chose her as their foil. So instead of raising a red flag, she blithely posted, "Feeling much better. Thanks!" She felt an illicit tingle when she responded to Evan's introductory message.

It all seemed so innocent to her. She was curious. She wanted to know more. She didn't know anyone, she thought, who'd been sent to Hell. She believed every soul had some modicum of goodness that could be nurtured, even if she had to do the nurturing. And with each message, with each coy reply, walls began to topple. She was falling in love.

Evan began to dream he'd be the one to catch her. And message-by-message, day-by-day the farfetched dream began to develop a resplendent sheen of credibility. A guy from Hell and a woman from Heaven were becoming a couple. They were in love, and together they began dreaming of ways they could be together.

And that's how it started. An innocent flirtation had kindled into a conflagration that threatened to singe ethereal realms.

It had the potential to render the phrase Holy Hell as something more concrete than mere metaphor.

14

PAT FINDER

Pat Finder's grandfather had been her Sunday school teacher and embraced a strict interpretation of the Holy Bible. The Father, Son and Holy Ghost. Forever and ever. Amen. God had created the world in six days. The stated fact had always amazed Finder, and she was curious to see how long it would take the Almighty to solve, say, a Rubik's Cube. She was taught to believe God created Heaven and Earth. But in her dreamy moments she was always eager to sincerely ask God who or what created Him. So having the opportunity to discuss Evan and Elle with God had seemed mighty prestigious. She wanted to snag some selfies. She was hoping to make a good impression and made a mental note to ditch the chewing gum.

And that's why Lyberty and Turner's surprise burst of giddy laughter left her feeling confused.

"What's so funny?" she asked.

"Pat," Lyberty said, "no one's ever — ever — seen God, and Jesus has been occupied since 1962."

Finder was perplexed. What, she asked, did she mean no one'd ever seen God? This was Heaven, was it not? And not seeing God in Heaven seemed to her tantamount to going to Disney World and not seeing Mickey Mouse.

They'd been talking for hours. It was always going to be that way with Paige. Conversation to him was akin to breathing, a necessary biological function not to be stifled. Lyberty, who was perfectly content with either silence or chat, suddenly felt like stretching her legs. She suggested a barefoot stroll on a sandy beach. Turner recommended Baia do Sancho in Fernando de Noronha, Brazil. They blinked and Lyberty and Turner were there. Pat Finder was not. So Lyberty went back. Pat was struggling with her Portuguese.

"Take my hand, child," Lyberty said. "We'll go together."

And, like that, they were there and Lyberty resumed without interruption the conversation.

"No one's ever seen God. It's never happened," she said. "The Bible mentions Moses and Abraham seeing visions of God, but just visions. Actually seeing God is like actually seeing the wind. Just because you can't see the wind doesn't mean you can't see evidence of the wind's existence."

"That's not to say one day we might see God," Turner jumped in. "People in Heaven are both content to believe we may one day see Him and patient enough to realize that may not happen for another, oh, million years or so. Seeing God may literally take an eternity, but an eternity is what we got, so everyone's content to be patient. We all have plenty of time."

Pat was feeling cheated. A million years? She wanted to meet both God and Jesus right away. She was learning she was too impatient for eternity. "Well," she asked, "where is He? Can I at least see where He lives?" She was thinking of trick 'r treating come Fall. Or maybe Halloween would offer her a better shot of meeting the Holy Ghost allowing, of course, that spectral logistics might rule out selfies.

No God in Heaven? Turner shared one popular theory: In the beginning God created the heavens and the earth. "'And on the seventh day God finished his work and on the seventh day He rested.' Did you ever think maybe He's still resting? The Bible doesn't say, 'And on the 8th day He invented bowling.' Who's to say He's not all tuckered out?"

"Maybe He'd bitten off more than He could chew," Turner wondered. "Making Heaven and Earth sounds so grandiose when you boil it down to just those four words. But think about the nitty-gritty. Think about making clouds — and let's start there because they're relatively easy to lift. But how many clouds are there? There's cirrus, stratus, cumulus, cirrostratus, cirrocumulus and the T-Rex of 'em all, the cumulonimbus — the weather whopper.

"Think how much work just went into creating clouds. And weather in general. Rain, snow, hail, tornados, sunsets, sunrises. And then there's the sun, the engine of the whole shebang. Imagine the calculations it took to figure out the size of a sun so it wouldn't singe. A little bigger and Earth burns to a crisp. A little smaller, and it's too cool for humans. He's doing all this in six days. Six! It's incredible. And it's not just our sun, but countless suns in numberless galaxies," Turner marveled.

"Then take it down to things like corn. Its familiarity makes it seem deceptively simple. But, oh, man, it's not. All that luscious silky hair, enough to make Marilyn Monroe envious. And sweet as can be. Delicious. You can pop it, boil, roast or eat it raw. You can't go wrong. Then there's cornstarch, corn syrup, and, ah, bourbon whiskey. Oh, corn is there anything you cannot do?"

The sky above Baia do Sancho was flecked with tiny strands of pinkish cirrus clouds that looked to Finder like tiny bits of cotton candy snagged on the sky. She couldn't resist and wished into her hand a fluffy cloud of actual cotton candy. It was delicious. She enjoyed it blissfully unaware that it contained multiple corn byproducts.

The more Paige spoke, the less pronounced became his Cockney accent. Lyberty noted almost no accent at all. When he was speaking praise for the Almighty, he spoke in the voice of all men and women.

"Then you get to humans. Imagine the calculations that went into creating something so magnificent, and in your own image, to boot! Imagine imbuing your divine creation with the capacity to love, to hate, to create life and to end it. Mankind is truly a marvel. This here's a lovely place, one of the most beautiful in Heaven and Earth. But nothing is as beautiful to me right now as the two magnificent creations with whom I'm blessed to be strolling."

His flattery was sincere. He truly loved his fellow men and women.

"So on the seventh day he rested? Well, I ask how long is a God day? Because He sure did a shitload on Monday through Saturday. Yes, perhaps He's still resting. He's earned it for a job well done."

Lyberty stopped to pick up a particularly lovely sea shell. She examined it, showed it to her friends, and then set it back down for someone else to enjoy.

"Then there's the theory that on the seventh day He just vamoosed," she said. "Maybe He went somewhere else to start all over. Really, He gave us everything we needed, and He gave us free will to do as we wished. Think about it, Finder. How different was a perfect day on Earth compared to a perfect day in Heaven? Really, without all the terrible headlines, was there much difference? God gave us all the Heaven humans could handle. It takes some people getting to Heaven to realize just how close to Heaven they had it."

"Aye," Turner said, "and how close to Hell, too, sometimes on the very same day!"

Pat Finder let the surf run clear up to her knees. "Well, what about Jesus? Where's He been?"

"Like we said, no one's seen Him since 1962," Lyberty mentioned, her eyes drifting to the distant horizon.

The year rang a bell with Pat. She remembered her fundamentalist grandfather using the date to rail about the decline of American values. It was all down *hell* from there, he'd said. Yes! She remembered: "Oh, 1962 was the year the government took prayer out of public schools!"

"True," Turner said. "But that's not the reason why He's been occupied. He's been busy writing a book."

A book? What book? Scout asked.

"It's Bible II, The Sequel," Lyberty said. "Word is He's been working on it since 1962, and the date is completely unrelated to the school prayer thing."

"Well," Pat said, "how come I haven't heard of this. You'd think Jesus writing a sequel to the Bible would upend all of Earth's great religions."

"You'd think," Turner allowed.

"Well, why hasn't it," she asked turning to Lyberty.

"Jesus can't find a publisher."

~

OF COURSE, Jesus was having trouble finding a publisher. He may have been The King of Kings, but that didn't mean He had the pop culture heat or requisite number of Facebook likes to attract any big-shot interest. Turner had seen it coming.

Prayer in schools was eliminated in 1962, three years before Barry McGuire released "Eve of Destruction," one of the grimmest prophecies for humanity since the Book of Revelation, and it was three years before John Lennon said the Beatles were bigger than Jesus. But that was 17 years before Mark David Chapman became Hell-bound when he fired five hollow-point bullets from a Charter Arms .38 Special, coincidentally, perhaps, forming a crude wound-crucifix on the former Beatle's back.

Such cruel irony. The man who became famous singing "All You Need is Love," died because instead of love, what he really needed was a bulletproof vest.

This all happened way before Facebook came along with its perfectly simple way to quantify who's bigger than whom. Like totals of their respective Facebook pages?

The Beatles: 43,090,121 likes.

Jesus Christ: 12,808,589.

Even John Lennon's posthumous page ranked higher than Jesus'. It had 15,631,259.

Turner didn't think Jesus wouldn't have minded. Jesus was rumored to be a big Beatles fan, although it was said he preferred Paul's more melodic stuff to John's militant anthems. The exception being "Give Peace a Chance," a sentiment it was assumed He wholeheartedly endorsed and in four nifty words Cliff's noted the entirety of the New Testament.

Had He been competitive, it might have provided some ego-soothing balm to know His page outnumbered Paul's (6,931,272), George's (3,664,972), and Ringo's (2,275,431).

A bemused Turner often pointed out when Lennon made the statement it was 1966 when The Beatles were really, really good. "But so was Jesus!" he'd exclaim.

Still, it was all about the Facebook likes. Even the people who killed Jesus had notable followings. The Judas Iscariot page has 2,424 likes; Pontius Pilate has 1,320. Mention of

Pilate always caused Turner to wonder why some creative hand sanitizer company hadn't adopted the Biblical character as a celebrity spokesperson: "I'm Pontius Pilate! And when I need to wash my hands of a really dirty job, I use Dove!"

It mystified him that Yoko Ono had 402,722 lost Facebook souls liking her. "Chapman killed John Lennon, but Yoko killed The Beatles!" he'd provocatively exclaim.

He was fascinated by the like tallies and would point out how Satan had 194,508 likes, a third less than Santa (308,768) and that Facebook listed Jesus, Santa and Satan as "fictional characters."

Just like Harry Potter! (74,186,101 likes).

"But what if something happens?" she asked.

"He gave us all we need to deal with anything that happens," Lyberty said. "We have everything here we need to ensure peace, contentment and joy will endure throughout eternity. And nothing that could threaten to upend that heavenly tableau has ever happened."

"Until now," Turner said. "I think we all understand the gravity of the situation. For the first time in history, we have a woman who is hinting she'd rather go to Hell and spend eternity with a condemned soul than be in Heaven without him. We could be faced with having to decide whether a beloved angel goes to Hell or, perhaps, risk the consequences of having an unrepentant killer from Hell possibly infect Heaven with his sordid ways."

Lyberty noted a twinkle in Turner's eyes as he laid out what for many was a doom-filled scenario. She asked why he appeared so mirthful.

"Aye," he said, "I'm what you Yanks used to call 'feeling jazzed.' For the first time since I've been here it seems we're on the verge of an honest-to-goodness caper, one with pivotal consequences. It's apt to be historic."

Pat Finder said a jiffy little prayer to the God whom she was told was nowhere to be found and to The Son who was busy crafting His manuscript for which He could find no publisher. Grasping at straws, she weakly made another suggestion.

"Well, you think maybe we could ask the Three Wise Men what they think we should do? I mean, they are Wise Men, right? They ought to have some good ideas."

Lyberty looked at Turner and noted his face blushing a shade not dissimilar to Rudolph's nose.

"Yes," she said, "a wise man sure would be useful right about now. What do you think, Paige?"

"Aye, but where's a Wise Man when you need one?"

"He's just being modest, Pat," she said. "Just last year, Turner was officially declared a bona fide Wise Man. All the committees decided he has the keen intellect, the fierce curiosity, and the gentle prudence to join Melchior, Caspar and Balthazar as Heaven's fourth Wise Man. It's a great honor and well-deserved, I should say." She playfully kicked a toe load of sand at her friend.

"So, in Heaven there are now, not three, but Four Wise Men," Finder said, sounding incredulous. "And you happen to be one of them? Tell me, if you're so bloody wise (Paige noted the mimicry), how come you need me and Lyberty to figure this all out?"

"A truly wise man knows the value of sage company," he said. "And neither of you is too shabby in the wisdom department. Especially, Miss Lyberty here."

Raised to believe in equality, Finder couldn't contain her pique. How come, she asked, that "none of the Wise Men were women." "You mean in all history not a single woman exhibited any of the smarts to be deemed a Wise Man? It doesn't seem right."

Turner guffawed heartily. "You've got it all backwards. It's true only four men in history have earned Wise Man distinction and I happen to be one of 'em. Sure, others — Abraham Lincoln, Nelson Mandela, Winston Churchill and Confucius come to mind — have been judged worthy and but they all declined the responsibility. They'd had enough. But it's not that there are just four Wise Men. What's startling isn't only four men currently qualified. What's apt to startle you is there are only four Wise Men, but that in history there've been a grand total of 4 million or so females worthy of Wise Man designation.

"And Miss Lyberty here is one of 'em."

15

HELL'S GATEKEEPER

Not many people considered "One Flew Over the Cuckoo's Nest," the 1975 Jack Nicolson film, a prison flick. Evan did. It had it all. It had Nicholson being held against his will in deplorable conditions. It had soul-devouring depredations and a wing of inmates ranging from crafty to just plain nuts. And it had Nurse Ratched — pronounced RAT SHIT — who in the end literally steals the soul of Nicholson's Randall P. McMurphy by ordering him to undergo a crippling lobotomy that turns his once-vibrant brain into a baked potato.

Evan could on so many levels relate.

A villain like Nurse Ratched was, Evan thought, essential to any good prison escape movie. The villain would need to be cruel, laconic, remorseless and intent on perpetuating systematic evil, a walking Mephistopheles in starched institutional garb.

She was Boss Godfrey in "Cool Hand Luke," the nameless warden in "Escape from Alcatraz," and Evan could see despicable traces of her in sadistic Capt. Byron Hadley, from "The Shawshank Redemption."

Lots of guys in prison, Evan felt, could relate to "Shawshank" and main character Andy Dufresne. Guys like Dufresne truly believed in their innocence — given that their crappy public defender couldn't get all the extenuating circumstances admitted in court. Bastards.

It was different in Hell where most men and women were at peace with their evils. Some of them, in fact, reveled in them trying to one-up — or one-down — one another over who was worse. Those bull sessions never lasted too long, though, as participants soon realized every single story was doomed to devolve into dead-end discussions of how Hell was hell.

Evan was not like them. He was truly remorseful for all his sins, even as he believed he could persuasively convince fair-minded jurors of his deserving a second chance.

He wondered what Jill Keyes would say. He wondered that a lot because it was rumored she'd only spoken only one word just one time in her entire 40-year stint in Hell. That word was, "Yes." It was in response to when Satan asked her a startling question coming from the confirmed bachelor with anger management issues: "Jill, will you marry me?"

"Yes."

He divorced her after two months. Judas said Satan told him she just wouldn't shut the hell up.

It was true. She deigned to talk only to those she believed were her equals in looks, intelligence, and in evil. Even on Earth, she was the girl who attracted the most so-you-think-you're-better-than-me challenges. And every time, guaranteed, she'd make it clear that she thought she was far, far better than her interrogator.

In fact, she was downright loquacious when asked about fashion or games of chance. But she felt no need in Hell to opine. Being quiet gave her an advantage among morons eager to hear the sound of their own voices. She enjoyed her reputation.

Keyes was Hell's Nurse Ratched. Hers was the first damned soul everyone who came screaming through the gates of Hell saw. As monsters go, she never looked the part. She stood 5-foot-6, was impeccably postured with small, but perky breasts and a nicely rounded tush. She kept her shoulder-length light brown hair in a spritely pony tail that tousled in the breeze every time Hell's gate whooshed open to admit another one of the damned.

Her eyes were a not-unpleasant gray-blue like the unbloodied parts of a Confederate soldier's rebel uniform. But if eyes were the mirrors of the soul, then Keyes clearly had lost soul. It was said looking straight into them could drive you mad in moments, that the view was a panorama of distant, lost solar systems where nothing holy could persist.

Judas said he knew a guy who swore she had the fetid death breath of a dozen rancid monkey butts. But Judas knew the guy was lying. The woman who never closed her eyes never opened her mouth. She'd been in Hell since she'd died (been killed) in a 1978 South Carolina women's prison riot where she'd been serving two life sentences for drowning her sons, ages 3 and 14 months, by driving her 1967 Honda Civic into bucolic Lake Thurmond.

She told police she'd been carjacked by a gun-wielding black guy. It was a lie, one that led to vigilantism and escalated racial tensions. When the car was found nine days after it was reported missing, detectives determined she'd jammed the seat belt latches with bent roofer's nails that had made escape impossible. The boys were awake and aware the whole time.

The county prosecutor described her as "pure evil," a

description eventually agreed to by both the South Carolina jurors and the one true connoisseur of pure evil. The judge imposed two life sentences and, for good measure declared they would run consecutively. She declined comment when the judge granted her time to speak. In fact, she never spoke another word for the entirety of her mortal portion.

She was the lone fatality in a prison riot at the Leath Correctional Institute in Greenwood County. She'd been shivved right in the carotid artery by cellmate Betsy Justice in the prison rec yard. Justice had been serving a 6-to-10 stretch for dealing drugs that led to the ODs of four Myrtle Beach addicts. She hated Keyes and her sepulchral silence and the way she could possess her soul with her otherworldly stare.

Killing Keyes earned Justice another 15 years, but she felt never seeing her again as long as she lived would be worth it. It never dawned on her how her everlasting soul might have to confront her in Hell. She'd never considered all actions have consequences. She couldn't have guessed that Keyes sought and was granted gatekeeper duties solely because she was waiting to assign Justice to the vacant upper bunk in the cell she was saving just for her.

Evan and Judas used to wager — $20, $50, sometimes a $100 — on the sinfulness of each entrant to Hell. How many did she kill? Did he molest little girls in the park? Was he a politician who took Big Pharma bribes to allow the opioid pestilence to flourish? It was all just a way to kill time. Winning or losing even several hundred dollars meant nothing to Evan or Judas. There were always ways to earn illicit dough in Hell. Money is the root of all evil, so Hell was flush with it.

As theater in Hell went it was pretty compelling. The squeaky gate — there is no WD-40 in Hell — would creak open and the next damned soul would slink in. Keyes' two assistants would begin a methodical beating, the severity of which they would intuit from what they could discern from her mood. Keyes betrayed no emotions, conveyed no orders. Each fresh victim — earth bullies all — would glance beseechingly at her behind her desk, but few made the mistake of trying to hold her gaze.

As welcome wagons go, it was pure Hell. But the beating, the forlornness, the feeling of being truly God-forsaken wasn't the worst of it. No, the worst was the terrifying feeling that it could instantly get worse. Keyes had the power to take anyone for any reason and order them into Time Out. It was the Hell described in the Bible. It was the Lake of Fire, the eternal torment of damnation. It was so bad even Satan stopped going there. Too depressing.

Yes, even Hell has a Hell, and Jill Keyes decided whose souls were sent there.

Sometimes she'd send a Ponzi scheme architect and let an unrepentant serial killer slide. She'd go a week without bestowing the sentence and then she'd send the next six to their doom. And through it all, she she maintained her Sphinx-like mien to the grisly proceedings.

Judas and Evan were among maybe two dozen observers who'd crowd the bleacher seats overlooking the desolate courtyard where the proceedings took place. Evan was reading that day's score card with all the vital information about that day's arrivals. Evan was always struck by the incongruity of the death notices being posted on earth, all sentimental hogwash, and the "death" notices in Hell.

Typical was this:

"Frank Lamont, a Latrobe, Pennsylvania, boozehound, died of the massive heart attack his friends had been predicting since 2007. Married and divorced three times, he was an emotionally distant husband, was mocked for his Moe Howard haircut, and was known to area waitresses as the town's worst tipper. He failed to pay child support to four children who are now dysfunctional adults nursing substance abuse problems of their own. He cheated at golf, sent annoying ALL CAPS e-mails and frequently drove in the passing lane with his left turn signal on. He worked at Kennametal. He's been sent to Hell for deliberately shooting his lieutenant in the back while fighting raged outside Khe Sanh, Vietnam, on June 11, 1968."

There were no niceties, no sentiment, no gentle nods to humanity anyone could place an unsoiled doily upon. Just mean base facts of brute lives.

Evan called them "oBITCHuaries."

He was about to wager on the next Hell-bound entrant when Judas gave him a sharp elbow in the ribs, and hissed, "Dude. Don't freak out, but Keyes is staring right at you."

He looked up from the daily obits. She was. He boldly stared back, understanding staring back from a distance wasn't as dangerous as being within the tractor-beam pull of her Manson lamps. It felt empowering. He wasn't afraid. Not the least bit unsettled.

Then she did something that sent a chill up his spine.

She winked.

16

LOLA & ELLE ENJOY A HEAVENLY PICNIC

Lola and Elle took turns on who would bring the two bottles of wine and who would bring the sandwiches, fruit and pastries. On this spectacular Northern California afternoon, Elle had disrupted the routine and had brought not two bottles of wine but three.

By the time the first one was near empty, Elle had begun complaining about the lack of convenient recycling bins in Heaven. She was adamant that she be taken seriously. "It just makes sense," she said. "We need to nip it in the bud before it gets out of hand and Heaven becomes more like Earth — and not in a good way."

Lola was amused by how fastidious Elle was about recycling. She did it with the plastic forks they took on picnics, she did it with the newspapers and magazines she brought with her and she without fail did it with the empty Cabernet bottles they both brought with them whenever they met. And by now they were meeting four or five times a week.

When Lola correctly pointed out that there was no pollution in Heaven and that all litter disappeared on its own, Elle became a cheerful skeptic, asking, "Well, where does it all go? It has to go somewhere. It doesn't just disappear."

"In fact," Lola said, "that's exactly what happens — and even if it didn't they're never going to run out of space in the landfills. Unlike Earth, afterlife space is infinite."

"They used to say that about Earth! And have you seen Earth lately?"

Elle was the kind of person Lola called "earthy" for reasons that had nothing to do with mortal earthiness. On Earth, an earthy woman was someone who enjoyed coarse banter, heaping plates of comfort foods, plain clothes, dirty sex, and was casual about shaving hair in places like her armpits. Like Lola!

It was different in Heaven. To Lola, Elle's earthiness meant she still felt a peculiar preoccupation with Earthly mortal doings back on Planet E. It was very odd. She just couldn't shake her humanity.

It showed in ways large and small. For instance, she'd rather read a competent daily newspaper from anywhere in America than lunch with Johannes Gutenberg, the actual inventor of the printing press. She'd skip a star-gazing session conducted by Edwin Powell Hubble in favor of watching remote reports of drunken eclipse parties along the path of totality. Lola knew it was becoming a real problem when Elle said she would rather watch the afternoon results from the Arkansas Derby than go horseback riding. The horses?

Seabiscuit and Secretariat!

Lots of people in Heaven maintained an interest in Earth events, but mostly for reasons of pure entertainment, the way mortals did with their reality TV programs. No one in Heaven would fret over wars, climate change, pestilence, tyranny, COVID-19, injustice or the fact that style mavens were predicting Capri pants were once again becoming de rigueur that Spring. They understood all trifling Earth suffering was momentary and would soon be rendered mortally moot upon the soulful ascensions to everlasting glory.

In the other place, not so much.

Not Elle. She'd become outraged that even one Earthling had to endure pain, injustice, want, tumult, depression, loss, forlornness, and that any monster would, for heaven's sake, declare Capris were ever anything less than perfect for summer casual wear. She'd grown up believing in Jesus and that He would one day return to Earth and preside over Paradise. She'd been convinced it would one day happen just as the Scriptures promised. But when?

Didn't He know He was needed on Earth? Right away. Didn't He know babies were burning? Didn't He know His children all around the planet were slaying innocents in His name? It infuriated Earthy Elle, and whenever she'd vent to Lola about it, Lola always said the same thing: "Looks like someone should consider making a trip to the suggestion box." The suggestion box in Heaven was always full and always ignored. So the suggestion box in Heaven was like the earthly equivalent to prayer. Elle had lots of suggestions on how to improve Heaven.

Those were just some of the topics covered during the first bottle of wine, a heady Opus One 2015, described as "initial dark fruit, spice and baking aromas interwoven with seductive notes of violet, black tea, and sage."

"And that's a $350 bottle of wine we're drinking. So, I propose a toast to Heaven where even all the good stuff's free. Cheers!"

Lola had become something of a wine snob since ascending to glory. She enjoyed reading the descriptions on the bottles aloud the way she enjoyed reading liner notes about insider band facts on the old vinyl records she collected. She called the label blurbs "winer notes." Elle was content with boxed wine or domestic beer — as domestic as any beer could be when it was brewed in Heaven.

Lola truly loved the girl time she spent with Elle. She was so earnest. In just the past two weeks they'd met to picnic in Key West, Martha's Vineyard, Santa Fe, Hatteras and Biloxi. Lola kept trying to get her to go "overseas," to enjoy the beaches of Phuket in Thailand or maybe check out some of the exotic moons of Jupiter. But Elle wouldn't hear of it. She was committed to seeing all of America and reveling in its wonders. Truly, she was an American girl.

She was hoping to hear it one day from no less an authority than Tom Petty himself.

And while she enjoyed seeing new places, there was something about the Golden Gate Bridge that exerted a peculiar pull on Elle. It was always her first suggestion. And Lola didn't mind. She loved it, too.

By the time they'd begun their second bottle of wine, Earthy Elle would begin asking questions of Lola about what it was like to be a truly earthy woman back on Earth.

When did she decide earthy was the way for her to go? Did being an earthy person ever leave you feeling dirty? And did she ever resist the urge to jump in a hot bath tub and enjoy a good scrubbing?

What did earthy mean to Elle? It meant natural, nothing artificial. It meant speaking your mind. It meant honesty, forthrightness, organic foods and deep musky natural scents instead of perfumed perfections. It was an ethos she could embrace, albeit with maybe one hand pinching her nostrils shut.

Some aspects of earthiness were still a bit off-putting to a girl who'd been raised to be refined.

"You have to understand, I lived two lives. I was a child bride to Rusty Lee, and that nearly killed me. He controlled every aspect of my life. He told me how to dress, what to eat. He let me know who I could or could not talk to. And if he didn't like some of my independent decisions, he'd beat the hell out of me. He was brutal. I'd wind up in the hospital."

She told how seeing her son stand up to the bully had inspired her to press charges. Elle listened intently as Lola said her Evan, just 14, had vowed he'd never again stand by while Rusty laid a hand on Lola.

"He said he'd kill him before he let him hurt me again. And that's exactly what happened. He tried to kill me, and Evan killed him. Killed me, too. And my cat. Then he killed himself. It was one really screwed up day. But I owe that boy for freeing me from Hell."

She was just 32 when she left Rusty and you can do a lot of living when you're 32, single, and still give off an optimistic vibe.

And lots of living is just what she did. She learned French. She took lessons on film criticism, the harp, landscaping and the cultivation of bonsai shrubs. She dabbled in still-life painting, sushi preparation basics, and volunteered for the local hospice angels.

Yes, a woman who twice in her life had been beaten right to the edge of death's door began devoting 12 hours a week to assisting others through it.

And of what, Elle asked, was she most proud?

"I learned how to love," Lola said. "I never loved Rusty. I was young, clueless, really. And I knew a lot of women from the shelters who went through what I went through and never again trusted another man, much less themselves. I didn't want that to happen to me. I wanted to believe in romance and that there was a knight in shining armor for every woman on Earth."

She never again let another man mistreat her, but she didn't harden her heart against every man either. She gave herself freely to the possibility she could find love each and every time she walked out her front door. She'd never remarry, but she found honest deep love with three different men. And she'd found lusty passion with bar strangers enough times to appreciate the animal nature of what it means to be human and horny.

"It was like what Wade, the local golf pro, told me. We dated for three years before he went back with his wife. I loved him, and he loved me, I know, but his wife got cancer and her getting sick healed them. I admired that. I died before she did or I think we'd have gotten together. I haven't seen either of them 'round here, and I can pretty much guarantee neither of them are going to Hell. They're good people.

"But I remember laying in his arms, and him saying, 'Three of the 10 best times I've had in my life involved golfing with my late father or friends. The other seven involved having sex with the woman I love or with women I'd just met.' I punched him 'cause I thought he didn't mean me, but he just laughed. Then he rolled me on over, and we did it again!"

She'd allowed herself to get lost in romantic reveries when she looked up and saw her virgin friend blushing. She'd gotten a big gust of just how earthy Lola could be when her guard went down.

Recovering, she asked if Lola had ever found him.

"Found who?" she asked.

"Your knight in shining armor."

"Life can be funny like that. It wasn't what I'd expected, and I'm not talking romantically, certainly, but my knight in shining armor was always my son. Even with all the tough times we had, he was always there for me, always with a smile and something to make me laugh. Right up to the day killed me. And now he's in Hell."

Elle got up from her chair and looked down over the edge. She'd just finished the last drop of the second bottle. She took the corkscrew and deftly liberated the cork from the tapered neck of the third bottle. She poured a glass for herself and one for Lola.

She took a drink and then a deep breath and turned to Lola and said simply, "I'm in love with your son."

Then over the next three hours and four more bottles of wine — they were wish ordered — she explained how that was possible.

17

HELL ON EARTH

Meanwhile back on Earth, all hell was breaking loose. It was breaking loose in Kyiv where Putin's stooge fighter pilots were dropping barrel bombs on their innocent neighbors. It was breaking loose in Somalia where pro- and anti-government forces were engaged in ritual mutilation, gang rape and the mutual slaughter of one another. And it was breaking loose in Afghanistan, Yemen and in places around the globe where my-God-is-better-than-your-God arguments had flourished for bitter century after bitter century.

The phrase "all hell's breaking loose" was coined by 17th century poet John Milton in his epic book, *Paradise Lost.* All hell had been breaking loose since well before that and it had been breaking loose ever since. There was plenty of hell to go around. It became so common, it no longer made sense to tell anyone to go to Hell.

Sooner or later, Hell comes to you.

And there was never any evidence of all heaven breaking loose. It was like Hell was a limber, deep-pocket developer capable of buying out neighboring properties, but Heaven was confined by some zoning board intent on reducing sprawl, even desirable sprawl.

So all hell was breaking loose all over the world. There was genocide, torture, jihad, threats of nuclear retaliation so vivid you could close your eyes and with all your senses imagine all the earth as ash. There were random shootings, assassinations, suicides and numberless hearts broken through all the collateral damage.

It was a desperate time to be alive, a time when many doomsday prepper parents were teaching their kids how to kill, how to bunker in, and how to look out for #1 for when the world goes to Hell. They failed to realize that if it wasn't for all the good-hearted parents teaching children to love, to share, to be kind, and to work together, Hell would already be here.

Earth was becoming a bloody hell. For souls who missed programming like "Ozark" and "Dexter," it made for some terrific television.

Aziz Ahl always had it on in the office when he was in there doing paperwork and ensuring Dog regulars had all their favorite libations. In fact, it was on most TVs most of the time in Heaven. There was zero violence in Heaven. No crime, envy or want. In that way, it was like Hudgeboro, one of those coastal California towns where there's a veneer of perfection and ease and fulfillment over a layer of more or less vague discontent. But, hey, the weather's nice and my hair always looks good, so whatever ...

But people were somehow nostalgic for the time when life was dangerous, and violence could sweep into their lives and rupture or end them.

Paige Turner's office had three TV screens on the wall facing his mahogany desk. The one on the left was tuned to the bar entrance so he could know who was in the bar. He wanted to be able to greet guests like he did last week when Martin Luther King Jr., Gandhi, and Richard Pryor came in for karaoke. It was a wonderful night, especially when MLK sang an uproarious falsetto version of Shel Silverstein's "A Boy Named Sue." Silverstein was rolling on the floor laughing.

He often railed against having set No. 2 tuned to constantly updated news of all hell breaking loose on Earth — it offended the optimist in him. Yet, at times, he found himself getting sucked in. He was as a man who loved human beings and had loved being human. The round-the-clock, instantly updated and broadcast on crimson HD of so much wanton cruelty between people who shared so much DNA was endlessly compelling. He loved soccer, sure, but nothing was as riveting as the epic story of the common man and his and her struggle to endure.

With all that going on before his eyes, Ahl knew it was odd how often he found himself staring at the third screen. Odd because it was never tuned into any broadcast. It broadcast nothing. Just a monotony of constant rolling gray. He was struck by the contrast, the vibrancy and the dullness. He was moved by an ill-defined belief that there were forgotten souls roaming in just such a twilight existence. He'd heard stories — speculation, really — and he wondered about them. Could there really be that many souls of such forgotten indifference?

It was a mystery channel and people in Heaven watched it the way people on Earth stare at those mesmerizing 3-D posters of things like emerging space ships.

No one could detect the source of the broadcast. It wasn't Hell and it wasn't Heaven. It was like a fuzzy moving image of a crowd massed to get into a ball park on a stormy day.

They were human, but they weren't. Aziz could watch

for hours. He'd sometimes make out a face, an arm, shrugging shoulders. Were they folks? Were they distressed? Did they matter?

His innate curiosity was kindled by a Hi-Def picture that seemed wildly out of focus.

He wondered if he could find them, save them. It's exactly the kind of thinking you'd expect from a man who dedicated himself to ensuring the bar's recycling regimen surpassed heavenly standards. But mostly he was just curious if he could fill a void that had long tickled the intellects of people who'd made the heavenly cut: Where was the realm between Heaven and Hell? Some suspected it was a dimensional void, an afterlife no-man's land.

Ahl suspected it was just the opposite.

He believed it was a land with billions of men and women.

He resolved to find out.

On the floor beside Paige's desk gathering dust was a 4x6x4 cardboard box. It was an Earth birthday present he'd given Paige the previous March. They'd re-gifted the box so often, Ahl could not remember who was the rightful owner. Inside the cardboard box was a camera drone. They were very popular on Earth. Not so much in Heaven where there was never a bad day and all the views were always spectacular. Watching a drone-filmed heavenly sunset just didn't quite hold the same appeal as it did now that you were in actual Heaven.

He wasn't thinking about filming anything remotely heavenly.

He opened the box and piece-by-piece removed the contents and began assembling them. Because it was Heaven, assembly was uncomplicated and there was no wrap rage. And — voila! — within minutes he held in his hands an Eagle Eye 2100 Range Rover drone capable of infinite battery hours and transmit distance of 11 dozen parsecs.

Or so the box claimed.

He leaned back in his chair and shouted, "Noel! Oh, Noel! Can you come in here, please? Noel? Noel!"

It took about two minutes of that before in sauntered waiter Noel Neetles. Seventeen years old, he'd been in Heaven just six months. His parents had been die-hard anti-vaxxers, which had been unfortunate for their son who'd died hard from an easily preventable case of measles. His death sparked a national outrage across America and an internal one in young Noel. He died two weeks before his senior prom, an event his girlfriend had promised would be the conclusion of his nagging virginity.

He was thrilled with Heaven, but saw no conflict in spending hours filling up the suggestion box saying dead virgins should be given a priority opportunity to screw. If anyone ever read his notes or anything else in the suggestion boxes, there was no evidence.

Turner'd hired him as a waiter, but demoted him the next week when it became apparent he was incapable of remembering who'd ordered what and where they'd been sitting. As a busboy, he was proving his incompetence was omnibus. He was good for breaking one glass or plate per hour, a rate of consistency sound enough for gambling legend Bobby Riggs to have begun laying odds.

When Ahl complained to Turner about his astounding ineptitude, the boss would say, "'He's a nice boy. He'll get the hang of it. Give 'im another 200 or 300 years. We have to find something for all stupid and clumsy people who are Heaven- eligible to do, too."

Noel tapped twice on the door and said, "You wanted to see me boss?"

He looked up from his desk. Noel's storm of red hair looked like it could have been styled in a blender. The buttons on his black uni-vest were misaligned. His dress white shirt had come untucked after having spent the better part of the last hour bending over to pick up beer mugs he'd dropped to their consequential doom. His casual attitude extended to his posture so that he resembled a walking question mark.

"What are you doing this afternoon, kiddo?" Ahl said.

"Nothin'."

"I want you to program this drone to transmit exclusively to this smart TV right here."

"Can do."

He was a whiz with tech but sought work waiting on tables because he liked people. And people like Ahl liked him, although he felt a stab of chagrin every time he heard another glass explode or another customer shriek.

"Then I want you to take it down to a place called Desolation Row and send it straight to Hell."

"Desolation Row?"

"Yes, it's named after the Bob Dylan song."

"Bob who?"

"I'm going to pretend I didn't hear you say that, but hustle your ass to the jukebox as soon as you depart here and play H10. 'Desolation Row' is the 11:12 epic finale to Dylan's 1965 masterpiece 'Highway '61 Revisited.' It's also the name of the most sparsely maintained section of Heaven down by the Southern border. There's no wall there. I want you to go there and release the drone —"

"I heard they were going to build a wall."

"You heard wrong. This has a range of —"

"I heard we need a wall to keep the bad hombres out."

"All the bad hombres are in Hell and can't get out. This should be programmed —"

"I heard it was going to be a big, beautiful wall."

"Please try and focus here on the matter at hand —"

"And I heard Mexico was going to pay for it."

"Will you shut the hell up about the stupid wall!"

Ahl's outburst secured Noel's attention and held it without further interruptions. He told Noel he believed the drone was powerful enough to reconnoiter a forbidden region where he suspected the mass of humanity's soulless beings dwelt. He told him it was possible that what the drone beamed back could re-write the entire afterlife map with existential implications for both Heaven and Hell.

Noel nodded his understanding. And later that day arrived at Desolation Row, newly enriched by his knowledge of Bob Dylan, and ready to fulfill his mission. And as he released the drone into the setting sun for its date with destiny, he was consumed with one thought.

"I still think this would be a dandy place to build a wall."

18

APART: EVAN & ELLE

"I miss the days when I knew I'd hear from you every day by 5 p.m.," she said. "This has been the longest we've ever gone without even so much as an emoji. It's been almost two months."

"It's been one month, 3 weeks and 4 days," he said. "You and I have been corresponding for 1 year, 8 months and 12 days. That goes back to the day I pranked you and all those angels. And, again, I apologize for that. I'm very sorry if I hurt anyone's feelings. Of course, I'd do it all again because it's what led me to you. And without you, I swear, I'd kill myself all over again."

Elle was sitting in her sun room sipping her third cup of coffee. The night before she'd been the drunkest she'd ever been and now she was feeling the rumblings of her first hangover. She was nauseated, and her head felt like it was about to explode.

She could have wished the hangover away, but the hangover had her feeling earthy, human. In Heaven ,everything was perfect and that's why any imperfection felt so good to rebels like Elle. Any imperfection in Heaven felt like you were sticking it to The Man, which was odd because everyone in Heaven knew The Man was God and God, being God, could never really be The Man.

Evan kept nervously glancing over his shoulder. If he was busted corresponding with an angel in a loving way, it was clear he'd buy a stretch in Time Out. The threat alone was significant enough to keep most of the worst in Hell on the straight and narrow.

His computer skills earned him privileges as long as it was understood he used them for nefarious means. Trolling angels was his designated priority. Get busted writing one of them love letters meant real trouble. So, he spent one tedious morning constructing an early warning system that involved rigging with string, pulleys, ramps and a near-empty can of generic cola — it was impossible to find an authentic Coke in Hell.

But the Rube Goldberg contraption, while it had been satisfying to set up and operate, soon began defeating its purpose. Rather than giving him more time to chat with Elle, it began eating into it by requiring him to set it with every deconstruction. So now he had a simple bell, string/tripwire system that was virtually foolproof to everyone but the guys who knew how to set it up.

He remembered seeing his Dad do it when, coincidentally, he wanted a little alone time with his Earth porn. With all the interruptions, he was often stuck looking at porn, too, when all he really wanted to do was woo Elle. He yearned for her. He thought about her his every waking moment. That was not an uncommon emotion in Hell. Men and women openly wept for the loved ones they'd never see again. It was more acute for Evan. All the others had zero hope.

It seemed irrational even to him, but she was convinced

someday they'd be together. What the hell that meant he had no idea. He felt he could even endure Hell, as long as he had wifi and unfettered access to Facebook. He didn't see why it couldn't continue indefinitely, although admittedly a hot spot in Hell, with its Lake of Fire, was different from a hot spot on Earth, which tended to be near places that hawked coffee.

His blog, urged on by Judas, was thriving. Readers loved his self-deprecated musings on life in Hell. He had a real knack for illuminating the banal aspects of Hell without raising the ire of the censors who, in fact, rarely bothered to censor anything. In that way, they were like Army mechanics on Earth who spent the majority of their time pretending to fix truck engines that they knew were already functioning properly.

Judas assured him the blog would one day earn money. Evan was suspicious, yet he persevered. He tried to write three posts a week; never fewer than 10 per month, and once did 20.

Still, he equated committing to writing a blog with having a goofy imaginary friend with multiple dependency issues. He couldn't abandon it for too long or it would likely die from lack of attention. But like having a needy friend, he spent a lot of time wondering if the damn thing's holding him back from more productive pursuits and wondering if, geez, would anyone really care if the SOB just died?

But it gave him an excuse to spend time on the computer, primitive as it was. Most of the library computers like the one Evan used were dedicated exclusively to pornography, which made perfect sense because so was the entire library. Every book, magazine, and VHS video depicted some human being dripping or shooting some love juice on some other human, animal, robot or exotic plant.

The books were roughly catalogued based on the bodily fluids, a real Screwy Decimal System.

In the background playing for the 113th consecutive time was "Bicycle Race" by Queen, a song he genuinely liked the first 30 or so times they'd played it. Even in the library it played at uncomfortable volume for the full day. *"Shhhing"* in Hell's library didn't help.

Evan's renown with computer skills earned him what amounted to one of the few private offices in Hell. Like most offices, it was mostly cell-like: three walls, no windows, a flimsy door that made a telltale *crrrreeeeaaak!* when it opened or closed. The computer faced the opposite wall. It was supposed to be private, but many of history's worst villains were always poking their heads in and wondering what Evan had done to make him so hellishly special. It was distressing enough that he rigged a little trip-wire and bell system that afforded him two seconds of warning of approaching villains. Just two seconds, but they could be crucial. In that span, he could without any due romantic fanfare pull the plug on Elle and switch screens to some Satanically approved porn.

The bell had saved his ass numberless times. People in Hell weren't just evil, they were nosy as hell, too. The alarm system was simple, but effective. It was a trick he'd learned from his Dad when the old man needed a morning jerk-off with his stash of porn. So he could be pouring his heart out to Elle one second and — *ding!* — like that be pretending to be an inmate lusting over illicit videos of a man putting it to a gentle pasture lamb.

"So you have an honest-to-goodness hangover, eh?" he asked bemusedly, recalling the nearly two decades he'd woken up most every morning either hungover or already drunk.

"Yes, I do! I could pray it away, but I've decided to wallow in it," Elle said. "Being sick, feeling like I'm going to throw up, reminds me what it felt like to be human. And I miss that."

"What was the occasion?"

"Oh, I've got a new friend," she typed. "I think you'd like her."

"Who is it this time?" he replied, only half mocking. "Rosa Parks? Joan of Arc? Dinah Washington? Mrs. Claus?"

One of the things he really envied about Elle being in Heaven was her endless access to really cool people and by really cool people he didn't mean "Laverne & Shirley" actress Penny Marshall, although she was, indeed, her own kind of cool. No, by cool, he meant like the Biblical Noah, who ran a combination zoo- waterpark not far from town.

"No, she's no one famous. She's just really, really cool. We have a lot of fun together. I'm sure you'd like her."

"Well," he typed, "who is she?"

Just then the tripwire tightened and — *ding!* — followed by the telltale *crrrreeeeaaak!* of a closed door opening. Then Evan, with gunfighter reflexes of a bad outlaw reached for the mouse and triggered the click. Like that Elle's sweet, smiling face disappeared and was replaced by the image of a giant hairy ass humping the school crossing guard. Evan swiveled his chair around in time to see Soviet butcher Josef Stalin approaching.

"Ha! I'd heard you were short," Evan taunted, "but I didn't know I could fit you in my shirt pocket."

On Earth as the tyrannical ruler of one of the most heinous and godforsaken regimes in history, a man responsible for the deaths of 20 millions In Hell, he was just another punk. Evan told him to buzz off. He watched as Stalin slunk away. He didn't resume his computer date until the door — *crrrreeeeaaak!* — signaled it was all clear. It would take him as much as an hour to reestablish contact with Elle. The modems in Hell were all dial-up.

∼

THE NEWS that Elle had befriended Evan's mother and that now the two of them were getting roaring drunk together on iconic bridges in Brooklyn, Santa Fe and San Francisco hit like a stick of dynamite in a popsicle statue art garden. What were they talking about? Where they scheming?

It was unsettling to Lyberty and Paige, less so to Pat Finder.

"To me, it just looked natural," she said, "like two girls dishing and having fun. If I hadn't been undercover, I'd have thought about joining them."

That Elle and the Lola woman hadn't invited her to join them was to Paige evidence that they were totally engrossed in their conversations. He surmised Elle was too polite to exclude someone like Pat Finder, a delightful girl, but likely as inept a spy as any who'd ever donned a fake mustache, which she had, in fact, done. She and Elle knew one another casually, and that Elle excluded her from their tete-a-tete meant the topics were grave, too momentous for a winsome youth.

Lyberty gave a respectful little whistle. "How could they have even found each other? And what could they be discussing? Certainly, Elle must know that Evan is in Hell for killing Lola, 36 other people, that whatzizname cat and himself. That's a lot of death for one day. She knows all that, right? She'd certainly done all her homework."

"Maybe part of that is what appeals to her," Turner said. "She'd led a very let's say pristine life on Earth, Patsie, am I right? Maybe she's taking what Lou Reed calls 'A Walk on the Wild Side,' as if Heaven even has a wild side."

"You're forgetting," Lyberty said, "the Wild Side upon which she's choosing to walk isn't exactly in Heaven."

Paige asked this, oh, so, wise woman what she was inferring.

"Clearly, there's an intense infatuation going on," she said. "It may be one-sided or it may be mutual. But I think what we're seeing here is the first case of a man or woman who's found Heaven lacking. She's discontented and it looks like it's going to be up to us to determine if this condition is acute or chronic. Then it'll be up to us to convince her she needs to forget about this Evan Lee."

"You think he's a lost soul, do ya?" Paige asked.

"You know me better than that. With Jesus as our savior, anything is possible."

"Anything?" Finder asked.

Lyberty stood and with the rapturous cadence of a preacher began, "Yes, hallelujah! Anything."

She told the story of the loaves and the fishes and about the time Jesus turned water into wine — good stuff, too. Not that cheap swill they sell on Earth in cardboard boxes.

"He healed blind, deaf and mute men and women. He allowed the lame to walk. With just a touch of his hand, he restored the severed ear of Simon Peter on the very night the Roman Centurions came to arrest Him in Gethsemane. He brought Lazarus back from the dead. And by dying on the cross, He saved the eternal lives of every believer who ever lived."

Lyberty was practically aglow with the Holy Spirit. She was blessed with a mirthful disposition, and now here as she related the story of her own blessed salvation it emerged with halo-like lucidity.

Born into slavery, she was first raped when she was 15. She never played with dolls. Never put on make-up. Never played in a sand box. Never allowed herself to dream there was a better life, much less a better Afterlife. She toiled in the cotton fields in the scorching sun, her life as hellish as any day in actual Hell. Did she ever even once smile as a child? She'd think about it even now. Was it when her sister had a baby? She loved babies. But even that had been a hard smile to coax.

Laughter? Not once, of that she was sure. There was nothing funny about life as a pre-Civil War slave. Being in Heaven and being able to enjoy so much joyful laughter was, to her, the best part of Heaven. And yet for all life's torments, she never once was sorry she'd suffered through them.

"So, no, there's nothing Jesus can't do. He took a lifeless girl like me, a soul bereft of even the simplest joy and restored it to zesty fullness. If He wanted, He could forgive this Evan Lee and bring him right to Heaven where, hallelujah, he could if he chose spend eternity with his true love. I believe it could happen."

Paige snorted. "Now, that'll never happen."

"And, pray tell, why not?"

"Too much paperwork."

She hadn't thought of that. Every heavenly entrant had to be vouched for, documented and processed in triplicate with one copy going to Immigration & Naturalization, one to Eternal Internal Affairs, and one to the CCB (Celestial Census Bureau). It was a real bureaucracy. Sure, Jesus could forgive sins, but there had to be some order to the whole process.

There was Heaven and there was Hell. No one could come and go as they pleased. There were consequences to earthly misbehavior. If there weren't, The Ten Commandments weren't worth the granite into which they were chiseled.

So, Lyberty knew Paige was right. But still …

Paige said, "As much as I'd love to sit here and listen to you rhapsodize about the glories of Heaven — when you tell it it always feels like it's the first time I've ever heard it — I propose we devise a plan.

"First we need to get Lola in here. Finder, that'll be up to you."

"What do I tell her?"

"Tell her the truth. Tell her — no, no, that never works. Invite her here to The Dog for dart night or something. You're a clever girl. Just make something up."

"Lyberty," he said, "I'd like you to head over to the library and research precedents. Is this a first? Have we ever seen anything even remotely similar, who was involved and how did they handle it? And while you're at it see if you can see any news of anyone ever having busted out of Hell."

The mirth left Lyberty's face, replaced by surprise. "You're kidding aren't you? Hell's the ultimate high security prison. No one's ever escaped. Remember this? 'Abandon all hope ye who enter here.' Sound familiar? It's preposterous to think the powers that be — in Heaven or Hell — would permit a prison break from Hell. And how would you do it? There are gates, guards, moats —"

"You don't know that."

"Well, I've read."

"In the history of Heaven and Hell, there's not been one eyewitness account of anyone from Hell eyeballing Heaven or of anyone from Heaven eyeballing Hell."

"It just can't be."

"Then it ought not to take you that long."

He told them to take the rest of the day off. "We've been hitting this pretty hard and it's only going to get more intense. So take the rest of the day off. Have fun, relax, do something heavenly. I hear Ben Franklin's giving a lecture on the role foolishness plays in enlightenment.

"What do you plan to do, Paige?" Lyberty asked.

"Well, I might go to that Franklin lecture just to see how he can make any sense of that. After that, I have a big job on my hands that must be addressed before I can do anything else. It can't be put off a minute longer."

Pat Finder wondered wistfully if perhaps Paige was destined to meet with Jesus about these issues in which they were about to be immersed: "What is it?" she asked.

"Paperwork," he said. "I'm getting way behind an' the Liquor Control Board is getting way up my ass about it. They gave me a deadline and said if I don't get it to them by then they'd revoke my liquor license. Can you believe it? Sometimes the pressure is just too much."

"How much time did they give you?" Lyberty asked.

"A measly 250 years," he said. "Can you believe it? How stressful! Of course, me being such a procrastinator, I'll probably end up pulling an all-nighter in ... ohhh ..."

∾

It took Evan in Hell another two hours to reestablish his link in Heaven with Elle. During that time, he'd been rudely interrupted by in succession Ty Cobb, George Wallace and James Earl Ray. Each looked at Evan like they were ready to kill him for hogging the computer, and kill him they would have, but he was already dead. Plus, his perks had been earned.

Each time, he'd been saved — *ding!* — by the little bell

and the door's *crrrreeeeaaak!* It wasn't like that when he and Elle were just getting to know one another. His heaven-hack had earned him special computer privileges that became instrumental in their courtship. They got to know one another and fell in love, true love.

He knew her favorite color was blue, her favorite movie Pixar's "Up" and her favorite songs — she couldn't have just one — were Tom Petty's "Won't Back Down," Tom Petty's "The Waiting," and "American Girl," by Tom Petty.

Her favorite musician?

Tom Petty!

He knew her favorite book was John Steinbeck's *Grapes of Wrath* and that her favorite passage was the part where the author steps back from the story and reveals the raw cruelties of wanton greed. Key line: "… and in the eyes of the people there is a failure; and in the eyes of the hungry there is a growing wrath. In the souls of the people the grapes of wrath are growing heavy, growing heavy for the vintage."

The words, the denunciation of inhuman injustice struck at her very core. She'd read it during her junior year of high school and the book's sentiments became bedrock principles for her. The girl who'd built a curb-transcending baby duck ramp would be forever eager to improve the human condition, just as she would the infant fowls'.

An exquisite tension to their typed conversations began to arise as Evan's computer privileges began to erode and people — *ding!* — began to trickle in without knocking. He was confident the alarm system would give him sufficient notification any time anyone tried to sneak in. But it meant an abrupt end to any meaningful conversation with Elle and then out of politeness would have to resume an hour or so later. When Elle told Evan she had an interesting new friend in her life it took about five computer sessions before she could identify the person.

She didn't mind the wait. She had some take-out sushi, a bottle of cabernet, and she always had Wordle. Plus, she had all the time in the Afterworld.

∽

PAT DIDN'T NEED to be told twice to enjoy Heaven. She left The Dog and stopped at the apartment she was sharing with Anne Frank to see if she wanted to enjoy an afternoon adventure. Frank was a very popular roommate and Pat knew she was lucky to have her, however briefly. The two'd agreed to a 500-year lease.

"I wish I could," Frank said, "but a boatload of Syrian refugees just sank in the Mediterranean and I told Gabriel I'd be there for the welcome reception. I'm playing harp." She was very proud of her harp playing. She asked what Finder had in mind.

"I'm thinking Everest," Scout said.

"Oh, you're going to love it," Frank said. "Be sure to do the inner tube down the South Face — and hang on tight or kiss your ass goodbye! Have fun. Oh, and don't forget to snag some hot cocoa from Tenzing Norgay's snack shack and tell him Annie F. says, 'Hey! HEY! Hey!' He'll know what it means."

Pat said goodbye and just like that she was roaring down Everest, failing to heed Annie F.'s wisdom about holding on tight and kissing her ass goodbye. It was a blast.

After that and in order she rappelled down El Capitan, white water rafted down the Colorado through the Grand Canyon and topped off the day with some beignet and an iced latte on the porch at the Cafe du Monde in New Orleans. Nearby Louis Armstrong was singing "It's a Wonderful World." She'd never heard the song before and asked the waitress about it. She said she'd introduce her to Armstrong.

She was having the time of her Afterlife.

∾

SHE FELT the familiar tingling sting of excitement as she saw his IM begin to dance across her screen. "So," he wrote, "you gonna tell me who it is?"

Elle said she wanted him to guess. She was enjoying the tease of playing out the revelation.

"Okay" Evan said, "let's see ... long dead or dead in the last 10 years?"

"Last 10 years."

"American or other?"

"U.S.A."

"President George H.W. Bush?"

"No, I met him, but that's not who I'm thinking of. And, yes, he's wonderful. He's taking me fishing next week. You're going to be shocked. Here's another ... this person is someone you — "

ding!

He heard the door behind him *crrrreeeeaaak!* Damnit. Who was it this time? He turned to see approaching one of history's worst monsters. Lucius Clay, a silver-tongued former soda executive who in 1985 persuaded Coca-Cola, a company that at the time was earning profits of $189 billion from a tried-and-true original beloved recipe dating back to 1886, that it needed a "new" Coke.

Evan loved Coke; despised Clay.

"Well," he said, "if it isn't Mr. New Coke. You know you're not allowed in here."

"I just stopped to see if you'd let me have a quick peek at some of them young ladies enjoying the intimate company of all the other young ladies."

"Not a chance," Evan said. "Get out."

Putting men and women in Hell for failed inventions or misguided attempts at advancement struck many as extreme. Not Evan. He knew most were motivated by simple greed. They'd replaced a perfectly satisfying product with an inferior alternative. It's why he'd always express shock to Judas that Steve Jobs wasn't in Hell. He kept repackaging the same product with new colors and minor tweaks when Evan thought he should have helped humanity by directing his genius to re-inventing the internal combustion engine to run on all the discarded iPhones he'd already duped everyone into buying.

No, he just kept tinkering with a device that held 8,000 songs until it could hold 10,000.

"The world is going to Hell," Evan was fond of saying, "but at least we'll be groovin' when we get there."

He'd say that back when he was still mortal. He'd sometimes hear himself say he was glad he'd died young, that the destruction of the planet, the corruption of morality and the diminishment of simple human joy were combining to kill him when he was still alive. Then he'd look around and realize he was in Hell and become sad about the slapstick episode that led him here.

He was sadly nostalgic for newspapers, Mom 'n' Pop video movie stores, getting birthday cards in the mail, and phones that were still phone-shaped. The internet was to blame. Technology, he'd decided, is the willful and agreed-upon demolition of charm and all that was once beloved as quaint.

And he'd take it out on men like Clay, who'd defend the gambit, even as he knew it had led him to Hell.

"Now, our market research showed the consumer was open-minded to —"

"And how much money did you spend on deciding to name this, oooh, 'new' Coke 'New Coke?'"

"— new product. And time is proving me correct because today's consumers have the choice of purchasing —"

Neither man was listening to the other. Happened all the time in Hell. It was a lot like the political chat shows on the Earth cable news networks.

"I want you out of here."

"— Diet Coke, Coca-Cola Cherry, Coke Citra, Orange Vanilla Coke —"

"Out! Now!"

"— Coca-Cola Zero Sugar, Coke Life, Coca-Cola Vanilla —"

"I ... said ... OUT!"

"— Diet Coke Caffeine-Free and Coke Mango!"

Evan turned and started to get up, but Clay had vamoosed. Evan'd been at the computer for four hours and had yet to learn the identity of Elle's exciting new drinking buddy. Oh, well. No one ever said Hell was a day at the beach. He shut down the computer, waited for it to power back up and then doggedly resumed his attempts to make a heavenly connection.

∼

Meanwhile back in Heaven, Lyberty was waiting in line with four other star-struck girls of various ages and dance experiences, but on this stage at that moment all shared the same dream. The girls were all dressed in nearly identical lime green cocktail dresses, splashes of sequins reflecting the spotlights. Each had gone to the trouble of getting themselves coiffed in page boy haircuts favored, they guessed, by page boys from the 1920s. Their expressions were a mingled mix of desperation masquerading as either honest indifference or hopeful arrogance.

Not Lyberty. She did everything but beg for the role. It meant a lot to her. She'd done, she thought, her best yet, her best ever. Would it be good enough? The star himself was the final-say evaluator and here he was mounting the steps.

Just meeting him had been a bucket-list achievement for her. He was so dashing, so dreamy. And here he was with those kind, almost apologizing eyes, one-by-one dispatching the other girls until it was just the two of them — Lyberty and a friendly girl from Idaho. Lyberty thought she'd lost when he turned to her and started out saying, "I'm sorry …"

Heartbroken, her lower lip began to tremble. "You think YOU'RE sorry? What about me? I've been trying to crack —"

"Darling, you didn't let me finish," he said. "I was saying, 'I'm sorry. Will you tell me your name?' See it'll help me if I know the name of my co-star. I want you to play the Debbie Reynolds role in my remake of 'Singin' in the Rain.' Do you accept?"

Gene Kelly, his dazzling smile beaming like daybreak, had just offered her the role of a lifetime. That it didn't occur during the time while she was alive mattered not one bit. She couldn't wait to tell Paige and Pat.

"Yes, Mr. Kelly! Yes! Yes! A thousand times yes!"

"Fantastic. Rehearsal starts tomorrow. Be here at 7 a.m."

The sudden rehearsal schedule put Lyberty in a bit of a bind. She knew she'd be occupied. She asked if it would be too inconvenient if they put things off just a bit.

Kelly asked for how long.

"It could be a week, but it might be a year or two. Is that a problem?"

"No, that's fine," Kelly said. "How about we put things on hold for a year, and you touch base with me in six months? Sound good?"

"That'll be great Mr. Kelly. You're a peach."

"So what's the big deal?" the star asked.

"I'm not sure it is a big deal, but if it all happens like we think it might, it could be a real blockbuster."

"You're not working on that new Hitchcock picture, are you?"

"No, sir. Nothing make-believe. I'll either let you know about it, or you'll hear about it as it's happening."

"Lyberty, you have the gift of suspense."

She was just given a heaven-sent gift, the role of a lifetime. But given what she thought might be awaiting her, Paige and Pat, she wondered which was the bigger role.

∽

WHILE FINDER WAS ZOOMING down Everest and Lyberty was realizing her dream to star in a Broadway musical with Gene Kelly, Paige was in his office immersed in paperwork. There were license updates, orders and stacks of job applications. It was just like Earth, but with more relaxed deadlines.

Still, it grated on him and one of the first things he always did when confronted with massive stacks of paperwork was to write a note about its needlessness and have it dropped in the suggestion box with all the others seeking some allowances for sexual relations in Heaven just like the kind people enjoyed back on Earth.

He did some office work involving renewals, capacity requirements before giving priority attention to the applications, which were often amusing if for no other reason than trying to discern the fake from the genuine. He was thinking that as he mused over the application from a man named Bart Ender who was applying to become The Dog's morning tap yanker.

Was it all a big prank? He thumbed through the applications and concluded the answer was yes.

Women named Kerry Z. Plates and Sue R. Vesmilles were applying to be waitresses. Then there was the Korean guy responding to a job-seeker ad to be the new Dog dishwasher. Name: Soo P. Waters.

In the end he hired them all, turned off the light, closed the door and headed down the adjoining hall to the library where he would for the next six hours he would revel in what he loved best about being in Heaven.

A man named Paige Turner loved having the time to read.

~

Evan's biggest concern was the routine would lead to carelessness. He took what he thought were sensible precautions to prevent anyone busting while he composed soulful love notes to one of heaven's angels. He'd come to rely on the *ding!* and its comforting warning signal, followed shortly by the door's *crreeeeaaakkk!* Together they were telltale touchstones of advancing trouble.

But he wasn't thinking of this when he was playfully messaging back-and-forth with Elle about the identity of her exciting new friend. He thought he was zeroing in and all signs were pointing to Petty.

Then he heard the bell *ding!* but instead of the creaking door, he heard a thoughtful tapping, so instead of abruptly severing the cranky connection he merely minimized the screen and replaced it with a grainy video of a man in rodeo costume having sex with a donkey. He told the door knocker to enter, already knowing who it was.

"Can I get you to please bookmark that for me?"

It was mass murderer and pop music critic Hugh Thanizer. Outside of Judas, Evan had little patience for even mundane interaction with Hell folk. They were surly, aggrieved, rude, and petty, and practiced the casual grooming habits of railroad hobos.

Thanizer, however, was tolerable, a guy Evan could rap with — and Thanizer kept proposing they actually rap together at the annual "Hell's Got Talent" show, the most egregiously misnamed program in entertainment history. Hell had no talent.

Thanizer'd been in Hell since 1978 after he'd hanged himself in the Statesville Correctional Center in Crest Hill, Illinois, where he'd been serving 15 consecutive life terms for the so-called mercy killings of 13 residents at the nearby Sunny Rest Assisted Living Center. The victims ages ranged from 32 to 89. All but two of the victims were in their 80s and suffering from painful conditions that were bound to kill them, but only when they were good and ready. Those killings took place over nine years and nearly went undetected. There'd been no investigations, no scrutiny until Thanizer killed a colleague and his supervisor. The colleague kept changing the classic rock channel to disco so Thanizer felt stabbing him in the heart was justified.

He offed the supervisor for being nosy about the disappearance of Nurse Dance Fever, and because he'd bummed $50 off her and she was getting impatient about the repayment, so she had to go.

He hated prison and with knotted sheets sought the supposed serenity of suicide. He never dreamed his earthly misdeeds would lead him to Hell, where his refined musical tastes would be assaulted by songs like "Muskrat Love," "Billy Don't Be a Hero," and, yep, disco hits like "Last Dance," "Disco Inferno," and "You Should Be Dancing."

Hell is particularly hard on people who aspire to musical tastefulness.

Evan enjoyed talking music with Hugh. He could push pause on his forbidden courtship for a few minutes — as long as Thanizer didn't lapse into his psychotic repetitions. During his trial, his defense attorneys noticed he'd been developing a habit of latching onto one phrase and working it into every sentence.

"Guess who I had lunch with yesterday?"

"Who?" Evan asked.

"John Wilkes Booth. Talk about surly. The guy is just miserable. And he hogged the salt shaker the whole meal. Bastard."

"What did you talk about?"

"Murder and music. He didn't start warming up until I told him I was in Hell for killing a guy over disco. He gave me props for that. He's obsessive about The Beatles. He's friends with Charlie Manson and you know Manson's just nuts about The Beatles."

Thanizer said both Booth and Manson were eager for Mark David Chapman to get to Hell in a hurry. The pair kept a list of all the people Chapman should have shot instead of John Lennon. It was a really long, thorough list.

"There were men like Kim Jung Il, Saddam Hussein and other tyrants. But the stupid list had a lot of basic jerks who I don't think are worthy of ballistic ventilation. The guy who invented the car theft alarm horn's on it. And what beef Booth ever had with him, I don't know. He's never even heard a car horn. But the worst is Mitch Turner. Does the name ring a bell?"

It did not.

"Sure it does. He was that wobbly place kicker for the Detroit Lions. His scattergun field goal attempts cost gamblers a small fortune back about 20 years ago. Does that ring a bell?"

"No. Does not ring a bell."

"But the worst thing about the list was their argument that Chapman should have shot McCartney instead of Lennon. You know why?"

Evan shook his head.

"Well, these two geniuses said because if he'd have shot Paul then the world would never have heard that awful that McCartney ditty, 'Simply Having a Wonderful Christmastime.' Now, don't tell me that doesn't ring a bell. One chorus concludes with Sir Paul singing, *"ding! dong! dong! ding!'* and on and on. Certainly, that rings a bell."

"Hugh, if you keep repeating yourself, you're outta here."

"Now, that rings a bell. I have this habit of repeating myself over and over again and again and I can't help it. So asking if I'm saying 'does that ring a bell?' rings a bell with me. Loud and clear."

"You have to go."

Then, as if by black magic the song changed from "Seasons in the Sun" to the 1978 Anita Ward disco song, "Ring my Bell."

> *You can ring my bell, ring my bell*
> *(Ring my bell, ding-dong-ding)*
> *You can ring my bell, ring my bell*
> *(Ring my bell, ring-a-ring-a-ring)*

"Boy," Thanizer said, "does *that* ring a bell. 'Ring my Bell' is the song that was playing when I stabbed that stupid orderly through the heart. Man, the memories I got going through my head. Small world. Even Hell, man, these coincidences. That's really ringing my bell."

Evan stood, turned around and escorted the now-babbling Thanizer out. Evan thought he was acting like a real ding-a-ling, but tried to clear bellish descriptor from his mind. Then he returned to his computer and enlarged the screen. He typed: "You there?"

She was. He felt momentarily justified in not severing the connection for security purposes.

"I give up," he typed. "Who is this exciting new mystery friend? My guess is Tom Petty. Am I right?"

"No, you're not even close," Elle informed.

"No more guesses. Who? Who?"

"Okay. Ready or not. It's L ... O ... L ... A!"

The classic rock reference confused him and he typed, "Ray Davies?"

He could almost sense the exasperation in in her typing. "How many Lolas do you know?"

Well, he only knew one Lola, but he couldn't believe it could be her. He couldn't believe the girl he'd fallen in love with in his star-crossed long-distance unconsummated love affair could be partying in Heaven with the mother he'd killed. The very idea was so bewildering he failed to pay any attention to the *crreeaaakk!* of the door, alone as it was without the telltale *ding!* of the bell.

And by then it was too late. Because he felt his breath on his ear and before he could turn around, he heard him say.

"Lola who?"

It was his father. He'd disengaged the simple alarm system and was holding the key component in his hands.

On this occasion, Rusty did not ring a bell.

19

IN THE DOG HOUSE

Lola Lee was seated at the conference table marveling at framed philosophizing by a genius unknown. The plaques, two dozen of them, were nailed snugly to what Turner called his "Wall of Enduring Wisdoms." The rarely used conference room could comfortably accommodate a dozen conferees, but hadn't been used in 15 years, back when Dog regulars had been petitioned to lower the pub drinking age from 18 to 15. It was rejected by a 6-5 majority vote with philosopher Socrates casting the deciding vote based on his belief that, even though it was eternity, he didn't want to have to explain liking Bob Dylan all over again to another generation of youthful innocents.

NONE OF SOCRATES'S sayings were deemed wall-worthy. Instead there were unattributed ones that read:

"Fools pray for money and get nothing.
The righteous pray for wisdom and need nothing."

"Honesty without tact is like brain surgery without anesthesia. The operation can succeed, but the cure could kill."

"We are all born free and spend the rest of our lives constructing prisons around ourselves."

She was moved by the profundities, and when Paige, Lyberty and Pat Finder entered the room asked about the source.

"It's a riddle none of us have been able to unravel," Paige said. "I found them in stack of old newspapers at a garage sale about 100 years ago. I have more in the back room. I asked Socrates, Plato, Mary Wollstonecraft, Aristotle — all the usual suspects. None of them claimed authorship. We even put Sir Arthur Conan Doyle on the case and he couldn't sleuth it out."

Lyberty watched him carefully to see if his poker face would crack. She knew he was the author, but he was always coy about owning up. She suspected he'd tried in vain to get them published, but had been defeated by mass rejection of the cruelly indifferent publishing industry. In Heaven you could basically have whatever you wanted but — on Earth as it is in Heaven — it was near impossible for a non-celeb like Paige to get even a great book published.

He never admitted to anyone that the quotes were, indeed, his, a rare example of a Wise Man playing dumb.

"But that's not why we invited you here, Lola," Paige said. "Do you know why?"

She did not. She'd answered a crisp knock on her apartment door and opened it to see Pat Finder. She recognized her as the girl she'd espied spying on her and Elle. She didn't find it suspicious. Elle was adored, and Lola knew many were envious of the time she spent with her. None of that was mentioned in the somewhat formal invitation for her to join the trio for drinks and appetizers at The Dog. She assumed it was just another opportunity to be social, have fun and make new friends and in Heaven that happened all the time. In that way, Heaven reminded her of a Carnival Cruise she took to Punta Cana the week after her divorce settlement with Rusty dropped anchor in family court.

"We know you and Elle Lavator have been spending a lot of time together, and we know she's in a relationship with your son in Hell," Paige said.

The blunt revelation startled her. Everyone knew she and Elle and been spending lots of time together. But how could they know that Elle was in love with Evan in Hell?

"Is she," Lola asked with a nod in Finder's direction, "spying on Elle and me?"

"Elle's been careless on social media," Paige said. "I must say, this may be the land of milk and honey, but the truly sticky stuff was coming from Elle's computer."

"But, how could you?" Lola asked. "I mean there are passwords, firewalls, redundant security systems, not to mention the ethics of sharing such snoopery outside of the involved parties."

"C'mon, Lola," he said, 'it's Facebook."

Facebook privacy in Heaven was notoriously porous.

"Well, just how is any of that your business?"

"It's everyone's business," Lyberty said. "Her infatuation could taint all of Heaven. We fear a domino effect where others seek to contaminate our splendors with all these killers and scumbags, and when that happens Heaven will become just like Earth. People condemned to Hell need to stay in Hell. We can't have these bastards bringing any of their ruin to paradise."

Lola stewed for 12 seconds before saying, "That's my son you're talking about."

"He killed 36 innocents and one guy who had it coming," Lyberty said, reluctantly.

"And don't forget that cat," Paige interjected. He'd felt bad about the gambling nuns, the erratic bus driver, but the Copycat was utterly blameless.

"But he's a good boy who just had one really bad day," she said. It was a vivid display of how a mother's boundless love extends beyond even elemental metaphysical boundaries. "And these are just two kids trying to figure it out out. I believe they truly love each other and are wistful for a kind of love that's unique to what happens between two consenting humans on Earth."

"Lola, this isn't Romeo and Juliet," Lyberty said. "It's not even 'Joannie Loves Chachi,'" an obscure pop reference that sent Pat Finder diving for her smartphone. "This has the potential to corrupt Heaven, to degrade it. It could soil all we hold dear about the place, all we prayed about and struggled for on Earth. And the more time she spends encouraging him with this ill-fated on-line flirtation, the greater the risk."

"You're wrong," Lola said quietly. "There's no chance of that happening."

"And just what makes you so sure of that?" Lyberty asked.

"Because Elle told me she sees no future in any online courtship between herself and my son," and shooting a nasty look at Lyberty threw in, "And he's NOT a bad boy!"

"Well, tell us," Paige said impatiently.

"She's going to unfriend him as soon she figures a way for them to be together," Lola said.

"And just how does she expect to make that happen?" Paige asked.

"Elle's going to Hell."

20

LOLA SHARES ELLE'S PLANS

Elle spilled the beans shortly after she'd spilled the beans. She'd been tipsy after the third bottle of wine and nappy after the fourth, which was fine with Lola. They'd left the Golden Gate Bridge in a giddy stagger with Elle repeatedly darting to the railing to gaze down at the waves.

"I didn't think it was odd," Lola said. "She'd never been drunk when she was alive and she was into it."

Lots of people were. Beer on earth was thought to be 5,000 years old; wine was even older. Evidence of the first wine-producing facility was found in Armenia dating back 6,100 years. The wine snobs all said roughly 4081 B.C. was a very good year.

In Heaven, there were no dastardly or shameful consequences to getting good and drunk, and unlike their human counterparts, people didn't drink to get drunk or fill an emptiness in their soul. Their souls had no holes. All souls were wholes. And they didn't drink to go out of their gourds. Their gourds were gone, entombed in some weed-strewn graveyard back in another world.

Drinking in Heaven was purely social, an act of convivial beauty, an expression of communal joy, all without the risks or negative outcomes. You could get as drunk as you want and not worry about getting pulled over. You could guzzle hootch 'til your heart's content and not get hungover.

Or you could. It was Heaven and you could do whatever the hell you wanted.

It's just that no one else ever did. People were overjoyed to bask in the rewards of having lived exemplary human lives. It was unbecoming, they knew, but many angels would admit to a certain smugness at having made the heavenly cut, like being in Heaven meant the Judgment Day referee had ratified them the winner of all those Facebook fights they'd gotten into with erstwhile friends over things like Trump's border policies.

With that in your quiver and all your wishes coming true 'round-the-clock for eternity, who'd want to spoil the party by getting all gooned up and making an ass of themselves?

Elle Lavator, that's who.

She was the first soul in heaven anyone could remember who acted like she played by the rules regulating earthly conduct. Acted, in fact, like she preferred it. She reminded Lola of the kids in junior high experimenting with their first drink the weekend the folks left them alone and forgot to hide the key to the liquor cabinet.

"She'd get really drunk, lay down and nap, wake up and either have some more or make coffee. She woke up drunk and tried to make coffee, but spilled the beans so instead of coffee, she poured another glass of wine while I made her some coffee."

The combination seemed to give her focus, she said, because she became articulate, more expansive, more profound. Or as Lola put it, "She started laying down some real deep shit."

She was talking about all the souls with all the holes. It was very upsetting to her. And when something upset Elle, she made it her mission to go wherever she had to go to ease suffering. On Earth, that meant she did church mission work in hellholes like Syria, Ethiopia and Yemen. She'd told her mission planners she'd wanted the worst-of-the-worst, the godforsaken places of doom, the ones that housed the hopeless.

Given Elle's background, it didn't take Lola even a second of her eternity to puzzle out the location of her next proverbial hellhole.

"'Everyone in Heaven is a Christian,' she'd say. 'We should be doing all we can to help save lost souls. If I learned anything on Earth it's that the people who are often most difficult to love are the ones who need love most."

She wasn't referring to her son, Lola said, but she by now knew Elle well enough to understand her grand scheme was masking a more basic mission, one that had less to do with the soul than the heart.

"She'd mentioned it all before," Lola said. "She was saying it wasn't fair how many people go Hell who never had a chance. She'd say how she was lucky to have been raised by two loving parents who'd stayed together, been good role models, avoided most of the more debilitating recreational drugs, and encouraged us to be well-rounded and ambitious individuals."

And, consequently, she figured if one was as graced as she was with so many advantages that bestowed her with an afterlife leg-up, then those who'd been thusly disadvantaged should have been given maybe a bit of a break, an afterlife sort of Affirmative Action.

Elle'd calculated from her experience that as many as a third of human beings existed without souls. They shuffled through life never once bending to the sweet breezes of humble humanity. Perpetually glum, morbidly morose, they were blatantly indifferent to anything that might tickle a vibrant intellect. If life is a dance, their every move was a mope.

"She thought some of them were simply defectives, that they'd been born with some essential switch left turned off, thus consigning these defectives to bland lives under what she called beige rainbows. Even more upsetting about the ones who through neglect or carelessness misplaced their souls or, worse, had them beaten out of them."

Lola said she'd naively countered it was impossible to kill souls. Souls were the very essence of humanity. Kill a soul? It'd be like trying to put a bullet in a ghost.

Her offhand appraisal caused Elle to show her a side Lola had not seen before. It was a flash of ferocity, justification, righteousness bound by determination.

"Don't think you can kill a soul?" she said. "They're killing them all the time. You kill one when you tell a kid he's not cool enough to sit with you in the cafeteria. When a boy laughs in the face of a girl who'd just used up all her courage to ask him out, her soul dies a little bit. When co-workers make out-in-the-open plans to meet after work right in front of Nick and then don't bother to invite him, that kills some soul.

"When someone paints a picture, writes a book or crafts a lop-sided little vase on a potter's wheel and people mock or ignore it, a little bit of soul dies."

Souls could be wounded or killed on purpose or merely through neglect, she said. Soul killers could be as gargantuan as a totalitarian government or as intimate as a 6th grade snub.

Elle sat back in her sofa and grew silent. Lola mistakenly thought she was finished and began to tiptoe to the door when she heard Elle in soft, spent voice call her name.

"You know another way to kill a soul? Tell a young girl who's in love that she'll never — never — for all eternity be able to love her dream guy because he's just all wrong for her.

"You kill her soul when you tell her she can't love him because he's the wrong color, the wrong religion, doesn't have the right job, that he comes from a bad family or that he's from the wrong side of the tracks.

"That's a sure way to kill a soul."

21

AZIZ AHL SEES SOME

Meanwhile, down the hall from where Paige, Lyberty and Scout began asking Lola questions about Elle and her alleged soullessness, Aziz Ahl was sitting bolt upright trying to blink away the surreality of what he'd just seen.

The Desolation Row drone that he'd asked Neetles to release near a wallless sector of Heaven had been beaming back shocking results. What he'd initially dismissed as static had turned out to be a large roving mass of what appeared to be idly roaming twilight souls. Part dawn, part dusk, these leaderless, herd-like roamers seemed to move like amoeba through a purgatory Ahl had thought was purely metaphorical.

It was mesmerizing. Millions of discarded souls moving without will or whim like one of the groovy lava lights that enjoyed momentary popularity every 20 or so years. Gray, expressionless faces uncreased by joy or sorrow, Ahl wondered about their origins. How did they get there? Did they ever serve a purpose? Could any of them ever be redeemed? Would they ever expire?

So many shades of gray, so much grim monotony, so much drab, bland conformity — and then ...

He nearly missed it, a fleck of red, no bigger than a period on a page. He was reaching out to wipe the imperfection off the screen when a face beneath the speck turned upward and began speaking to the drone.

The red was a splash of color like a lifeboat in a vast gray sea. Ahl zoomed in. The hat was one of those big floppy red-and-white toppers like The Cat wears in Dr. Seuss's "The Cat in the Hat," the eternally joyful ode to silly rhyme. Ahl was suddenly on fire to know who the cat in this hat was and what he was trying to say.

He focused on the man and spun the dials on the control panels until he attained the best clarity. The man appeared to be in his early 20s. Unlike those marching around him, his face was alive with expression, and he had something to say.

Just what Ahl couldn't discern. The drone had no mics or equivalent sound features. He needed an expert lip reader.

Instead, he got Noel.

"I need you to see this, and I need you to keep this between just the two of us," Ahl said. "Can I trust you?"

"Sure, you can," Noel lied. He'd posted an account of what Ahl had been up to on his shadow Facebook page before the lunch rush. It went viral instantly.

"Good. This is the feed from that drone. It located a sort of purgatory, a place where souls of indifference go when they've wasted their lives in mundane nothingness. They're not good enough for Heaven, but too good to warrant eternal damnation.

"Now, I remember you saying you're a lip reader, correct?"

Noel confirmed he'd said just that, which didn't make it true, but he did say it like it was.

"Yeah, I can read lips. Test me."

It seemed as silly as Seuss, but Ahl figured it couldn't hurt so he soundlessly mouthed, "You better not be foolin' me," which Noel translated into, "Shoe header hot tree rulin' tea."

"Okay, genius, what is this guy trying to tell us?"

He cued it up again and hit play. Both Noel and Aziz stared at the screen. The man did not appear to be distressed. More like bemused. Noel stared at his moving lips. He asked to see it again. And again. And a fourth and fifth time. He then announced, "It's pretty clear the man is addle-brained. Why else would he be muttering such gibberish?"

Noel then announced with the utmost confidence that the cat in the hat was saying, "My name is Bother Thou sand bill you bingy a bear."

Ahl told him to resume busing tables and decided to try and crack the puzzle himself. He couldn't be sure, but he thought the man was telling anyone who cared his name.

His name wasn't Bother Thou.

His name was Arthur Thou, and he was asking the drone to bring him a beer.

22

CHRISTMAS IN HELL

Christmas in Hell was always a real drag, like being in Buffalo from 1990 through '94 when the Bills lost four straight Super Bowls. Life was a constant reminder that you'd backed a loser, things weren't going to get any better and it was still godforsaken winter in Buffalo.

And although no one would say it aloud, everyone missed something about Christmas. They missed decorating the tree, opening the presents or sneaking a smooch 'neath the mistletoe. For some of them, Christmas was the only good memory of a life that led them straight to Hell, a place where celebrating the Savior's birth was considered faux pas — faux pas enough to earn the Yule celebrant a stint in Hell's Time Out.

No one was supposed to talk about Christmas, but Evan thought he could trust Judas. So they talked about Christmas as they watched Jill Keyes silently terrorize the new fish.

"It drives him crazy," Judas said of Satan, "that Jesus's birthday is such a big deal on earth and that no one even knows his birthday. He thinks there should be anti-Satan parades, protests and greatest hits movie marathons of things like 'The Omen.' He craves attention. He's outraged no one knows his birthday."

Evan hadn't really thought about it. He had no clue. He asked his friend.

"It's February 29," Judas said. "He's a Leap Year baby."

"That explains a lot," Evan said. "I had a leapling cellmate back in the Athens County joint. He blamed all his troubles and misbehaviors over feeling shortchanged on his birthday and his parents not knowing whether to celebrate on Feb. 28 or March 1. He was serious, too. Jury didn't buy it. But he always said leaplings got cheated, like babies born on Christmas Day, but I guess that wasn't really a problem for Jesus."

The observation sent Judas into a reverie about the old days before Jesus became the Savior — and when Judas said "Savior," he always said it with air quotes like he was discussing some international conglomerate such as Brown & Root or Monsanto. Being the "Savior" to Judas meant big business. He always clung to the intimate personal recollection of when Jesus was still a sort of Mom & Pop shoppe.

"Remember — growing up there and then with Jesus was vastly different. There was no Black Friday, no big doorbuster sales. What you know as Christmas was just another day. And Jesus was just another guy. A lot of illiterates had no idea what one day was from the next. Calendars were unheard of.

"It was the same with birthdays. Most people didn't know if they were Sagittarius or Pisces. They didn't have any hallmark birthdays. It wasn't like turning 16 meant you could run out and get your driver's license. It was almost as near the advent of the motor vehicle as it'd been the advent of the wheel.

"Were we a bunch of primitives? No, we were not, but they were simpler times. Would I have preferred being born and living during more exciting times? Absolutely not. I prefer simpler times, simpler things. All these fancy gizmos I hear people talking about, well, they're not for me."

Besides being the Biblical betrayer of the Son of God, Judas was also a bit of a technophobe.

The birthday talk sparked in Judas a vivid memory of the night when Jesus turned 30. He and the rest of the apostles had hired an innkeeper to throw a lavish feast. Besides being Savior, Jesus was a really great boss. The innkeeper went all out, he said. There was wine, fish, fresh vegetables — all of it first-rate.

"I'll never forget," Judas said, "the innkeeper took this circular flat bread and ladled on some spicy garlic tomato sauce. The she took some cheese and cured meats and sprinkled them on top of the circular flatbread. Then she threw it in this old wood-fired oven for 20 minutes.

"When she thought it was done, she removed it from the oven and sliced it into these little triangular pieces. It was delicious. I never before or since had anything like it. I remember asking Esther — that was her name. Or was it Irma? Anyhoo, I asked her what she called it. Esther/Irma said she called it 'circular flatbread with spicy garlic tomato sauce topped with cheese and cured meats.'"

Evan told Judas that he was describing pizza.

"Pizza? You don't say? Man, that was good. Everybody loved it. Jesus asked her to bring another one, but this time he asked her to put some anchovy on it. Ruined the whole damn thing. Jesus had the whole rest of that circular flatbread and spicy garlic tomato sauce topped with cheese and cured meat and anchovy whatever meal all to himself.

"I'm not going to deny it. I was pissed. That was more

than 2000 years ago. I never got another bite. You know, I'll bet if people knew there was no pizza in Hell they'd be a lot better behaved with their souls hanging in the balance."

Evan said nothing, but was in full agreement. Fewer people would wind up in Hell if they knew there was no circular flat bread with spicy garlic tomato sauce topped with cheese and cured meats once they got there.

Judas asked what he missed about Christmas. Evan didn't have to even think: "Christmas in Indiana, Pennsylvania, at The Jimmy Stewart Museum. My Mom thought seeing 'It's A Wonderful Life' every Christmas should be a national obligation. The Stewart Museum is perfectly charming. Every year all day they screen the movie in their cozy little theater. Such a happy memory."

He wondered if he could rig an illicit "Wonderful Life" screening for just him and Judas. He might be able to pull it off, but getting Judas the technophobe to watch on a computer seemed unlikely. Evan thought Lola could persuade him to watch. She believed, he said, the message — that every life has enormous worth — is one that needs constant reinforcing. And the movie is just perfectly entertaining. It's funny. It's sentimental. And it gives the heterosexual men an annual opportunity to fall in love with Donna Reed all over again.

"I'll never forget this one time the audience included a woman who I thought must've have escaped from the local lunatic asylum. She laughed hysterically at even the mildest laugh lines. She roared when George was shopping for luggage, she cackled when Harry Bailey was carrying plates on his head, and when the floor to the pool opened up she laughed so hard I thought the building would collapse. It was excessive and I figured the woman, about 40, was probably nuts. I whispered that to Lola — that's Ma's name — and she glared at me.

"She said, 'Or maybe she was just one of those perfectly nice and joyful people, the kind of person you'd imagine Jimmy Stewart was all the time. Either way, it's pretty clear she's the kind of person who won't cut in line, ruin your day with road ragery or cause a nasty Facebook fight over pointless political differences."

Evan remembered he had started to backpedal, but Lola was just getting started.

"Insane? We should all be so insane," she said. "We need more like her. For that reason alone, I hope she carries the movie's message with her throughout her every day. I hope she wakes up realizing her joyful exuberance is making a difference throughout the world, that she is an inspiration to those who struggle and that by finding happiness in even little things, she is making everything better. Because she matters. A lot. We all do. Because it's a wonderful life. It's a pretty darn good movie, too."

It was a beautiful speech and Evan's heart warmed at the memory. And at that moment, if he could have made any wish come true it would be to take his friend Judas to Indiana, Pennsylvania, to see "It's A Wonderful Life" at The Jimmy Stewart Museum with Lola and Elle.

And because he knew it would never happen right then and there at the very gates of Hell, Evan felt an utterly alien emotion. He felt like he was going to cry. He'd been resigned to his fate throughout his life and his afterlife. Now he felt an aching poignancy for the roads he didn't take, for the bartenders he didn't shoot, the nuns he did not run off the road, etc. He felt a singular woe, a combination of past regrets and future dread. He felt cornered. He'd never feel lower, more vulnerable. He felt a need to reach out, to unburden, to confide. Fully aware of the historic irony, he turned to the only man in Hell he thought he could trust.

He turned to Judas.

"Hey, man," he said, "I have some things I have to get off my chest. I need someone to talk to. Can I trust you?"

"Jesus did," he said, "and you saw how that worked out."

They both looked over at Jill Keyes. She was fully engaged overseeing the welcome-to-Hell tortures of a Big Pharma executive who'd made obscene profits on drugs proven in test trials to save the lives of pregnant mothers, but who died when they could no longer afford the pills. He used the profits from the drugs to buy a Major League Baseball franchise, sold off all the quality players and stole the hope of long-suffering fans. He upped the price of beer, too, thus assuring his status as a first-ballot Hell of Famer.

There were many gaudy perks to being a white-collar criminal on Earth. In Hell, not so much.

From what he remembered of his bewildering arrival, entrants were required to mill about for days on end outside the gates in a stifling-hot warehouse-sized waiting room before being summoned. Many mistakenly believed the waiting room was Hell. It was hot, confusing and full of evil men and women. There were TVs, but the clickers were all broken so it had to be Hell. By then, all the anxiety and deprivation made the summons a welcome distraction. It was so bad in that warehouse, you almost forgot that bad things can always get worse.

Keyes was scrupulous about her duties. The gate was never allowed to open for more than the split second it took to admit another one of the doomed. Then the beatings commenced. Could he bust out during the brutal commotion?

Not without help.

He put thoughts of escape deep in his head and turned to Judas: "It all started when they gave me that computer and asked me to hack Heaven," his brown eyes dancing mischievously on his face animated by mirthful recollection. "They wanted me to disrupt their perfections, stir up trouble. I did all that, but wound up falling in love. It was a long-distance relationship, sure, but residential differences aside, we have so much in common. It's the first time I've ever known a girl where I didn't have sex like right away. And by right away, I'm talking like in the ladies' room about eight minutes after our first howdy-do."

It was a match made in Heaven, he said, knowing full well the statement was freighted with boxcars full of obvious logistical inaccuracies.

He hadn't realized how much he'd been enjoying the courtship of his heavenly angel until he shared it all with Judas. He told him about their first IM conversation the way other young lovers talk about a first kiss. He told him about how her playful earnestness led him to lower all his defenses, and how he'd managed to maintain discreet if sporadic communications with his angel.

"She's convinced me that someday we'll be together," he said. "For the life of me, I don't see how, but she says with love anything is possible. Now, I believe in love like I never dreamed I could."

And he told of the terror he felt when he noticed Rusty's fetid breath dampening his shoulder the day his secret was exposed. He shared with Judas every morsel of his and Elle's budding romance and how he lay awake at night dreaming of escaping Hell and ending up in Elle's soulful arms and making love in a way he never had before.

He was so lost in dreams of a future that may never in all eternity happen that he barely felt Judas's elbow nudging him in the ribs until it was done with sufficient force to leave a faint bruise. He'd been too distracted to notice that Keyes had been staring at the both of them.

And now he could see she was mouthing words at the pair.

"What's she saying?" Evan asked.

"She's either saying, 'I can read lips!' or she's wishing us a Merry Christmas!"

23

LUNCH IN HEAVEN

It was a meeting of the utmost import if for no other reason than one of the topics involved the potential import of a hellish contaminant. Their decisions could leave an eternal dent in Heaven's quality of life. Every aspect of the consequences of their decisions could have everlasting impact — or at least until Jesus got back from His authoring sabbatical and straightened it all out.

To make matters worse, their every meeting was now being broadcast to an ever-growing multitude eager for distracting novelty. This was really the first authentic reality show in the history of Heaven. Others strove for authenticity, but fell short.

How could they do otherwise as long as Jeff Probst's human heart was still beating?

Viewers said they watched because they sensed they had a vested interest in the outcome. Whatever was going to happen to Evan and Elle was bound to alter the very character of Heaven.

Wanna know what you're playin' for?

Paige was prepared to begin the program laying out the

vital questions that needed to be addressed: Could a soul in Hell be paroled (there was a first time for everything); was one of the most popular women in Heaven really so unhappy in Heaven she might, in fact, consider soulicide (the word was coined by heavenly wit, Mike Royko); and could a soul be allowed to, in effect, under its own will defect to Hell?

And because this was Heaven, Paige, Lyberty and, to a lesser degree, Pat expected a certain level of sophistication. Therefore, the most pressing question was of where to enjoy that day's pre-broadcast lunch.

It, too, was filmed. Viewers enjoyed the behind-the-scenes and the off-the-record commentary. Paige in particular was acquiring a cult following for his easy banter and Cockney conversation

Paige argued persuasively in favor of a little roadside lobster shack in Wiscasset, Maine. "It's called Red's Eats," he said. "The lobster roll is all lobster — no celery or lettuce or any of that other crappy rabbit food. Just pure lobster. It's $9.99, a little pricey, but it's worth it."

Lyberty almost won the argument by proposing Pascal's Manale on Napoleon Avenue in New Orleans. "We all start with a cup of gumbo and then share an order of Pascal's original Barbecue Shrimp. Mmmmm ..... mmmmm ... mmmm. You just can't beat it. Mmm!"

But in the end, they went where they'd been for four of their last four weeks. They went to Disney World! EPCOT, specifically. They did this because it was fun, the food was good, and they did it out of deference to Pat. She was proving herself as able and affable as any of the scouts with more historic pedigrees. And unlike, say, Kit Carson, Renegade Pete "Four Fingers" Gustovson, or Danny "One Ear"

Herald, Pat Finder didn't require a fresh mule. She just used her imagination.

She'd already ingratiated herself with Lola sufficiently that she was acting as a trusted go-between for the moment when Paige and Lyberty were ready to approach her. And that moment was nearing. But first they needed to establish the ground rules for any powwow. Who'd be there? Who could ask questions? How much ground were they prepared to surrender?

That ostensibly was the agenda for these working lunches. But despite the evident urgency of their gatherings, the lunches all seemed to cascade into the trio spending the three-plus hours of unstructured jolliness. Paige insisted any civil lunch be a minimum of two hours and watching Paige get progressively drunk became must-see viewing. The highlight was when he'd lapse into Cockney limerick-doggerel involving the fable of Evan and Elle in Heaven and Hell.

"If Evan and Elle from 'eaven and 'ell thought life would be a lark,

Then Elle 'n' Evan from 'ell 'n' 'eaven would find life but a walk in the park."

He'd then move on to rhymes about Larry and Carrie from the Township of Derry; Tim and Kim from the village of LaLimme, etc. Lyberty could see Pat was enjoying the nimble-mindedness of Paige on a roll, but cut him right off when he started a dubious limerick involving a lad named Brock and a lass from a town called Medinah.

"Whoa! That's enough, Paige," Lyberty said. "You're veering into tastelessness."

Pat sat there alive with interest as her mind raced through her own versions of the recreations that would ensue when a boy named Brock met a girl from a town called Medinah.

The bibulous lunch ended without the whole point of meeting even being brought up. The only decision they'd made was to extend the silly siesta to Maine for lobster rolls at Red's Eats followed by gumbo and Barbecue Shrimp at Paschal's Manale in New Orleans. The day ended after much laughter, much fellowship and an increase in camaraderie that was commensurate with a relative increase in phantom cholesterol.

None of it mattered. They were in Heaven and almost everyone in Heaven was having a hell of a good time.

And later that night at home while watching a Jimmy Stewart movie marathon, Lyberty wrote up a detailed proposal, complete with multiple bullet-point affirmations, that offered detailed and fair solutions to every eventuality that might arise from a civil confrontation with Elle Lavator over l'affaire Evan Lee and sent copies to Paige and Pat Finder. Upon awakening the next morning, Paige gave the proposal an approving scan and a quick assent. Didn't change a word. Lyberty's document covered all the bases. Paige trusted her implicitly. The Wise Man was, indeed, a wise man.

All was proceeding as planned. It looked as though embarrassing cataclysm would be avoided, a PR disaster averted.

Who could ask for anything more?

They were soon to be introduced to the one who would in the very near future ask for so much, much more.

24

EARTH MATTERS

Meanwhile back on Earth, the corporeal humans spent their every waking moment unwittingly doing deeds that would determine their stark afterlife destinations. The stakes were becoming less and less clear, the lines of demarcation more and more muddled, as the mortal realm was increasingly becoming an arena where Heaven and Hell mingled like chili on the simmer.

It was Veteran's Day, a day dedicated to commemorating man-made carnage, when armies from around the world rushed to the Philippines to try and alleviate some of the God-made kind. The typhoon had killed 100,000. At first glance it seemed like mankind had entered an enlightened age where our great armies were mobilized for strictly humanitarian missions.

If only the trajectory of man's collective reaction to human suffering were that simple.

Because in five years there was always a chance future veterans would be steaming to those very same ports to annihilate the same poor bastards their heroic predecessors were once determined to save.

Cataclysmic events were piling up with dizzying frequency. It became a cosmic certainty no one would ever again experience what used to be described as a "slow news day." It was 24/7 genocide in central Africa, famine in Asia and raging all around the world were the typical my-god's-better-than-your-god wars that never went out of fashion.

And many in positions to help began succumbing to the worst disease ever to strike mankind:

Indifference.

They'd see 100,000 dead in the Philippines and think, man, there's not a thing I can do about that.

They'd say their prayers that God will help the godforsaken, but there's zero evidence He'd heeded any of the many prayers they'd said asking that He stop with all the deadly earthquakes, volcanos, hurricanes and other calamities the bloodless insurance industry describes as "acts of God."

The only thing more efficient at killing than Acts of God were the Acts of Man.

Connoisseurs of killing needed to only look back on the instigation for Veteran's Day. That would be World War I, the conflict that confounds students of history as maybe the most insane of them all.

In about four tidy years, the war killed 8.5 million soldiers and about 14 million civilians.

The armistice was as maddening as the bloodshed that preceded it. The armistice was signed at 5 a.m. that day meaning the war was over, but the carnage continued for six more bloody hours until it technically went into effect on the 11th hour of the 11th day of the 11th month. During those six hours after the truce was signed, 2,738 from both sides were killed and another 8,000 wounded.

The first and last soldiers to die in the war were killed within a few miles of each other and coincidentally buried in the same Saint-Symphorien, Belgium, cemetery — just seven yards apart.

History students are still having a tough time making sense of it all.

Pestilence, famine, hurricanes, earthquakes, volcanic mayhem — these were acts of God, a vicious, vengeful and arbitrary meanie of a God.

The drumbeat of doom was becoming so relentless it was easy to forget that a giant redwood, a wondrous sunset, and a magnificent first kiss were all Acts of God, too, as are the births of all our children.

We shouldn't hold it against God when some of those kids turn out to be hellraisers. One of them was Randall P. "Rusty" Lee, who at that very moment was in Hell wondering just where the hell it had all gone so wrong.

25

RUSTY DOES CARD TRICKS

It was mesmerizing the way the cards remained in motion. Like dry leaves being elevated by an autumn gusts, they'd flutter and dance in mid-air and somehow land stacked in order and in defiance of the laws of both chance and physics. With card shuffling skills and deceptions like that, he'd have been a fine con man.

And Rusty Lee had been just that. He'd worked lucrative scams across the Midwest. He was a gifted grifter. But he'd been born lazy and had, against his nature, been raised mean. His father, Carl, had been a railroad engineer who was home only long enough to each month to traumatize his son. He was the son of a son of a bully. Mean dispositions were the only thing one generation of Lee men bequeathed to the next. That and the racism, misogyny, grievance and belief that a somehow the deck had always been stacked against a family of card sharps.

For any man handy with a deck of the devil's pasteboards, it was a tough contradiction with which to deal.

He always wondered if he would have been a successful "art" artist had that side of him been encouraged. He thought being an artist would have been easier than being a bully, which was so stressful he'd become an alcoholic by the time he was 20. He'd always thought he'd have been a good one.

His paintings in school showed a sensitivity toward gentler things, still lifes, meadows, and butterflies. His hand had a light touch and the brushes gave faint, but vivid dynamics when his hand danced across the canvas. Even all these years later, he wondered just what he'd been thinking the first time he'd shown an early landscape to his father.

Sure, the beating had hurt. It always did. But he was surprised by the bitter sting he felt from his father's cruel mockery and how when he'd snapped the brushes it had felt like he'd snapped the bones in his hands. The hands involuntarily formed tiny fists and the fists were all that remained.

The first time he beat Lola was because she'd sassed him. It had felt natural, an Old Testament sort of spousal communion. He'd at one time truly loved her. This ceased when she began to encourage him that he could be better than himself, that he could still become the man he dreamt of becoming back before it had been beaten from him.

The thought of squandered opportunity infuriated him.

She never brought it up again. Neither did he.

Beating Evan for the first time had felt different, unnatural. Even as he drew back his fist, he remembered thinking, man, does the kid really have this coming? No, he did not. But neither did he. And by then, the proverbial bullet was already speeding down the barrel. And you can't boomerang a bullet. He didn't even know what the kid had done to deserve the beating, but maybe that was the whole point.

Senseless violence was senseless for a reason.

It made no sense in his experience, either.

He thought about asking his old man — he'd been in Hell since he died in 1963. But Rusty and his father hadn't spoken since 1947, and it didn't look like they'd ever speak. He was in Hell, too, sure, but the impenetrable silence that existed when they were alive extended to the grave and beyond. So, no, he didn't talk to his father, who didn't talk to Rusty's grandfather who didn't speak to his great grandpa, etc.

In fact, the only kin he spoke to was his own son, his executioner, and all they did was bicker.

The cards tumbled between his knuckles. One after another the aces popped up. Then the kings, queens, jacks — a veritable conga line of chicanery. Evan hated his father and felt no remorse for killing him, but he admired the way he could make a deck of cards come alive. His dexterity was like that of the great Andres Segovia, the classically trained Spanish guitar virtuoso. His mother had taken him to see Segovia in Athens. He hadn't wanted to go, but wound up glad he did. The great Segovia was a marvel. He imagined with such nimbleness, his dad could have been a tremendous guitar player. But as he did his card tricks Rusty looked bored, detached, aloof from his mastery.

Evan never knew what made his old man so uncommonly hateful. He didn't care. He believed no one was a prisoner of their past. He couldn't imagine ever laying a hand on a woman, much less a child. He may have had a roll in dispatching 37 souls — not counting Copy — but he still felt morally superior to his no-good, wife-beating, child-pummeling father.

And now his old man knew the one secret that could get him in the kind of trouble that in Hell could lead to real trouble and in Hell that really meant something. Judas had told him all about Hell's Hell, the place where Satan himself oversaw the sadistic beatings, the kind that made Jill Keyes' welcomes seem like playful tickle-fests in comparison.

So, he knew the stakes. Anyone trying to escape Hell was doomed to spend a lengthy stretch in Time Out. But he remained confident it could be done. He just knew he'd need a lot of luck and a lot of help.

And now he'd need to secure the cooperation of the man who hated him for murdering him. And just how much did Rusty know? How long had he been standing there? Did he know about Lola? Elle? He'd been unusually quiet since his surprise interruption.

Evan could only guess.

But what he should have known was that his father hated him. He hated him for standing up to him. He hated him for succeeding where he had failed. He hated him for murdering him. And he hated him for his theft.

Evan had stolen from him his last shot at redemption. He always felt if he could get a little money, he could turn his life around and maybe stop the crooked hustle. That's what he was doing on that ill-fated day. He'd heard Lola had won a bundle. He was going to plead with her and the boy for a cut to stake a new life. It was his sincerest wish. In fact, it was destined to become his dying wish.

Because the music was too loud, neither Lola nor the boy could hear him knocking. It made him mad. Already drunk, he pulled his pistol — never hurt to be safe — kicked in the door and barged in. He didn't know who was in the house nor the threat level of the occupants. He crept toward the music.

He saw the stupid cat first. He didn't shoot, an act of restraint which he thought qualified him for responsible gun owner status.

Then he saw the boy charging at him. In hindsight, it may have worked out better for him had he sacrificed his son, all for the greater good and all. At least his own greater good. Because he could have pleaded, truthfully, the boy was trying to kill his ex-wife.

But he did not. He lowered the gun. In a split-second, quick as a blitzing linebacker, the boy was on him. He didn't know it, but he'd be dead in three seconds.

Because Evan, unarmed and fearing for his life, a likelihood that would have ended his in-motion plans to kill his mother, charged at his father and shoved him backwards down the spiral staircase. He became the first victim of the worst spree killer in Athens County history.

He remembered waking up in Hell to endure a terrific beating before the pitiless

eyes behind Hell's Welcome Wagon. It turned other men to quivering piles of Jell-O. Not Rusty. He'd endured beatings before.

His most dominant emotion that day was one of denial. His dad-murdering son had denied him his last shot at human redemption. And now he was in Hell with no chance of turning his life around.

All he had left was revenge, and his dad-murdering son had just innocently showed him the best way to even the score. He mindlessly re-shuffled the deck and ran through another mesmerizing round of tricks that bored him and enthralled everyone else.

26

MEETING AT THE DOG

It was a busy enough Tuesday that both Paige and Aziz were pouring drinks and Bart Ender had agreed to stay after his shift in case he was needed to bartend. Kerry Z. Plates and Sue R. Vesmilles were waitressing while Noel Neetles bused tables and kept Soo P. Waters busy at the back sinks.

Experience-wise, the crew was fairly green and prone to the kinds of mistakes that added hours to the dining experience, but no one minded. Eternity had a way of softening the edges of dining flops that on Earth would have earned the offending establishment a pissy tsk-tsk Yelp review before the desert menu even landed on the table. And no matter how long dinner took, no one ever complained about dessert, not when Kaye K. Baker was at the oven

And clientele at The Dog were always in an upbeat mood because you never knew who you'd see there. As it was connected to the Carnegie Library, it attracted a more upscale, more erudite clientele — the kind that wouldn't look confused if Paige described them as "erudite."

On this Tuesday, customers at scattered tables included

authors John Steinbeck, Dorothy Parker and Joseph Heller; renown artists Georgia O'Keefe, Pablo Picasso, Mary Cassatt and Norman Rockwell; chefs/cooks included Julia Childs, Col. Harlan David "KFC" Sanders and Jehane Benoit; and taking strategic turns dominating the quarter jukebox were the giggly trio of Martha Washington, Princess Diana and the always-irrepressible Gilda Radnor.

As always, there were no fewer than three former U.S. presidents, and a table with Tom Petty, Roy Orbison, George Harrison and two empty chairs awaiting their Traveling Wilburys bandmates. Aziz Ahl, in particular got a kick out of watching Richard Nixon nearly every night approaching the table, pulling one of the reserved seats and being told, sorry, that seat's not for you, then watching Nixon skulk back to sit with Millard Fillmore, Herbert Hoover, John F. Kennedy and the other presidents.

So it was a heady crowd and few paid all that much attention when Muhammad Ali and Frank Sinatra walked in.

They'd almost stopped watching then Ali went back and made a big show of holding the door for a woman who'd never once on Earth ever been asked to sign a single autograph.

In through that door walked Elle Lavator. She was smartly dressed with summer yellow capris and a blooming daisy print blouse, her soft, chestnut brown hair bound in a ponytail that bounced the way a real Thoroughbred's mane did as it was crossing the finish line during a springtime "Run for the Roses."

And everyone in that celebrity-laden watering hole, both the erudite and the inane, rose as one and began to cheer. Not one of those momentary hoots like when the opposing pitcher walks in a run in the second inning, but a sustained and reverential applause like when a war hero passes by during a hometown holiday parade. And this star-spangled parade element was walking straight toward Lola.

Lola instinctively rose from her seat and greeted her friend with a kiss on her cheek and a tight squeeze. The cheers began to subside, but the buzz remained steady. The room had changed. It had been electrified, charged with ions. An energy had been bestowed.

It began to course through Lola, who couldn't stop beaming.

"Did you see Tom Petty? He was on his chair whistling! He nearly fell into Roy Orbison's lap."

Paige had seen the whole thing. It was the first time he'd laid eyes on Elle and he was impressed. Ravishing figure of a Gretsch Country Gentleman guitar and the luscious hair like the kind you see in the shampoo commercials. Yes, it must be noted there were still commercials in Heaven. How come? People still needed time to run to the frig.

Her beauty was evident and Paige, to his shame, took lascivious note. He knew it was wrong to judge any soul on his or her looks and, further to think impure thoughts. He knew angels were supposed to be more mature. In his defense, for Pete's sake, he was only 128- angel-years old. It was like he was still in angel puberty.

And more than her looks, he admired her intangibles: poise, posture, self-confidence, the way she seemed capable of making intimate eye contact with throngs of thousands. He'd met some of the best and most consequential men and women in history and she, he was sure, could roll with them one and all.

It baffled him. Here's a woman who could enjoy the company of humanity's finest — and all the time in the Afterworld to do it — and she was thinking of chucking it all, her very soul, for what amounted to a blind date in Hell with a mass murderer.

What was he missing?

He told Aziz to send over a free round of drinks and an invitation to join him, Lyberty and Pat Finder in the VIP room when they were ready to talk.

∽

AS GRAND MEALS GO, it wouldn't exactly bump The Last Supper off the first page of culinary lore. There was a plate of mixed veggies, a bowl of strawberries and a sloppily torn package of Oreo Mega-Stuft cookies. And because it was Heaven where when a cookie claimed to be Mega-Stuft it was MEGA-Stuft. Finder began to consume the Oreos with dog-like ardor.

As host, Paige made the introductions and set the tone. His countenance grave, spine stiff, voice no-nonsense. He cleared his throat and began: "Thank you for agreeing to meet with us, Elle. Miss Lee. We're here to learn directly from you, Elle, if what we've heard is true. It's a matter of the utmost consequence. It threatens the foundational attitudes about what it means to be in Heaven and Hell. And what would happen if those bold borders are ever blurred."

Elle sat there looking perfectly composed, poised to flawlessness right up until Paige shifted gears and asked her a question for which she was totally unprepared.

"And before we move onto these weighty matters, I must ask you a question," he said.

She straightened in her chair and said, "I have nothing to hide. Ask me anything you want. I'll respond truthfully. I'm grateful for the opportunity to tell my side of the story."

His first question caught her off guard. He wanted to know why the grass farmer crossed the road.

Elle blinked and leaned forward as if she'd misheard. "I'm sorry," she said, "but did you just ask me why the grass farmer crossed the road?

His eyes never leaving hers, he nodded affirmatively.

"I don't know. Why did the grass farmer cross the road?"

Paige leaned forward, chin high, and said, "The reason the grass farmer crossed the road was he wanted to get to the other sod."

And no one laughed. Elle's face went totally blank, Lyberty rolled her eyes and Pat Finder was too transfixed to move, even as the ivory smear of cream-filling from the MEGA-Mega-Stuft Oreos clung to her chin.

So it was Lola who made the first dent in the silence. It sounded like the sound you'd get if "Ha!" and a "Whoop!" got together and had a really giggly little baby girl. Either way, the sound was a real ice breaker because the welcome chirps of budding laughter began to percolate.

And soon everyone in the room was laughing.

"This is a serious matter," Paige said. "But that doesn't mean we must be serious people. After all, we did make it to Heaven and we've earned the right to fill our lives with joy and love throughout all eternity."

And that, he said, was what he wanted to impress on her; that this was Heaven. She could have anything she wanted for as long as she wanted. She could dine with Elvis, talk religion with Joan Of Arc and philosophize with Socrates.

"You talk poetry with Maya Angelou and Shel Silverstein. Golf with Arnold Palmer."

She picked up the thread. "You're saying I can ski down

Everest, Hang 10 at Diamond Head and sip mimosas with Eleanor Roosevelt on the banks of the Seine?"

"Yes! All that and more! In Heaven, you can have it all. You can meet and experience all the best the world has to offer. And when you run out of that — and some angels never do — you have the whole universe to explore. You can go anywhere. Do anything that'll make you happy."

"I can do it all! I can have it all! I can have eternal happiness, right?"

"Yes! Yes! That's what we've been saying!"

"One question," Elle said. "What if I don't want to be happy?"

"Not happy?" Paige said, genuinely confused. "What conceivable alternative are you seeking?"

"I just don't care about being happy," she said. "I just want to be human."

Silent for so long, Lyberty blurted out in exasperation, "But you can't be both! C'mon! Trust me, you can be divinely happy in Heaven. And you experienced the inhumanity of being human firsthand. Or have you forgotten?"

Elle nodded coolly, her fingers absentmindedly drifting to the exact spots where the killer's bullets had penetrated her torso. No, she had not forgotten.

"I forgave him the instant I saw him kick down the door. And I feel like I could've helped him."

Paige leaned forward in his leather chair and exhaled. "What can we do to make you happy?"

"Nothing," she said. "It's something I have to do myself. Yes, I'm in love with a boy who is condemned to Hell. He's there because he had a role in killing four people, a bus full of gambling nuns and one cat. Not to mention a surly barkeep. It's because of all those nuns he's not forgiven. I want him freed and given a second chance."

Viewing monitors all around Heaven reported this was the moment that by now nearly every set was tuned into the show.

"He's really a very good boy," Lola said. "I've forgiven him." That Lola was serving as a quasi-character witness in her son's quasi-trial had left her elated.

"I figured this was something you'd be interested in so I did some research," Lyberty said. "In the known Hell history, we know of no one who's ever broken out of Hell, much less done so and snuck into Heaven. The metaphysical obstacles are insurmountable."

"I'm not talking about sneaking him into Heaven," Elle said. "I understand that can only be earned. At this point, we can't be together here in Heaven."

"Well, you can't mean sending you to Hell, do you?"

In fact, she'd considered exactly that. That was the depth of her despair. For love, she was willing to send her soul to Hell. The Lake of Fire, the brimstone, the tormented souls and the crappy wifi — it was something she'd been willing to risk, but Evan Lee talked her out of it. He knew he couldn't live with himself, or rather afterlive with himself.

"No," she said, "that's not what I want. I want to be with him at a place where we can figure it all out on our own."

"Are you talking about raising Hell?" Paige said.

"I think she's talking about lowering Heaven," said Pat Finder.

"Well," Paige said, "which is it?"

"I'm talking a place that's equal parts sacred and sinful," she said.

A light went off in Pat Finder's head. She knew exactly where this was going. She remembered her grandfather talking about it. She remembered him railing against the wickedness, the soul-crushing despair, the naked appeals to wanton lust. It was humanity at its most craven.

He and his old Army buddies went there at least once a year — strictly for missionary purposes, he swore.

Equal parts Heaven and Hell, it was all human.

"Guys," Pat said, "don't you see what she's talking about? Even a dumb kid like me can tell she's talking Vegas, baby."

Paige was silent for a moment before it began to sink in. "You mean Las Vegas? Nevada? Back home?"

"Yeah, Vegas,"

"Vegas, baby. Vegas."

"Vegas," Paige said with a telltale hint of sad resignation. "Please tell me you're joking. Not only do you want to leave Heaven, you want to resume human form and go to Las Vegas. Not only is what you're asking impossible, it's beneath banal."

He pointed out she could have all Vegas had to offer right there in Heaven. The thrills, jackpots, buffets. "You can have front row seats for Elvis and then go out for midnight waffles with him and the band after the show. This. Is. Heaven, Elle. Heaven, baby. Heaven!"

"Oh, yeah?"

"Can I bet the mortgage on black 13?"

"Yes, you can!"

"But if I lose, I know I'll still be here in Heaven. Betting it all is pointless when the stakes don't matter."

Paige had to admit there was a difference.

And, she asked, if she got really, really wildly out-of-control drunk, she'd naturally get a hangover, right?

"Naturally."

"But I could make the hangover go away if some friends invited me to brunch — and I wouldn't want to feel nauseated."

"In the blink of an eye, you'd feel good as new."
"No consequences?"
"Not a one!"
How about me and Elvis? she asked.
"I think you two'd really hit it off," he said.
"I would hope so, 'cause I'd like the night to end with him inviting me back to the Jungle Room where I strip off his sequined trousers and tickle The King's cock."

Paige's surprisingly prim streak rose up. He said, "Miss Lavator! Please, some decorum. There are children present."

The present child was at the moment fully engaged. This was the first disagreement of any kind she'd seen in Heaven. It was as electrifying as it was unexpected. She watched the color drain from the old pub master's face. He took a moment to compose himself then continued.

"Now you understand there's no sex in Heaven. It would just complicate things. I'd advise you to write a thoughtful note and place it inside one of the many suggestion boxes conveniently located throughout Heaven."

"I apologize for succumbing to the urge to shock, but I want to be as emphatic as possible," she said. "I was a good girl on Earth. I didn't drink, smoke or swear and I'd never had sex. Ever."

Paige interrupted, "Oh, and now the good girl dreams of being the bad girl."

"That's not it," she said. "The good girl just wants to be a girl. She just wants to be human, and to experience all that means — both good and bad."

"I give up," Paige said. "Lyberty, do you have any wisdom you can share?"

"This is a real toughie," she said. "She makes some good points, I'll say that much."

Paige concurred, albeit to himself. He was a devout humanist and reveled in the spirit of the common man — and woman. He was the kind of man who'd earnestly counsel youths to avoid alcohol and promiscuity even as he'd declare seven of the 10 best times he'd had on earth involved gettin' drunk and gettin' laid.

"I'm reluctant to admit it," he said, "but I think this is a case where we'd be wise to consult a higher authority."

Pat Finder perked up. Could it be?

"I agree," Lyberty said. "It's not within protocols, but on this case, I don't see us having any choice."

Paige made deliberate and bracing eye contact with Elle, Lola and Pat Finder. Then he cleared his throat. He apologized to the viewers and said the team was going into "executive session" and that would be it for that evening's broadcast.

This particular executive session would be privileged to include Pat, Lola, Elle, Lyberty and Paige.

"Ladies, circumstances merit you follow me and Miss Erdeth to a place where we'll be seeking an aged wisdom superior to ours. So follow me. We're off to ... The Orchard!"

∽

IN AN INSTANT, the five of them were on a bucolic country lane resplendent with fall colors. And on both sides of the road, for as far as the eye could see, were apples as big as Civil War cannonballs. There were Gala, Honeycrisp, Jongagold, Fuji, Red Delicious, McIntosh red — all of them glistening like Christmas ornaments dangling from the muscular-looking trees.

The cameras were gone. The show was on hiatus. It was just the five of them.

They stood there momentarily disoriented by the bounty. Each felt a core urge to leap over the split rail fence and snag an apple.

Each felt tempted.

A weathered hand-painted sign by the entrance read:

Adam's Apples
No Reasonable Offer Refused

Together they entered, not in single file or in a line like a football team approaching the line of scrimmage. More of a confused little clump of humanity, not exactly sure of where they were going nor what awaited. One hopeful, one forlorn, one bewildered and one with a primal eagerness to engage even the thorniest of problems so they were fairly representative of the human population at large.

27

JUDAS MAKES A PROMISE

The bocce courts were too shaggy to bowl, the darts were bent, and spiking the flaccid volleyballs was like trying to swat an airborne bag of stale microwave popcorn. The pool cues were all warped, the footballs had all been deliberately deflated below league-mandated levels, and the damned Zamboni was always either laying down too much water or never enough, leaving the hockey surface either too swampy or too spotty.

In Hell, there were plenty of diversionary games, but each of them had some inherent flaw or equipment failure sure to frustrate the participants into squabbling.

All but the ping-pong. Sure, the balls had their share of dead spots, the net was limp and the playing surface had dents from vanquished opponents, but the game in Hell was the one that most closely resembled its mortal Earth namesake. You could play back home and sense a sporting kinship. But there was one key difference.

In an Earth match, you could be playing a spouse, cousins, or any of the neighbor kids old, and coordinated enough to swing a paddle. In Hell, it was pretty much guaranteed you'd be playing either one of two:

Judas or Satan.

The pair were demonic juggernauts.

Well, one of them was.

The pair individually were by far the best in Hell. No one came close. And they hogged the only table. Nobody ever beat them, and they had priority serve whenever they wanted to play.

Satan had a fierce forehand, a crafty return and a devastating serve. He was terrific. He could beat anyone.

Anyone but Judas.

"Are a lot of people too intimidated by him to play their best?" Judas asked rhetorically. "Sure. But I'm not. We've been through so much, he gives me my space."

Judas and Evan were between games. Judas was up three games to one. Evan suspected his friend, history's most indelible betrayer, had gone soft and let Evan win one — and that was partly true. Evan was sneaky good. The game he'd won was legit. Judas blamed it in part on his opponent's skills as a conversationalist. The kid sure could talk, talk in a way so engaging Judas would let his concentration slip. He didn't beat himself up over the occasional loss of one game to Evan.

After all, he was a man who didn't beat himself up over his role in the torture and murder of the Savior, so what was a lousy ping-pong game compared to that?

Apples and oranges, sure, but still ...

He'd been pondering the overlapping quality of the two when Evan's voice brought him back to reality.

"Well, did you?"

"Did I what?" Judas said annoyed but more with himself than Evan.

"Did you ever use your apostle-ship/friendship with Jesus to score with the babes?"

"Oh, sure. I think we all did. I remember telling girls, sure, babe, stick with me and you'll meet Jesus. All but Philip, but he wasn't into girls."

"You mean there was a gay apostle?"

Judas shook his head. "I didn't say that. I said he wasn't into girls. He seemed most content being in the company of other men. Real manly men. Fit men of strength. Men who built things and sang songs about men they admired."

"Sounds kind of gay to me. Maybe he was in the closet."

"No way. We didn't even have closets back then. There were just hooks on the wall. So, no, Philip was never in the closet. All I can say for sure was I remember how his eyes would light up when he'd sing a song about a man with a hammer."

Judas cast an appraising eye on his young friend. Average height and nothing especially outstanding about his (average) looks. But his eyes flashed with a playful mischief that appealed to all who caught its gaze. He was blessed with ample charisma, Judas judged, and he was a man who knew a thing or two about charismatics.

He wondered why he didn't use his personality to raise his Hell standard of living. Certainly, he could have his pick of women, although even the best women in Hell could be real bitches.

"And what about you?" Judas asked. "I never see you with a woman. A good-looking guy like you. What are you, off the hook?"

Evan looked quizzically at Judas. Off the hook?

"It's what we used to say about gay dudes back before we had closets."

No, that wasn't it, Evan said. He wasn't gay. He wasn't stuck up. He didn't think he was better than anyone else.

"I guess what it comes down to is," he paused to pick his next comment with what amounted to reckless care, "I guess I'm in love."

Judas had been in love once. It had been a long time ago — and Jesus didn't count, although love Him he did. He didn't love Christ in the physical sense, even as He found Him vividly charismatic.

Judas loved a simple maiden who cleaned for Pontius Pilate. She was at the time considered one of the great beauties of the region. She had poise. She had a good figure. She had great hair. She had 11 teeth!

To Judas, she had it all.

But working for Pilate was a glaring conflict of interest. He told her she had to choose. She did, and when Pilate was washing his hands of his role in the Crucifixion, she was in his kitchen washing his dishes.

When he was tying the noose around his own neck, his final thoughts weren't of regret over his betrayal of Christ, but of longing in vain for her. So, he understood Evan Lee and his heavenly love.

And that's when he vowed to Evan he'd do whatever he could to help him escape Hell. He promised Evan his enthusiastic support, even as Evan expressed initial skepticism.

"For any plan to succeed, it will require the utmost secrecy. If word gets out then it's you and me both being dragged off to Time Out. Can I count on your secrecy?"

"I'll not tell another soul."

Evan continued to press. "When things seem their most bleak and I look over my shoulder to see who has my back, will you still be there?"

"Yes! I got your back!"

"We need to absolutely be of one mind, closer than any brothers. Two men/one brain. Any less commitment than that and the consequences are unfathomable. So, I'm going to ask one more time. Are you 100 percent certain I can trust you?"

"You can trust me ...or my name ain't Judas Iscariot!"

28

ADAM

They walked for what seemed like miles. So transfixed were they, their little march had turned into a browse. It was a side of Heaven none of them had ever seen. There were waterfalls, unexpected and rugged rock outcroppings and noble stands of imposing Sequoia formations that raked the clouds. Natural thermal bath pools bubbled their cozy invitations to the troupe.

And everywhere there was wildlife — deer, rabbits, squirrel, a cuddly little honey bear — playfully darting near around them. In fact, it seemed a misnomer to declare anything so articulately docile as "wildlife." One doe ambled along so near and confidentially, Paige kept expecting it to offer them some tea and scones.

When Pat Finder saw what she swore was a unicorn she broke the silence. "This is paradise."

"No," Lyberty said, "this is Heaven."

"Then why does everything seem so much more heavenly?" Finder said. She wondered aloud where everyone was. Lyberty couldn't answer. The orchard was listed in all the guidebooks and, sure, most people talked about visiting, but on this day, it seemed they had this overlooked jewel all to themselves.

Up ahead in the distance, they saw a charming barn and a tidy little farm house with a dirt-rut driveway that led to a fruit stand where a little old man in bib overalls was seated reading a book beneath the shade of an old beach umbrella.

They quickened their pace and when they neared they saw him slip a bookmark in the pages and set it beside a 1950s-vintage old, black dial-up telephone, which was umbilically tethered to the house with about 200 feet of phone cord.

He stood up. He wore a straw hat over thick gray, disheveled hair that reminded Paige of the British parliament as it argued amongst itself about whether or not to send troops into harm's way.

His name tag said, "Hello, My Name is ADAM," which he immediately rendered superfluous by announcing, "Hello, my name is Adam, and welcome to my orchard."

It was Lola who put it together before Elle and Pat Finder. To confirm her suspicion, she asked Adam a simple question: "Adam who?" she said. "What's your last name?"

"Don't have one. It's just Adam."

It fell to Paige to end the mystery. "Our man is just being humble," he said. "This is THE Adam. Human Numero Uno. The very first. The Adam of The Book of Genesis. And when you're first, you don't need a last name."

~

IT WAS safe to say that Paige knew Adam as well as anyone in Heaven. The first, First Couple had a reputation for being loners. So, people gave them their space.

Nonsense, Paige thought. He found Adam to be

informed, patient and curious about the afterworld, if a little absentminded. And Paige considered him an expert on relationships. He ought to be. He'd been married to the same woman for thousands and thousands of years.

Paige also admired his contentedness. Adam didn't feel the need to be zooming all around the known universe. He acted as if everything he needed was right there within a few thousand yards from where he'd been born.

Or crafted, as it were.

Paige'd curate library books for him and Eve; non-fiction for him, fantasy romance for her. Adam, a Civil War buff, was currently immersed in *Confederates in the Attic,* by Tony Horwitz. He didn't recall what Eve was reading or if she even had time to indulge in reading.

Eve was perpetually busy, in perpetual motion, always cleaning something that didn't need cleaning. It was odd to Paige because every inch of Adam's Apples orchards seemed pristine. Yet, she was always weeding the budding sprouts of nuisance vegetation invisible to all but her.

Then there was the laundry. Hamper after hamper full of it. In the washer, hanging to dry on the line. Like bales of hay piled on the sofa waiting to be folded, it consumed the house. Adam never could figure out where it all came from. It made him long for the days when wearing a fig leaf over her pubes qualified as formal wear.

Of all the wise men and wise women in Heaven, Paige valued Adam's insights above all the others. He was just so seasoned. Truly, he'd seen it all. Plus, in the case of Elle, he thought Adam could convey keen insights about marriage. He'd try to make a point out of stopping by once a year or so to chat, munch on an apple and see if the phone had rung, something that had only happened once and that was 61 years ago.

To Elle, Adam was smaller, dumpier — near gnome-like — than the mythical Adam. He was short. Firm. Squat. If this guy was created in God's image then the Almighty resembled a city fire hydrant. But his eyes, green as spring grass clippings, captivated Elle. They were kind and forgiving, sure, but they were also imbued with a playful mirth that indicated to Elle they were never more than a wink away from instigating an elaborate prank.

The aspects of his appearance that Elle found unflattering were the same ones Lola found appealing. She wondered if it was sinful to think impure thoughts about the first human, decided it was not and quickly resumed the dirty thoughts about jumping into bed with Human Being version 1.0.

Lyberty, the most enlightened of the bunch, never judged anyone until she heard them speak.

"Welcome!" he said warmly. "Would anyone care for one of our apples? First one's free. After that any reasonable offer accepted."

Lyb instantly liked him.

After wishing she'd brought her autograph book, Pat Finder soon began fixating on the phone. What the hell was it? And why wasn't it in the house? Big enough to cripple a cow, it just sat there, all antiquey looking. And what about the freaky long cord? Wasn't there wifi in Heaven?

"Let me explain why we're here," Paige said.

"No need," Adam said. "You want to hear my advice on marriage, yes?"

Paige smiled and nodded. He was hoping Adam could convey the warts 'n' all version of marriage, maybe dissuade Elle from her idealized vision of it. After all, who knew more about marriage than Adam and Eve? They'd recently celebrated their 50,000th wedding anniversary.

"Let me guess," he said. "One of you is thinking of getting married. Is it ... you?"

He was playfully pointing to Pat Finder. She blushed and unable to think of anything else to say blurted out, "What's with the phone?"

Adam let loose a bark of laughter. "It's a special phone," he said. "There's not another like it in all of heaven. It's I guess what you'd call a hotline. It's a private line between me and a most special being. Anyone care to guess the identity of the other party?"

With the exception of Paige, all their faces were blank. Paige knew and Lyberty had an intuition, but it seemed too preposterous to indulge aloud.

"It's a hotline to God."

Lola felt a distinct tingle. It was right there — right there — for her to reach out and touch, the answer to her every question.

Pat broke the silence. "Can I?" she said, her hand reaching out involuntarily.

"You cannot," he said sternly. "It's a very special phone. Many years ago, before even the invention of the first Earth phone, God appeared to me in a vision and said he was going to have a communication device installed that would permit us to discuss pressing issues involving His creation."

In the vision, Adam asked what was wrong with Him making His wishes known through more visions. "In the vision, He said it was not for me to question His will, and the very next day this burly, rather rude tech guy shows up and installs this phone you see here."

He said he thanked the tech and started out the door.

"'Whoa,' he said. 'Where do you think you're going?' I told him I was going to pick apples. He told me I should always keep the phone nearby. So he hooks up this cord. The phone's been by my side ever since."

"Call Him!" Finder said.

Adam chuckled. "No, no, heh heh. You don't just pick the phone up and call God. It's completely inappropriate. It just isn't done. Me, I'd never do it … at least not anymore."

"You mean you used to?" Lola asked.

Yes, he did, Adam said. Why not? After all, God had given him a personal phone with a direct line. Of course he was going to call Him. Lola asked if He'd ever answered.

"For the longest time, no. Then after years of trying every day, someone picked up and said, 'Hello?' I said, 'It's me, Adam.' Then the voice changed like it was someone trying to disguise it. They asked who it was I was trying to reach. I said, 'God,' and they said, 'Sorry, there's no one here by that name. G'day!' Then they hung up. It was the last time I tried to talk to God. He must have caller ID."

Lyberty asked if God had ever called him.

"One time," Adam said. "It was October 13, 1960. It was harvest. I was sitting right here in this very spot when the phone rang. It was God. He said, 'Did you see that? It's a miracle! I wouldn't have believed it if I hadn't seen it with my own eyes. A miracle, I tell ya.!'"

Confused, Adam said he asked what He was talking about. "The World Series," he'd said. Bill Mazeroski had just hit a walk-off home run to beat the great New York Yankees, who'd been heavily favored to trounce the Pittsburgh Pirates. Turns out God's a big baseball fan. And that was the last time the phone rang."

"That's quite a story," Paige said. "And you still lug that heavy phone around."

"And I always will," Adam said. "Always. If God calls, I want to be ready."

Out of the corner of her eye, Elle saw a flash of luscious blond hair peeking out from behind a nearby apple tree. The two made momentary eye contact, Elle swore she saw the smirking woman wink. Then she was gone.

Adam's mind had gone blank. "Now … where were we?"

"Elle wants to get married!" said Pat with the enthusiasm of a quiz show contestant answering a bonus round cash grab.

"That's right, Adam," Paige said, "but there are extenuating circumstances, ones that could render profoundly cosmic consequences."

"Well," Adam said, "this sounds too momentous a topic to tackle on an empty stomach. Eve, my beloved! Bring us plates heaping with your finest meats and cheeses! Bring wine and spirituous liquors. And bring cakes, sweets and sumptuous figgy puddings."

It was the woman from behind the tree. It was Eve.

Pat looked on in amazement as she saw Eve behind Adam's back theatrically mocking his regal request before sashaying off to the homestead. She returned five snappy minutes later with a tray of Saltine crackers and a party-sized jar of Jif peanut butter. Then she turned and was gone.

Adam seemed to accept this insubordination in good humor and offered everyone another apple. He had plenty. Like free firewood, Adam's apples grew on trees. That the First Couple were bickering was lost on no one, but they were all too polite to be nosey. All, but Lola, who bluntly asked, "So what's up Eve's ass?"

Adam snorted at the brash phrasing of her question. It was so disarming, he responded when he knew better than to air his dirty laundry, at least not when it's within view of his clean laundry, which at that moment was waving in the breeze on the clothes line just behind the homestead.

"She's mad at me, and when she gets mad she just shuts down," he said. "She's not speaking to me."

Lola, who'd once employed the same tactic against her erstwhile husband, Rusty, for seven weeks, asked how long he'd been getting the silent treatment. Adam exhaled, gazed skyward and began doing the math out loud.

"Let's see, last June made three ... or is it four ... ?"

Sensing an opportunity to seize the role of experienced senior over history's oldest human, Lola interjected, "Oh, that's nothin'. I once shut my old man down for almost two whole months. He came —"

"Oh, I'm not talking weeks," he corrected her. "I'm talking three or four ... thousand years!"

The little dinner party let that sink in. It was impossible to fathom. Paige, the oldest of the troop, had been experiencing eternity for more than a century and felt he had a firm grasp on the concept, but was anecdotally blown away that the poster couple for marital longevity were mired in Cold War that predated the crucifixion by several thousand years. Lyberty, a peacemaker who'd been denied her chance to inherit the Earth, but was enjoying the consolation prize, thought maybe she could preside over a reconciliation.

Elle was bewildered. She'd gladly go straight to Hell if it meant spending even one day with Evan Lee, and here were Adam and Eve in a paradise within a paradise, yet incapable of overcoming a multi-millennial marital rift.

Pat, who had no concept of eternity, but an innate zeal for salacious gossip cut right to the chase. She asked: "What'd you do to piss her off?"

"She busted me ogling Ruth down at the beach."

"Ruth?" Pat asked.

"Bible Ruth, the one from the old Testament," he said. "The paragon of fidelity. Her life decisions illustrate the benefits of loyalty, as told in the Book of Ruth. She remained faithful to the memory of her husband, even devoting her widow years to protecting her mother-in law. She was steadfast, but once she got to Heaven she developed a bit of a reputation as a bit of a tramp, a real party gal. A babe. Babe Ruth.

"And one day we were at Put-In-Bay and, I swear, she starts hitting on me — right in front of my old lady! Now, I didn't want to lead her on, but I didn't want to appear rude, either. So, yeah, we made out a little bit — but that's as far as it went. But Eve went nuts. We raged for almost a week. She called me every name in the book. Then she clammed up. Hasn't spoken to me ever since."

As it was for the rest of Heaven's occupants, sex was a distant memory for Adam.

"If missing sex makes me shallow, well, so be it," he said. "Now, I'd had a lot of sex. We did it all the time. Of course, this was before the invention of radio, TV, Gameboy. Heck, the candle hadn't even been invented yet.

"Me and Eve, we really didn't have the whole speech thingy mastered yet. Remember, in the beginning there weren't even any words for in the beginning. All we had were these young bodies with the factory settings stuck on 'Procreate.' And we couldn't keep our hands off one another. We were learning as we went along.

"The only downside was after we were spent I couldn't go down to the bar and brag to the boys about the hot sex. There were no bars, no boys."

Adam boasting of his sexual virility, and his looks, caused Pat to snort in derision. It was a good thing Heaven did not yet have the Cancel Culture. Still, she found herself admiring Adam's audacity.

"Hey! For many years, I was the Sexiest Man Alive. True,

those years coincided with the time when I was the *Only Man Alive*."

He began to point out the distinctions between *People* magazine and how he and Eve had joked about starting a *Person* magazine when it was just the two of them. They lived in paradise for so long and things were still great — even after the fall from grace.

"Yes, she was the only girl for me — and I'm not being hyperbolic. There were no other girls. Of course, the thing about monogamy is it shares a lot of the same characteristics as monotony. In fact, they're even spelled so similarly that if they were school students they'd be seated in the same row in the same homeroom."

Elle had heard enough. "My soulmate is in Hell. I'm considering eternal damnation just to be with him.Your soulmate is right across the yard, and you're involved in a tiff that's lasted more than 3,000 years? I can't figure if you're trying to scare me out of marriage or into it."

Suddenly serious, Adam said, "Neither. But I do want to stress that you'll get over this phase you're in. Just give it time. This is Heaven. Love is all around. You should just stop obsessing over this forbidden fruit. Believe me, nothing good can come from it."

He asked if anyone wanted another apple. Pat nodded her head.

"I feel like no one here understands me. I'm in love with a condemned soul responsible for the deaths of 37 mostly innocent souls —

"Don't forget the Copycat!" Paige interjected and immediately wished he hadn't after Lola shot him a look.

"Yes, and the Copycat," Elle continued. "I hear stories of what it's like to be human and am told how wonderful Heaven is, but I just don't feel it. I'd rather be in Hell with a chance at true love than in Heaven with a yearning I'll have for eternity."

"Please understand, my dear, we're all willing to do anything we can to help you," Adam said. "But there's nothing in the playbook about angels raising hell and the very thought of trying to lower Heaven seems extravagantly risky. In eternity, it's black and white, good and evil. There's no gray area. Well, maybe there is, but that's just a rumor."

The whole group fell silent. The only sounds were the chirping of birds, the croaking of bullfrogs and somewhere, faintly, the distant persistent hiss of a single serpent.

It was so peaceful Lyberty thought how wonderful the setting would be for a soulful nap. Then the serenity was shattered by Adam's thunderous exclamation: "I've got it!"

Everyone's spines straightened.

"It's so simple I'm surprised no one's thought of it before. It's the perfect solution. See, all we need to do is —"

That's when the phone rang.

Adam became transfixed. All other sounds ceased. He stared as the phone rang a second time. Then a third. Each ring seemed to sizzle like a lit fuse. When it rang a fourth time, the suspense became nearly unbearable. Adam made momentary eye contact with every one at the table. He then stood up at near-military attention and said, "I'm sorry for the interruption, but as I'm sure as you'll understand, this is an imperative call, one I simply must take. Please excuse me."

And on the seventh ring, he answered.

"Hello. You've reached Adam's Apples. Adam speaking. What can I do for you?"

His tablemates listened to the one-sided conversation, trying to divine if it was God and what He was saying. Was He intervening on behalf of Elle?

"Yes ... I see ... uh huh ... Well, yes, I can see certain advantages to what you're saying ..."

If Adam was talking to God, he'd adopted a very irreverent tone.

"See the problem is that you're trying to sell me something I don't need for something I don't have. Why would I need to extend the warranty on my vehicle's transmission when I don't even own a vehicle?"

He pulled a pencil from behind his ear and began jotting down notes right on the table.

"So now you're going to sell me a car, too?" He pulled the phone away from his head and pressed it to the shirt over his belly to muffle the sounds. "Sorry, this sounds like this going to be a while. Can you come back in a week or so? Maybe next month?"

They each said hasty goodbyes and began to depart, with Elle last. She couldn't be sure, but as she glanced back toward the farmhouse she could've sworn she saw Eve duck behind a curtain hanging in a second-floor window. And it looked like she was clandestinely talking into a smart phone.

Elle pretended she didn't see her.

"So, you're throwing in the floor mats, right?"

29

JUDAS, EVAN & RUSTY

Judas and Evan were months into strategizing their escape from Hell when they heard a telltale fart leak out from beneath the wall-mounted bed rack. It was Rusty emerging from beneath the bunk.

"I wasn't hiding," he said, his voice betraying hurt defensiveness at the unspoken insinuation. "My gum had fallen out of my mouth and it still had some good chews in it. I didn't want it to go to waste. Then I fell asleep while I was down there looking. Oh, and I found a Tootsie Roll, too."

Evan lunged for his father as Judas played peacemaker and stepped roughly between the men. In the background playing for the 105th consecutive time was the 1982 Michael Jackson/Paul McCartney pop hit, "The Girl Is Mine," so tempers were already short at a critical time. Then the fallen apostle began a series of measured questions as he sought to learn how much of a threat Rusty'd become.

How long had he been listening? Had he told anyone? Just how much did he know?

"I know enough to know that you need me," Rusty

hissed. "And now you're going to have to decide whether you're making me part of your little scheme — or else. 'cause if you don't take me, no one goes. Well, I guess you'll go somewhere ..."

Even Hell has a Hell.

And Rusty began to talk, critique, strategize. At times, it almost sounded to Evan like he was capable of making sense, and he'd have to remind himself that his father was a bumbler, and a mean one. Still, it was impressive the way he began to deftly impose himself on the cliquish twosome. He knew plenty. Judas and Evan had spent endless days surveilling the only way in or out of Hell. They'd done so surreptitiously, wary of attracting the attention of Jill Keyes, Hell's gatekeeper.

Satan had ordered her to serve as gatekeeper role nearly 'round the clock. Sure, she excelled at the job but Satan liked knowing where she was so he could avoid her. He did that with all 25 of his ex-wives. He'd never learned the four-time married Willie Nelson's Law of Matrimonial Cohesion which states: "There are no ex-wives; there are only additional wives."

Outside the door was a sign that read, "Abandon All Hope, Ye Who Enter," which had tickled Satan's fancy after reading Dante's 14th century *Inferno,* the book he eventually dismissed in 2-star Amazon review as "too presumptuous." Prior to that the sign had said, "Welcome to Hell! Make Yourself Right at Home." Satan liked that one for its cheery optimism that preceded the brutal beating Hell's welcome wagon extended upon arrival.

It was treated as gospel that in Hell, there was one way in and no way out.

It had all been tried.

You couldn't dig your way out. Dig all you want, Satan would laugh, you'll only dig your way to a more subterranean Hell.

You couldn't climb, catapult, chopper or slingshot your way out. Hell was a skyless bunker.

You couldn't chisel a hole in the wall and conceal it with a sexy Rita Hayworth poster you snagged from Red, the guy who for a carton of smokes, can get you things. There was no sewage pipe leading to freedom. There was no corrupt, Bible-thumping warden. No secret fraudulent bank accounts set up to finance a Caribbean frolic.

Hell is pure Hell.

They reached an uneasy agreement to work together. Soon, Judas and Rusty were cautiously becoming acquainted, and the next thing you knew there was Rusty teaching Judas the rudimentary principles at how to win at 3-card Monte.

Evan felt queasy. He'd vowed to bust out of Hell with two partners in crime, and the one he trusted most was the one who'd been sensationalized as the most treacherous friend in history.

Not for the last time he began to remind himself that Elle believed true love could overcome anything. The romantic theory would soon be put to the ultimate test and Evan knew the deck was stacked against them.

Now, he and Judas at least had a partner who was adept at dealing with stacked decks.

∼

IT WAS at about this time that Heaven began an unprecedented tilt toward madness. Mass impatience, a surreal yearning for snappy resolutions to tumultuous problems. Twenty-four-hour news channels experienced a surge in viewers and advertisers. Mental health experts were summoned to explain the phenomenon. People began picking sides. Afterlife-long friends began unfriending one another as innocuous observations became banal flash points for bitter judgements.

The angels were agitated; an unseemly quickening had come to eternity. Instant polls proliferated. Artist renderings of the couple united in both Heaven and Hell became staples of the craft circuit, and fan fiction with all kinds of fantastic speculations led to shelves of best-sellers and fame for the authors, as fleeting as the momentary solvency.

Evan and Elle were all anyone was talking about. Everyone had an opinion.

Roughly one-third thought Evan should receive what became known as the "Parole Option." This would involve his being, in effect, given a pardon and supervised admission to Heaven with certain conditions. Like Earth-parole, which often lasted as long as four or five years, an accommodation would be required. Many believed a parole of, oh, 500,000 years was just — with a mandatory ankle monitoring device.

How to facilitate his departure from Hell featured mostly the televised insights of men like Gen. George Patton, a darling of right-wing cable shows said, "You gotta hit him hard and hit him early. Get in there at dawn and kill! Kill! Kill! You can't let one sorry bastard like this ruin what the rest of us so love about the sacred blessings of all-out war."

When the host pointed out that no one was suggesting going to Hell to kill Evan, since Evan was already deceased,

Patton glared at him and suggested someone ought to off the host. He then stormed off the set and transported himself straight to Germany to urinate in the Rhine River.

The options for Elle were more diverse. Prior to the inevitable backlash, she was beloved. No one could bear the thought of Elle in Hell. Still, few could believe Evan was worthy of her so many of the heavenly biddies spent time trying to fix her up with their sons or nephews. The matchmaking attempts were mostly in vain due to the obvious redundancy where every potential suitor was described as a "real angel."

Then there were the conspiracy theorists who'd convinced themselves that Evan and Elle were in league with the Antichrist, who they suspected in opposition to all heavenly logic, was actor Jimmy Stewart. Some threads hinted Stewart and other Hollywood glitter shitters would meet in the basement of a family pizza joint and force children to watch "It's A Wonderful Life" over and over on holidays like April Fool's Day.

Just because they were deemed worthy of Heaven didn't preclude any number of certifiable kooks from getting in.

When Evan heard about the ruckus, he thought it was hilarious, a reaction he knew he must keep to himself. If anyone in Hell found out he was playing e-footsie with Elle, man, there'd be hell to pay.

Elle at first became both defiant and despondent; defiant because she truly didn't care, despondent because part of her truly did. All her life, she'd been proper, a uniter. To have her private life be so thoroughly dissected exasperated her goodwill.

They called her crazy. Whore. Ingrate. Fool. Bitch.

"And these are from the people judged in their mortal

lives to be worthy of Heaven," she told Lola, as she pulled the cork from that day's third bottle of cabernet. "These are the good guys."

"Seems like you're not the only one yearning to be human again," Lola said.

Elle asked her to explain.

Being confronted with the possibility of an eternity of being, yuck, nice forever, people who were up and aware the last 30 years rebelled. Being really good can be a real burden, she said. "Remember, many of the people arriving in Heaven are coming from a place where they weren't truly happy unless they were truly angry. So they'd contrive differences with old friends who would reciprocate and then they were off. It was neighbor against neighbor, co-worker against co-worker, etc., etc. It was very disruptive and led to a lot of painful estrangements, but people liked that. We were unified by our shared division."

"During our mortal lives, we used to argue about controversial political figures," she said.

"Now, here in Heaven there are no controversial politicians, so the only thing left to bicker about is —"

"I know —Me!"

The philosophers wondered how far it would go before The Father or Son stepped in to make things right.

Because acrimony and suspicion reigned, petty hatreds were emerging. The Creator was no where to be found. Some began to whisper that Heaven was starting to feel godforsaken.

So, a lot of people in Heaven were starting to feel right at home.

Lola finished the third bottle of wine, opened the fourth and helped drain it before saying goodbye as Elle uncorked bottle No. 5. She wouldn't see Elle again for another 10 days when Elle swore to Lola again and again she was sober and of sound mind and body. Elle swore this while balanced like a gymnast on the railing of The Golden Gate Bridge, peering 245 feet straight down into the frigid San Francisco Bay waters.

30

AZIZ AHL SEES ALL

No one was more surprised than Aziz when his channel devoted to 24/7 filming of the Roamer realm began to develop a sizable cult following among the heavenly set. Why? Who knew? Maybe because it was so throwback that viewers came to regard it as kitsch. And why not?

In Heaven all the screens were HD HD. Some were V(ery)HD, while others were so R(eally)VHD that it was like the viewer was right there in the room with the stars. And that happened, too. It was Heaven, and you could do that kind of stuff.

Maybe that's why Roamer Vision was so popular. It offered a bland, staticky alternative to flawlessness. It was old-school back when all the old schools used toxins like asbestos for insulation, gym mats and salad fixings. Everything was grainy, stark.

Or maybe it was the lurid appeal of seeing a Roamer who bore a striking resemblance to a tyrannical old boss, teacher or lover. Everyone understood that feeling gleeful and unsympathetic about a former acquaintance's afterlife lot was a base emotion, undeserving of angelic status, but they couldn't help themselves. They were only human. At least, they all used to be.

But Aziz thought it was all about the dude in the big red hat.

And he was correct.

He was the only Roamer to show a spark of animation. All the other Roamers trudged along in dirge-like monotony, dressed in the gray uniformity that was becoming a sartorial hallmark of this monotone land of the bland.

The red hat, among other fashionable flourishes, drew every eye to him. Clearly, he didn't belong where he was. There'd been some mistake. But it compelled nonetheless. Eighty-three percent of those surveyed who had favorable impressions of the channel reported watching at least two hours a day in the hopes of seeing the man in the red hat; and 51 percent admitted to feelings of depression if he went unseen.

And those who admitted to feelings of disdain about the show confessed to watching the show six to eight hours until they saw him.

His antics varied from moment to moment. There he was marching mockingly beside a stoic roamer. Then he'd jump on the back of another for an unbidden piggyback ride. And here he'd be locking arms with a beige-faced female for a square dance do-si-do.

Then, most poignantly, there were the times he'd look straight at the drone and mumble what appeared to be fervent prayers for ... what? Salvation? Re-assignment? Another chance?

But his beseechings were unheard over the herd. The

dominant noise was the steady low hum made by the base existence of multitudes who had nothing to say. It was a case of droning drones rendering an airborne drone incapable of picking up the sounds, a case — not of being tone-deaf — but drone-deaf.

Some old hippies called in to declare they knew him. They said he played bass for The Kick Stands, an Austin, Texas, garage band. Others swore he ran a Haight-Ashbury hookah joint. And yet another caller argued persuasively that because of his stylish appearance, he was sure he used to shop at Lapels Fine Menswear in Greensburg, Pennsylvania, as tasteful a designation as one could muster.

Dapper dress notwithstanding, Aziz knew he was none of those things. He suspected his boss was right.

"I have a hunch the man in the red hat is the legendary Arthur Thou IV," Paige said. "And if it is, we have a second existential question on our hands."

It was proving to be a heady time for a Wise Man entrusted to make momentous decisions. But it was all too much. It was making his head hurt.

For centuries, there'd been rumors of a realm where the gray beings were banished. It made sense because there had to be a place where those who weren't all good or all bad could be warehoused. Paige wasn't privy to who was making those decisions. He was just relieved all those excess souls weren't stumbling in and out of The Dog.

The possible appearance of Thou was another matter entirely.

He never bought the fables that a man had escaped Hell. The very idea was a smudge on rational thought. Escape Hell? It was impenetrable. And where would you go? Back to Hell? There were no extradition treaties. Satan frowned on diplomacy.

Turner told Aziz to keep him informed on everything Arthur Thou/The Whimsical Man in the Red Hat was up to.

Aziz and Paige had begun to understand the man could potentially play an as-yet undefined role in resolving any number of afterlife situations that seemed to be coming to a head.

Aziz wondered aloud if maybe it was time to turn to historic customs that people in times of strife rely on when situations spiral out of control.

Paige said, "Now hold on, my friend. I'm not sure if what you're suggesting would be helpful or an utter waste of time. With the holy trinity being on historic sabbatical, I wonder what's the use? I mean, the situation differs little than it did on Earth really, does it?

"I mean, we started off with paradise and two humans bestowed with free will. With all due respect to our friends in The Orchard they made a real mess of it.

"Doesn't it seem like history is repeating itself? Like at Eden, we've been given utter paradise, but no adult supervision. For God's sake, you could argue they left me, a Cockney publican in charge!

"Is it another test? Is there a real Heaven after this one? Does anyone really know? We're here for eternity and we're just a tick or two into it. I'm starting to think Heaven is a lot like Earth only with more time at the traffic lights to run the stale yellows."

Aziz was listening intently.

"So if you're asking me to join you in prayer, you're asking the wrong guy. I'm starting to think heaven is becoming just like good ol' earth. We're essentially on our own. Prayer don't help."

Aziz took this all in thoughtful stride then reached

behind the bar and pulled out an unopened bottle of Villa One and two shot glasses.

"Who said anything about prayer? I'm talking tequila."

Paige laughed. Took the two of them the better part of an hour to drain the bottle.

31

EVAN IN HELL

The less they communicated, the more lustily vivid his dreams of a life together became. It was a rich life full of tenderness and soulful companionship. In dreams, no detail was too picayune for soulful extrapolation. Her hair, her fingernails, the strength of her touch, the fragrance of her skin just below her ears — all these details and more were subject to dreamy adjustment.

The satisfying dreams almost always and inevitably concluded with the two of them making love. It could be in a bed or on a beach, in a car or on a couch, on a blanket beneath the stars, or on a bearskin rug beside a roaring fire.

The fantasies were odd and unattainable to boot, he knew. Odd, he knew, because he'd only seen her image through Facebook profile pictures. Unattainable, because, well, they both resided in different ZIP codes, so to speak. Yet, he did nothing to temper the potency of the serial dreams. What's the point of dreamin' if you can't have dreamy dreams? So — damn the torpedoes! — full dream ahead!

But in his most recent dream, there was no sex, only

visual evidence that there'd been sex. Funny, he didn't know if any of it involved him or not. What surprised him was his utter indifference to the understanding that he was not the father of their baby — and he did consider the baby theirs.

In the dream, Elle was aglow with pending childbirth. She shimmered with the precious life growing inside her. Evan saw himself enter his own dream and put an arm around Elle. She turned and smiled sunshine at her bad boy. He smiled back and put his free hand on her belly and gave it an exploratory rub.

Bingo! Evan could see that dream Evan had felt a kick!

Then the dream got inconceivably weird, as dreams are wont to do. The three Wise Men entered the dream and began high-fiving dream Evan. What was even more weird was that the Wise Men weren't the fabled Magi of Melchior, Gaspar and Balthazar. In fact, two them weren't even men. One was just a kid. The other female there was a stunning black woman. And the man looked like he'd be more at home serving half-off Happy Hour cocktails at the local watering hole. The depth of their collective wisdom was impossible to gauge.

But that didn't matter to either dream Evan or Evan the dreamer. He just sensed they were good folk. Regular people. They were supportive and caring about Elle and their baby. They would soon begin cameoing in more happy dreams and Evan always felt comforted by their appearance.

They said their names were Paige, Lyberty and Pat, names that Evan promptly forgot. He was never good with names.

So to Evan they were the Three Kind Folks, bearers of Klondikes, Cadbury eggs and the occasional 6-pack of Stoney's lager. Practical stuff.

What expectant mother wakes up in the middle of the

night with homicidal cravings for gold, frankincense and myrrh?

Maybe the dreams were especially poignant because of the dire contrast with his wide-awake reality, which was hell.

He had no way of knowing how long he'd been there. There was no calendar, no stars to chart, no sunshine to mark shadow designates on a sun dial. None of the clocks were synchronized. It was rumored that in Hell some days lasted 28 hours, others 16. There was no way of knowing. It ensured maximum sleep deprivation.

It didn't matter. And to those determined to lasso order amidst chaos, it didn't matter that it didn't matter.

One long-timer, a slave trader from the 16th century, was so determined to catalogue the simple passage of time that he counted out loud, second-by-second a full day, then measured the passage of give-or-take a day on a bedspring contraption he'd rigged. Then he'd take a piece of charcoal and — *SCRATCH!* — mark another day of torment. The problem was he soon had covered all four walls and both the ceiling and floor with so many dark scratches that the cell was very conducive to sleeping, and the experiment petered out.

Evan thought he could deal with the time fluctuations if he didn't have to listen to the 24/7 news. It was originally called Hellivision, but Satan thought that was too obvious. It had started out as cable news, but then the major channels faced off and began accusing their competitor of skullduggery.

So cable news became cabal news.

And what Evan saw made him sick to his stomach.

There were school shootings, political divisiveness, domestic violence, urban warfare and pandemic episodes.

There were genocide, chemical weapons, border disputes, toxic waste dumps, climate change and poll after poll showing the faithful had lost faith.

It made Satan very happy.

It made Evan something beyond sad. It made him sick.

Homesick.

The broadcasts in Hell and on Earth were eerily similar. Death was everywhere. Mean, cruel, forlorn, dreadful, wanton and blithely random death. The only difference is the mortals died only once.

In Hell, mortality itself was immortal. You could die daily.

The idea was killing Evan. He clung to his dreams with a desperation known only to the condemned waiting for a last-minute reprieve from the governor.

The call from the governor never came, but one from Elle did. She called to say she was ready to risk it all — goodbye in the hopes it would lead to hello.

32

PAT FINDER IN HEAVEN

She died 10 days before she'd intended to kill herself. She wasn't sure she could go through with it — she was afraid of heights — but she was determined to try. That dire step was rendered moot when she died peacefully in her sleep after her room above the garage filled with carbon monoxide from her now-dead, scatterbrained grandfather's cranky old jalopy.

And tonight, she and her parents were going to have dinner with the man who had — whoopsie-daisy — accidentally killed them all.

Funny how things had a way of working out, she thought. She thought of this as she was fixing her hair in the mirror which reminded her, as it always did, of her father's so-called "Reflections on Mirrors."

"Women look into mirrors and see flaws — flaws no one else can detect. Men look into those same mirrors and see perfection — no one else can detect!"

Oh, how she'd wished she'd have given the borderline Dad joke more consideration back before the mean girls had begun to circle, before their cold-shouldered indifference turned to red-hot hostility that made her life a living Hell.

Hers had been a sheltered childhood. She was raised by loving parents who encouraged her, read to her, constructed an awesome self-esteem and promised her the sun would always find a way to shine solely on her. It was the kind of upbringing every kid ought to have. So, it was doomed to be tested by hate and envy by those with feral upbringings.

In that way, she'd been just like Elle. Both were sure everything was going to work out in the end. She still felt that way. Even with all the tumult, the sensational coverage, the attendant circus and, yes, the scandal, she still wanted to be just like Elle.

Looking back, she wondered if it was her mortal naiveté had gotten the better of Pat.

All she'd wanted was to be included. She didn't think she was better than anyone else (she was). She didn't think she was smarter (she was), that the teachers favored her (they did), or that the boys found her more attractive than the rest of them (they did, too).

Her parents never warned her that there were sharks in the water, which seemed fateful that it had all started at swim practice. That's where the four cool girls had with their personalities constructed a fortress of impenetrable aloof. They were just that cool. And at 15, that's a monumental castle to cool. They were each attractive in their own way, supremely self-assured and clumped up all together in a little clique by the side of the high school pool as they waited for swim practice to begin.

Pat wore a shy smile on as she approached. She made direct eye contact with each, came to a stop and chirped out one word in a bird-like voice.

"Hello."

They pretended they didn't hear her.

She said it again.

"Hello."

It was as if she didn't exist. She walked away. The girls gave each other nervous little glances. Who does she think she is?

But Pat was nothing if not persistent. She made another lap and repeated her icebreakers.

It happened just like that three more times.

"Hello."

Nothing.

The girls shared mean little smiles. This was the point, she later reckoned, where she should have accepted defeat. But her feelings had been hurt, and she was not made of wax. She was a 14-year-old girl, thus one of the most combustible substances on the planet.

So, instead of accepting defeat, she nimbly pushed all four girls into the pool. Ignoring her ceased being an option the instant their feet hit the water. They emerged from the pool, their eyes stinging from chlorine, their composure evicted by splashy indignation. Still hysterical, they vowed they'd kill her, but later after they'd toweled off and cooled down, they reconsidered.

Wouldn't it be better, they reasoned, if they led her to kill herself?

As bullying goes, it was fairly simplistic. They mingled rumor with threat, intimidation with confrontation, mockery with ridicule. They were expert at their craft. Pat never had a chance.

That's how eight months after she'd pushed the trio into the pool, Pat found herself, weak-kneed, 245 feet above the pavement that surrounded the Pinckney, Michigan, water tower that helpfully announced the village population

(2,427). It was a great place to raise kids, even as the locals liked to joke you had to go through Hell, (Michigan, pop. 266) to get to Pinckney.

Funny, she thought, she went through Hell when she let Pinckney get to her.

She planned to jump the very night Abigail, Samantha, Bridget and Elizabeth were to enjoy their prom. An incident that had begun at a pool would conclude with a different kind of splash.

The pity was that Pat, with her youthful impatience, could not have known that the universe has a way of working things out. Her beautiful bullies' reign was about to end.

Abigail was the prettiest girl in Pinckney. Buxom, blonde, with a knack for picking just the right jeans, she assumed the attention she got for her fine appearance would never fade. About this, she was mistaken.

After 10 years, she and her high school sweetheart, a popular football player, will marry. He'll spend the next 20 years cheating on her with a succession of younger, prettier girls until divorce lawyers are summoned. She'll spend long hours looking in the mirror and realizing every day for the rest of her life it's all been downhill since the 2021 senior prom.

Samantha, the one with the cute ponytail, will become a successful administrator at a nearby university. She'll find satisfaction in her job, but she'll always wonder if something's missing. The first marriage didn't work out. He was a drinker, a mean one. She'll spend long nights at the office intermittently checking match.com profiles of men who'll invite prospective dates to come over and cook them dinner. She'll remember the guy who asked if she was good with laundry. She'll get together with friends for lunch once a month. They'll sit around and bitch about what jerks men can be.

The perky girl named Bridget will get married and raise a family. She'll love her children with fierce devotion, but as the kids get older and find their own diversions she'll wonder what happened to the man she married. He's so distant. He'll come home from work and turn on the games and never even ask about her day. How could he be so indifferent? Didn't he know how much it hurt to be ignored?

The fourth girl, Elizabeth, will get everything she ever dreamed of. She'll marry a kind, handsome man. He'll be a good provider, attentive to her emotional needs and will relish spending time with their two daughters. Together, they'll raise these bright, beautiful children with love and wisdom.

And some night, years later, she'll recall how cruelly she treated that awkward, open-faced girl who just wanted someone to acknowledge her existence. And there in that bed she'll share with the man she loves, Elizabeth will shed tears of soulful regret.

"How," she'll wonder, "could I have been so mean? What was I thinking?"

Both Samantha and Abigail for different reasons will find out that Hell was a whole lot closer to Pinckney than they'd ever imagined.

On the other hand, Pat and her family were given EZ Pass express aisle access to Heaven where Alex Trebek explained the perks (many, including having a famous game show host explain the heavenly customs) and the penalties for violating the ground rules (none; it had never happened).

So she spent her first night in Heaven dining with her family and Alex Trebek. It was so fun, so relaxing — so *heavenly* — they even needled Grandpa about having killed them all.

A world that had been so dark, so brutal, so menacing had suddenly filled with brilliant light. And Pat intended to savor every bit of it. She was going to ski, sky dive, ice skate, and volunteer at the local animal shelter. The need was great because, as everyone knows all dogs go to Heaven, and unlike their human counterparts, dogs were allowed to have sex in Heaven, which they did with canine gusto. When complaining humans asked how come dogs were allowed to have sex and they were not, they were told it was because when humans had sex it led inevitably to squabbling, petty jealousies and hurt feelings. When dogs had sex it just led to more dogs.

Pat decided the next day she'd have breakfast with astronaut Sally Ride — on the moon! Over butter croissants she told Ride she was looking for a mentor, someone fun, with a great imagination who wouldn't mind showing a kid the ropes.

Ride, correctly assuming she meant her, said "I'd advise you to hook up first with Lyberty Erdeth at Human Relations. She's a, shall we say, a very wise woman. She'll find something for you to do that'll help explain the lay of the land.

Then I'd advise you to reach out to this new girl. Name is Elle Lavator. She's just wonderful. Really doing it up right. Not only does she know how to have fun, she helps people. All the angels are starting to emulate her. Yes, everyone wants to be just like Elle."

That very night she vowed now that she was dead, she was going to live, really live.

And she vowed she was going to live forever.

Just like Elle.

33

DECISION MAKERS

The jalapeño poppers went quickly. But the quesadilla sampler proved difficult to resist, as did the English-style candied bacon. Paige was just a bit surprised the fried zucchini strips hadn't been more popular. Fried zucchini was a dietary compromise for those who liked to pretend eating healthy in Heaven was a sensible priority and those who realistically didn't give a crap, a decision that on Earth hastened by up to 10 years their obese ascension to Heaven.

But the shrimp cocktail was the clear favorite. Everyone finished off one shrimp-rimmed martini glass and expressed an interest for more! More! More!

It was the 10th time they'd met and the pressure for resolution was ramping up. The networks and websites worried that the drama might never crescendo, that the saga would surrender to the lukewarm satisfaction provided by the unyielding inertia of eternity.

There were no deadlines where nothing ever died.

So Lyberty and Paige just kept hosting these pub powwows, very low-key events where the cast outnumbered the crew 5-to-1. They were mostly redundant rehashing of the previous week's installment. There were no special effects, no stylish dress, no contrived shouting matches — just a story about two ah-shucks young lovers trying to overcome tremendous odds to be together.

It was a runaway hit.

There'd been talk of staging what was now considered to be a "show" at the Parthenon in Athens and bringing in celebrity judges Antonin Scalia, Ruth Bader Ginsburg and Roy Bean and have them mete out a ruling.

But the consensus among the primary five was all just a lot of silliness and people were just homesick for silly. Hosting these at the Parthenon, the U.S. Capitol or any place other than the conference room at The Dog, made no sense. Lyberty and Paige were too stable, too seasoned, to let pop culture determine the outcome of something so momentous.

What would have struck many as funny was that Lola knew Elle was going to do just whatever she wanted, regardless of any phony rulings that might or might not be issued.

Lola believed Elle was indulging Paige, Lyberty and Pat because she'd become fond of them. It was just her way. Despite being at the very first scandal in the history of Heaven, she didn't want to be seen as a selfish boat rocker. Paige and Lyberty sensed this and were counting on it to help them find a way out of the morass.

About this they'd made a serious miscalculation. Elle was not about to let personal relations get in the way of a personal relationship. It was the one boat this once- beloved angel was ready to truly rock.

Lola was most stunned by how fast the heavenly public turned on Elle. Where she was once more popular than the two Marys (Magdalene and Tyler Moore), her "Q rating" led her to share tenuous popularity terrain with Letitia Tyler, Sarah Polk, Jane Pierce and a few of the other more forgettable first ladies. Nice gals, sure. But none of them had the wattage of say, M.T.M.

Another element: people weren't merely indifferent to Elle. They actively disliked her. And this was Heaven where folks were just nice as pie. Until Elle, there'd never been any hate in heaven. But ever since Elle began asserting herself, people began questioning her motives, her authenticity.

"Who does she think she is?" asked one summarizing talk-radio caller. "Does she think she's better than the rest of us? I mean, if you can't be happy in Heaven, do you really deserve to be here? For all I care, let her go straight to Hell."

The angel was being demonized.

When the host pointed out she'd lived an exemplary life and had mere months ago been voted one of Heaven's most beloved angels, the caller sniffed "That's fake news." Then he called the host and his listeners "sheeple," hung up and went straight to his basement to begin calculating how many letters were in various iterations of Elle's name.

It saddened Lola because Elle was the purest soul she'd ever known. She was generous. She was vivacious. She was charismatic. She had no doubt she'd have changed the world had she survived just a bit longer. As it was, she was poised to change the afterworld.

∼

"SHALL WE BEGIN?" Paige asked. "Everybody get enough to eat?" Of course, they had. It was Heaven. Nobody went hungry. Everyone was just happy to be there.

Well, almost everyone.

Paige addressed the camera: "I want to thank those of

you who've been watching at home and on your precious devices. We'll be re-capping our journey in a moment, but before we begin I'd like to take this opportunity to remind you it's wing and rib night here at The Dog with drink specials all night. Plus, performing on our A stage will be Muddy Waters, Howlin' Wolf, Chuck Berry and the God Fathers of Rock band."

Some of the higher-ups objected that, in Heaven at least, the band name was at the least vaguely sacrilegious, but Chuck liked it and even in Heaven no one wanted to mess with Chuck. All blasphemies aside, Liberty had told Paige the pitch was a bit crass. Paige had to admit she was right, but what business owner could resist ignoring an audience that numbered in the tens of billions?

And interest in Elle's situation had led to the beanstalk sprouting of the monetization of Heaven. As on Earth as it is in Heaven, where there was interest there was profit. Now, there were novelty T-shirt sales, quickie bios of Evan and Elle, and there were subscription podcasts and radio shows like the one Paige had been talked into hosting.

"Now, here's Miss Lyberty to summarize where we are and how we got here."

She straightened her spine as the main camera turned toward her. She was never comfortable talking into the camera. Pointing a camera at anything, she believed, changes everything. It was a good thing she'd had some nerve-steadying shots of Wild Turkey bourbon whiskey before that evenings proceedings.

"Well, we had no idea this is where we'd wind up when we began this journey," she said. "If you recall, this all started when our young friend, Miss Pat Finder, reported that her idol, Miss Elle Lavator, had been conspiring romance with one of the condemned."

Elle bristled at the word conspiring and through a straw took a sip of her vodka & tonic. Paige had counseled against her drinking so conspicuously. He said people were using her alcohol consumption to pass judgment on her. She no longer cared. The woman who was in effect on trial for falling in love with one of the damned no longer gave a damn.

Her correspondence with Evan had slowed to a trickle, but the decreased communication had done nothing to diminish her illicit ardor. That many partisans now considered Elle to be irrational only bolstered her resolution.

A human in love is the very definition of irrationality.

And Lyberty continued: "And it isn't your run-of-the-mill condemned. "He's a bad hombre. He's responsible for the deaths of 37 innocents, including his own mother and father, their cat and a busload of nuns."

Lola piped up.

"If I may inject a little perspective," she said, "I was his first so-called victim — and he was acting on my request. I was suffering from advanced Alzheimer's and didn't want to live, so mine was a mercy killing. Killing his father was self-defense. The bartender? That was an accident, but it's my understanding he was a so-called 'Bad Hombre' who preyed on children so that kill could in hindsight be considered righteous.

"Now that busload of nuns, that gets us into a bit of a gray area, I admit. But the nuns have forgiven him and one of them told me the bus driver was texting before the accident."

"And, Lola," Paige said, not confrontationally, "what is your point?"

"I just want people to know he wasn't that bad a guy," she said. "Of course, this is his mother talking, but he still has much to give. I think Evan and Elle would make such a great couple ..."

Lyberty sighed. This was the 10th televised conference of what was popularly being called, "What To Do About Elle?" It seemed to Lyberty that they were spinning their wheels. Paige agreed and seemed to imply tonight he'd make some decisions to break the stalemate.

"No one's disputing that, Lola," Paige said. "The problem is there is no way in Hell we can ever get these two together. No way in Heaven either, for that matter. We can't send an army down there to start a war. We can't negotiate. Can't do a swap. The precedent would lead to disgruntlement, chaos, the very ruin of Heaven itself."

Turner said everyone knew someone in Hell, and many recalled them fondly, despite their being condemned for criminal acts that included murder, kidnap and a sinister potpourri of heinous misdeeds. The difference? Eventually, people stopped giving a crap. Sometimes it took a year. Sometimes 10 years. Sometimes 200.

But eternity is a stealthy seductress.

Why they seemed to have zero effect on Elle mystified Paige and Lyberty. If she would only open her mind and just give it time.

"Well, we're out of options," he said. He gave Elle yet another exasperated glance. She raised her hand to speak, but Paige cut her off.

"We have a caller on Line 1," he said. Adding phone calls hadn't been their idea, but they bent to the reasoning. "Go ahead, caller."

"Hi Paige, love the show. My name's Rita, and I have a question for Elle."

"Go ahead, Rita."

"Elle, you're from Wisconsin, right?"

"That's correct," said Elle, her mood teetering between indifference and surliness, but still instinctually polite.

"Well, my nephew just got here. He was a firefighter in Racine. Got killed in the line of duty. He's a great kid. Red hair. Big hands. I think you two would really hit it off. Can I bring him by to meet you?"

"Thanks, Rita, but I'm not dating right now."

"Oh? But he's just the kind of kid you're looking for, only he's not destined to spend his afterlife in Hell."

"I'm sure he's a great kid, Rita. I'm just not in the market."

"Oh, so you're too good for my nephew? Well, if that's the way you feel, you can just take your —"

Paige didn't need to see Elle making the slashing motion to cut Rita off. He was dismayed how even in Heaven, the cloak of anonymity seemed to bestow permission for decent people to spew the crudest oaths. Now, Elle, as strong-willed and independent a woman as there ever was, seemed to be bringing out the worst in the trolls.

"Calller on Line 2, Joe from Waco. Go ahead, Joe. We're listening."

"Yeah, thanks for taking my call. This Evan seems like a decent guy. What we need to do is build an army of our toughest guys, take us all to Hell and just kick ass. I'm talking kill everything that moves."

"Now, hold on a tick," Paige said, "Our man Evan, he moves."

"I'm not saying there won't be some collateral damage," Joe said. "But the tree of liberty must be refreshed with the blood of Muslims and ... er ... and ... ah liberals."

"Oh, who let you into Heaven?" Paige said. "You mangled the quote and conveniently turned it into hate speech. Begone! Next!"

"Hi! I'm Fred from Key West. I'm calling to see if Elle is interested in polishing Howard Stern's balls!"

The tone and unexpected wording left Paige confused. "I'm sorry, I couldn't make that last part out," he said, as Lyberty began frantically waving her arms.

"Polish Howard Stern's balls!" exalted Fred from Key West. "Shine 'em up!

"No!" Paige shrieked.

"Baba Booey!"

The call-in segment never went smoothly, but today was particularly aggravating. It was upsetting to Paige who'd vowed to take steps to speedily resolve the matter. After all, it couldn't go on forever. Well, it could, but ratings would tank and nobody wanted that to happen.

"All right, we're going to give this one more try," Paige said after gathering himself up. "Please stick to the subject. Don't promote any agenda or nefarious social movement. And don't try to liaise a romantic interlude between Elle and your fair-haired neighbor boy."

"And please understand," Lyberty said, "how we're all trying to do our best with the facts we have at hand. We're not monsters trying to impose some New Afterworld Order on the 'Sheeple.' We're dealing with something without precedent. We're dealing with an otherwise delightful young woman for whom Heaven isn't heavenly enough."

Elle was watching intently, but had already made up her mind. Paige wasn't the only one prepared to act.

"Let's try one more call," Paige said. "Hello, caller. What's your name and question?"

"I'm, uh, Patricia," she said. "I don't have a question. I just wanted Elle to know there are a lot of 14-year-old girls out there who have her back. Like me. We just think you're the best and when you're sad, so are we."

Elle had seen Pat surreptitiously slip away during the "Baba Booey" mischief. She knew Pat was crouching mouse-like in the supply closet down the hall. She'll be fine, Elle thought. She had her whole afterlife ahead of her.

"Thank you, Patricia," she said, looking around the table to see if any one else caught on. "I'm grateful for the love. It's my belief that finite Earth-time is superior to eternal perfection. The capricious wonder and whimsy of life itself surpasses afterlife."

So this, Patricia asked, is about more than just one guy.

"It started out as just one guy. I so want to put my whole heart into mortal love. But Heaven is pointless if you take away from that one special guy all redemption, forgiveness, grace and hope. Without those elements, eternal happiness is pointless really. Happiness in the presence of suffering is an abomination, Heaven a conceit."

Paige heard none of this, flummoxed as he was trying to screen the calls, monitor the mics, the camera positions, and produce the therapy session that had gotten out of hand. He wondered how he ever let himself get talked into something so far from refereeing simple pub trivia.

By now, Elle was saying we should embrace, not shun, the condemned. And not a soul should rest until every soul is saved. Then — and not until then — can we celebrate being in Heaven.

"So give me one more crack at humanity, one where I forgo material pleasures, and devote my entire existence to the improvement of my fellow man. I'll take that one fleeting span of abject misery over the comparatively hedonistic afterlife in Heaven.

"All I want is the company of that one good man to help show me the way."

Pat, still sequestered in her hiding place, wiped tears

from her eyes. She said: "That's beautiful. Someday, I want to be just like you, Elle."

"And someday, Pat, I'm sure you shall be."

Paige, indeed, was a Wise Man, but he was still at heart a man. That meant he was prone to fits of thought that for every complicated problem there was a simple solution. Hammer the square peg hard enough and the round hole will comply.

The beauty of it, he thought, was in its impetuosity. The idea came to him and — just like that — he acted upon it. Didn't even consult Lyberty. Didn't need to! He had his gut and his blessed impetuosity.

"We've reached a decision," he said, ignoring Lyberty as she began shaking her head and mouthing, "NO, WE HAVE NOT!"

"In what will be a first for Heaven, we will be meting out a punishment for a personal transgression. Not a sin, mind you. This is Heaven so therefore the very idea of sin is impossible. So let's call it a faux pas — and it's a doozy."

Elle looked on in disbelief. She'd thought she could trust Paige not to act rashly. She'd thought once she'd rallied public opinion to her side that diplomacy would prevail and she Evan would be united in, perhaps, some neutral realm.

"Hell isn't a concept," Paige continued, and those condemned to dwell there aren't some abstract fable. It's a real place full up with real sinners. If we start letting their kind into Heaven for pure matters of the heart, well, there goes the neighborhood. Thus, an example must be made."

Hoping to convey the gravity of the situation while clinging to the belief that impetuosity would rule the day, Paige looked at Elle — sweet, earnest, altruistic Elle — and settled on the only extension of her that could ever be considered villainous.

"You know we love you, Elle, but we can't have you in regular contact with Evan in Hell. The risk of unholy corruption is too great. And we can't add to the Hell firewall, 'cause then we'd all have to change our passwords and you know what a pain that can be.

"No, there is only one just solution ... Young lady, hand over your cell phone!"

Elle surprised him when she busted out laughing and slid the phone over without a fight.

"Now, you can have this back in, oh, let's see ... 500 years. Yes! I think by then you'll see the error of your ways. It'll be over before you know it."

Paige was feeling rather satisfied with himself when Elle revealed she was no slouch when it came to impetuosity. She blinked her eyes once.

And then she disappeared.

34

ELLE AROUND THE WORLD

The first call came in mere seconds later. It said Elle was on the sidewalk of the Humber Bridge at East Yorkshire in England. "She's looking out over the water," said the caller. A minute later, there was Elle looking out toward the Gulf of Mexico from the south-bound side of the Sunshine-Skywalk Bridge in Tampa.

It went like that for the next two frenzied minutes.

She was spied at the New River Bridge in West Virginia, the West Gate Bridge in Melbourne, Beachy Head at East Sussex, Niagara Falls and The Gap at New South Wales near Sydney.

"Why," Lyberty asked, "would she pick now of all times to visit some of the most popular wedding proposal sites?"

"Maybe," Paige said, still on an impetuosity high, "she took to heart what I was saying. Maybe she's thinking about new beginnings."

The door opened and in walked Pat looking tense. She stood there awkwardly. Lola was slowly rising from her seat in the corner.

"You're wrong, Paige," Lola said. "She's not thinking

about beginnings. She's thinking about endings ... Follow me!"

And just like that they were on the Golden Gate Bridge. The cantaloupe-shaded sun was setting. The foursome had materialized amid two wedding parties, families on a frolic and young lovers excited about their futures — both the distant and that night's. At that moment, all was right in the afterworld.

And then Elle materialized about 15 yards away in a pose Lola had by now seen dozens of times. It had never before troubled her, not like it did now.

She turned and showed a little ironic half smile. She said, "500 years, eh, Paige? You overestimate my patience with eternity by, oh, 499 years, 11 months and change."

Paige felt a soothing burst of relief. She wasn't, he felt sure, going to do anything rash. That she started off monologuing was a clue that this had become a negotiation. He felt that right up until the very next moment when he realized it had not.

The realization smacked him in the face as he and the others watched Elle, nimble as a gymnast, put both hands on the orange railing and with a pert little hop fling herself over the edge.

Half the observers screamed in holy terror while the other half froze mortified. A second later pretty much everyone screamed when they saw Pat run from a dead stop and impressively hurtle herself over the sidewalk safety railing.

Just like Elle.

∼

Those rare few bridge jump survivors have told suicide researchers they vividly recall the exact moment their fingers let go of the railing. One poignantly remembered thinking how everything he'd thought was unfixable was, in fact, quite fixable. It was an illumination that every wretched mistake he'd ever made was, in the grand scheme of things, just a minor whoops. Every wrong decision was just another thing that could be fixed.

Everything except the decision to let go of the railing.

Experts say that to the suicidal-minded, jumping into a large body of water is to the jumper subconsciously akin to the jumper returning to the womb. The facts betray that theory as fraudulent. Neither the womb nor the would-be returnee could withstand the 75 mph re-introductory howdy-doo. Nor can sentiment hold its own to simple physics. The typical bridge jumper can upon impact expect instant agony, disfigurement, pulverized internal organs followed by a painful expiration. It can be worse for jump survivors, some of whom report recoveries so torturous that some of them considered resorting to, well, suicide.

At least that's the way it worked on Earth. Things were decidedly different in Heaven.

That was the conclusion of one fascinated observer, Sir Isaac Newton, the famous thinker who'd revealed an object in motion will not change its motion unless a force acts on it.

"Thus," he said, "Elle should impact the water in .8 seconds. Yet, she continues to sail ..." He was learning either the Laws of Nature didn't apply to Heaven or else Elle was a true outlaw.

Elle had braced herself for pain. She'd read the studies. Had seen the autopsies. Knew what she was in for. None of it mattered. She'd already died once. Now she felt she was being killed all over again, but only slowly and without finality. Being denied love when love was all she'd ever wanted was sufficient reason, she felt, to succumb to a second death, albeit a grisly one.

And if suicide was the ultimate sin, then certainly the first suicide in the history of Heaven would lead her to uniting with Evan in Hell. She didn't expect it would be easy, but it would bestow her afterlife with real purpose. So, yeah, she was prepared for the pain.

What she was unprepared for was the pestering.

"Please, Elle, you can't do this! We need you! You're breaking our hearts! You can't die. You just can't!"

It was Pat. Utterly indifferent to the consequences, she had jumped off the bridge a split-second after Elle had. She'd vowed she'd follow Elle anywhere, but no one suspected such devotion would lead her over the side of a tall bridge. Her urgency was such that she had no sense she was speeding to her doom.

Together they fell like twin apples conforming to the pitiless laws of gravity.

And Pat kept talking, pleading and seeking resolution. It was like she was filibustering suicide. She talked for so long she began repeating herself — "Elle, you can't die! You just can't!" As their talk took a conversational tone, it finally began to dawn on them that time was standing still for just for the two of them. And they were enjoying themselves. Because falling is fun. It's the landings, the abrupt stops, where things get sticky.

Instead of slamming into the waters the pair were buoyed up by unseen breezes, and there in mid-air they began to frolic. It was Heaven doing what Heaven does best, surprising folks with joyful reminders of how great is to be alive. Or used to be.

At that moment, Elle was happier than she'd been since before she and Evan had begun their illicit correspondence.

Whoever or whatever was controlling them initiated a controlled descent as Elle asked Pat what had moved her to act so heroically.

"Oh, I didn't have time to think," she said. "I just knew you'd need help, and I guess I knew nothing bad was going to happen to us. This is Heaven. You can't die. You just can't."

They kept descending as if in a highrise elevator slowing as it reached its appointed floor.

Their controlled anti-climactic landing was pinpoint perfect on the bow of posh cruise liner. Within seconds of touching down a squad of tuxedoed waiters surrounded them with heaping trays of succulent Dungeness crab, calamari, sushi and Ketel One Bloody Marys.

Pat and Elle imbibed copiously (the younger virgin's Bloody Mary was correspondingly virginal). As they noshed the captain approached and said he was taking his passengers to Alcatraz Federal Penitentiary. Would Pat and Elle enjoy a VIP tour? Sure. What the hell.

Pat was struck by how many happy selfies free people took in places where incarcerated people spent so many miserable years.

Elle was struck by how a place that was once considered escape-proof had over time become an offbeat tourist attraction.

35

ELLE PONDERS ETERNITY

It was considered very good news that Elle was alive and well, although the sticklers would argue that, well, no one in Heaven was truly "alive." But they all saw it. Elle jumped and was followed immediately by the now-much heralded Pat Finder. And they didn't die. Quite the opposite. They appeared exhilarated, Pat in particular.

Soon jumping off The Golden Gate Bridge became a popular pastime with lines stretching down near The Presidio. The crowds were very well-behaved and exceedingly patient. In Heaven, moans of, "C'mon, we haven't got all day ..." were never heard. Because people did have exactly that.

They had all day all of the time.

And while it was good news that Elle had survived unscathed, the very idea she or anyone should feel suicidal in Heaven was decidedly upsetting. It was an emotion that had never before happened and it had a ripple effect, not unlike that of a pebble hitting the surface of a pond. Only in this case the ripples were a result of the pebbles *not* hitting the pond.

Elle briefly contemplated trying again, but figured it'd be pointless. She thought about renting a boat and taking it out to the open sea where she could chain herself to three cinder blocks and chuck them over the side. She was sure the blocks would magically transform themselves into flotation devices that would preserve her saintly safety.

That wouldn't be all. Bullets would turn into butterflies, poisons into Popsicles, big, long knives would turn into tiny tickle sticks — any manner of self-harm just wasn't going to happen in Heaven.

You were, like it or not, bound to be happy, by God, in Heaven forever and ever. Amen.

You weren't supposed to have bad days, question the prevailing wisdoms or betray any emotions other than the sunny sort. Sure, you could still swear, but only when the curse was part of the punchline.

Elle supposed she understood. It was, after all, Heaven, a celestial designation that hinted at perpetual paradise. Give it time, the thinking went, and she'd forget all about Evan. There were plenty of history's most eligible men and ample time for courting. But Elle didn't consider herself single. She'd pledged her heart and soul to him, and she was stubborn when it came to things like soul pledges.

Her love story — the story of Evan in Hell and Elle in Heaven — was one of the great love stories of all time. She believed it made Romeo and Juliet seem as puerile as "Joannie Loves Chachi."

But what if she was wrong? What if what she was putting paradise at risk for all the contented innocents? Was she being selfish? Foolish? Reckless?

She decided she needed collegial counsel from someone who'd withstood historic scorn in the name of love, someone who, rightly or wrongly, was held responsible for the destruction of something beheld by all as perfect.

But Yoko was busy, so she made up mind to talk to Eve.

"Sorry, Elle, but Eve doesn't see anyone," Adam said. He'd been sitting at the roadside table, distractedly staring between the God phone and a half-eaten softball-sized Gala apple.

"Really?" Elle said skeptically. "No one?"

"Honest. She doesn't even see herself. She got rid of all the mirrors."

Wow, Elle thought. That's commitment.

"She's seen just one person in the past, oh, about let's say 400 years.

Elle asked who.

"It was The King."

"Which one? Caesar? Charlemagne? Alexander? Martin Luther?"

"I said The King, not *a* king."

"Oh, Elvis. She have a thing for him, too?"

Adam raised an eyebrow. "Too?" he asked. "I thought you only had eyes for your Evan."

"What can I say? I'm only human. Or at least I used to be …"

"I'm sorry I can't help you. I suggest you reach out to Yoko Ono. She'll probably have some wisdom, albeit wisdom she's apt to dispense in incomprehensible haiku. Nonetheless."

"Well, if you see Eve and you're communicating, please tell her I'd like to see her and the matter is urgent."

Just then they both heard the menacing hiss of a serpent. near enough to make them both flinch. There was a rustle in the bushes and from it emerged Eve. She was wearing a string bikini. And a more voluptuous and desirable creation Elle had never before seen.

"Hello, Elle," she said. "I'll be happy to talk with you."

She shot Adam a contemptuous look. He seemed to flinch once again. Elle glanced his way and felt momentary pity. Adam was a simple farmer who'd been through a shot gun wedding with a vaguely incestuous relation. Despite the challenges, their marriage had flourished. Yet Eve had blossomed into a self-assured, poised and clearly provocative woman of the afterworld.

The first woman had become an Alpha female.

Poor Adam looked pathetic, weak, dominated. Of course, the guy hadn't gotten laid in something like 4,000 years. That had to grind on him, she felt. It was grinding on her.

— << >> —

The pair set off on a barefoot stroll. To Elle every vista looked fresh and magnificent. There were meadows, waterfalls, mesas that looked straight out of some John Ford movies. Elle asked about how so much wonderland could be so unspoiled.

"This is Heaven," Eve said. "Sure, it's all Heaven, but this is the original Heaven. This is what paradise looked like back when ol' Adam and me were dancing around in just our whoop-de-dos. It was absolutely perfect."

Elle wondered why more people weren't around to bask in the splendors.

"Oh, they're coming," Eve said. "Give it time. It's our nature. We can't resist trying to improve on perfection. People have been respectful, for the most part, and they're enjoying their theme park version of Heaven, but they'll eventually move on. It's the pattern of man. Depletion followed by discovery. We're basically parasites with personalities."

Sorry she brought it up, Elle changed the subject. She asked Eve to tell her about the early days.

"Oh, we had so much fun! Just two kids exploring the world and each other. Every discovery was utterly euphoric.

"Do you remember your first kiss? Imagine being the recipient of the very first first kiss. It took longer than you'd think. He kept missing. He'd kiss my nose, my eyeball, my forehead. Then — finally — we connected. A kiss on the lips. Wow. We just kissed for like an entire day. It. Was. Amazing."

Elle watched her disappear into a reverie so deep it felt like she was intruding.

"Then, ahhh, then we discovered his boner and through trial and error — learned just what it was for. And, boy, are we glad there were no camera phones around. People either! Once we figured out what goes where, it was 'Let the games begin!'"

She said at first they mistook the erection for a fatal defect (on reflection years later, she wondered if that first impression was spot-on). They both believed its explosive climax meant the end of Adam. The gush of fluid and the high-pitched barking sound he made upon climax had them fearful his collapse was imminent.

But then, she said, the erection resumed and the process repeated itself again and again before it dawned on them it was natural phenomenon. Pleasurable, even. Well, not the barking, but they learned to live with it.

"Of course, by then we'd found the ‚owner's manual and it was all there in black and white."

"Really?" Elle said, unable to conceal her surprise. "You

came with owner's manuals? You could read? Or was it all drawings?"

Eve gave her a wry smile. "Darling, I'm kidding. There were no owner's manuals. No YouTube instructionals. There was none of that. And think about this: No in-laws! I hear they can be quite nettlesome."

She thought about telling her about her relationship with Lola, but figured it could wait. She asked how Eve and Adam wound up back in paradise after being so famously and Biblically expelled.

"Oh, God forgave us," she said. "Almost right away. He said He'd overreacted, that we were mere children. Easy prey for wily serpents. But it cost us our innocence. Before that, we never fought. It was pure bliss. Then — *boom!* — just like that you have kids. One of them murders the other one. But you have to keep busy populating the planet just so, by the way, He can wipe it out with a great deluge. A few thousand years pass and before you know it you can't remember the last time you made love. Or spoke really."

Elle gushed how she couldn't fathom going more than a few days without affectionate feelings for Evan. Eve said that she and Adam were just experiencing a lull in what had been a strong resilient marriage, one that had withstood the test of time, of all-time, really.

"Well, in any marriage, there's bound to be rough patches," Eve said. "But as he liked to joke, 'I was the only woman for him and he was the only man for me.' We've been through so much together, and there's a lot to be said for that. We're in for the long haul. And we have that indelible bond. I was once a part of him. Like a rib. A real rib."

"Does it make me crazy," Elle asked, "to believe I'm part of Evan and he's a part of me?"

Eve thought about it for a long moment. "It does not.

Young lovers will always believe theirs is the first true love. But that's good for young love to be bold, brazen even.

"What might not be good for anyone is a love that crosses the metaphysical boundary that separates all the good people from all the bad ones."

Elle said, "It's complicated, I know. I just happen to believe no one is beyond salvation. That God's love will prevail, starting with Evan."

Eve asked if she'd told Jesus any of that. She had not. He'd not been around since the 1960's. I think it was the day after The Stones released the first studio version of "Satisfaction."

"If He reads the notes in the suggestion box, He's seen it. But no one's seen Him. It's like in Heaven He doesn't exist."

"Really?" Eve asked. "Just who do you think was behind the giant air pillow that saved your life and the life of your impetuous little friend? He has a plan. He's in control."

"Does He have time to call Adam on his Bat phone to negotiate a new automobile warranty for a car he doesn't even possess?"

If a woman who is historically depicted as being fully nude could be described as blushing that would be Eve. "Busted," she said. "I was just having a little fun. I immediately started feeling bad the instant he read me the security code on his American Express."

She'd seen Adam use the kitchen phone to check if the God phone was still functioning. To prank him, she simply hit re-dial and crouched behind the curtains.

Elle asked if the phone was legit.

"Yes, it is. When it was installed, He'd call once a week. Then one day He just quit calling. No explanation. No nothing. Poor Adam's become obsessive about never leaving its side lest he misses the call. All these years, just that one call. About the World Series."

"That call was legit?"

"Indeed, it was. God called Adam to recount how in 1960, Bill Mazeroski hit a walk-off home run to beat the heavily favored New York Yankees in Game 7. Said it was a miracle."

Was there some deeper meaning, Elle wondered. Some allegory? Something buried in Scripture?"

"Nope. Just that God was a Pirate fan. But that was a long time ago. I don't know how anybody can root for them after they let Andrew McCutcheon get away."

As they walked, her mind still on thoughts of young love, Eve felt her heart begin to soften. She'd been with him longer than Pluto'd been a planet. Together, they'd had kids, and those kids'd had kids, and those kids'd had kids, and on and on and on …

She wasn't going to let her temper fester another hundred years. She wasn't going to let it fester another minute.

And, suddenly, there was Adam, a rosy red Gala apple in each hand. Eve put a hand on each of his shoulders and pulled him in for a kiss so vigorous it looked to Elle like a prelude to a professional wrestling move, which in a way it was.

The kiss lasted 30 seconds, the first 10 of which Adam was too flabbergasted to manfully reciprocate.

"I've missed you, my little Mudbutt."

"And I've missed you, McRib," which Elle surmised — duh — was his pet name for her. "Elle, I don't know what you two talked about, but you're welcome to visit anytime you want. Anytime!"

She'd come to the orchard hoping for concrete direction.

Instead, she got a passionate lesson that for some couples love never dies. In fact, it burns ever stronger.

"Do you want to go inside?" Eve whispered.

"I'd love to, hon, but don't you remember? The Big Guy put a moratorium on physical love and put us all on the Honor System. We could get in trouble."

By now she was dry humping his fatal defect, rendering Adam incapable of coherent thought.

"C'mon," she purred, "We won't get caught. Elle won't tell, will you, dear?"

There was zero chance of that. Not only were they chipping away at one of her pet peeves, the last thing she needed was to become embroiled in another controversy. "Not a peep," she said. "Have at it."

Adam said, "My bonnie little temptress, you know I can never say no to you. Let's go!"

They turned toward the house and arm-in-arm began a slow but purposeful amble up the path, like lust-fueled amoebas being hastened along by breezes unseen. They were about 15 steps from Elle and the roadside table when they were jarred by an otherwordly sound.

The God phone was ringing.

Adam and Eve's faces became carnivals of consternation and anticipation. On the one hand, they believed the caller was God, the Alpha and Omega, the Creator of the universe. On the other hand, geez, they were horny as hell.

It was left to Elle to disrupt the stalemate. "For heaven's sake get back here and answer it!"

He was on it in a second. He took another second to compose himself and answered the phone on its fifth ring.

"Hello? This is Adam ..." His face betrayed his agitated nerve.

"Yes, I can explain, Father. See, Eve and I haven't been intimate since the 18th Century ..."

"What's that, Father? Yes, I can shut up for a minute ..."

"Elle? She's right here. Are you sure there's nothing I can do for — Yes, Father."

He then turned toward Elle, handed her the phone and said with an element of ice in his voice, "He wants to talk to you.

36

EVAN GETS A SUMMONS

Evan was in the middle of the rinse cycle when Bernie Madoff delivered the papers explaining why his presence was required in the executive wing office of The Minister of Factual Truths. The office was right next to Satan's. Its occupant: The only man in Hell whose poisoning of his six children was a mere footnote in his hellish bona fides.

Doing his laundry always put him in a good mood, a good mood at least for a guy who's in Hell. Compared to most of the condemned, Evan still had and took pride in a rather snazzy wardrobe. Sure, it was thrift shop refugee, faded and threadbare, but it was Hell nice.

Second, doing the laundry always gave him a sense of accomplishment. So many domestic tasks in Hell never came to fruition. There was no point in making the bed or cleaning the cell. A pristine bed was unnecessary because trash pick-up was so sporadic that the garbage just accumulated. No one complained because Hell's garbagemen were particularly surly.

Lastly, there was no one in Hell a man like Evan cared to

impress with household refinements. It wasn't like he was going to sing out, "The Manson Family are stopping by for sunset cocktails so let's put a little shine on the place. Wouldn't want the neighbors to talk!"

So just seeing Madoff approach began to piss Evan off. It was never good news in Hell. What he had to say was the worst. Well, second-worst.

"Mr. Evan Lee," Madoff said, "you have been served. Your presence is required — I stress 'required' — at Office No. 2 in the executive suite, today, at 10 a.m. Failure to comply will have hellish consequences."

"Are there any other kind?" Evan asked rhetorically. "Now, run along you waddling little punk, you, before I drop a pyramid on your scheming head."

Madoff scuttled off, no doubt happy to have momentarily, at least, avoided harassment of all the New York Mets fans who'd never forgiven him for his role in extending the Bobby Bonilla contract.

Evan glanced at the clock, instinctively aware time in Hell befriended no one. It was already 9:45 and it was at least a 25-minute hike to Hell Hall, HQ for the nether regions and the root source from which emanated everything that made Hell hell. Ensuring no one arrived on time, which was Standard Operating Procedure. In Hell, everyone had to have something about which to bitch, so ensuring someone was late provided a built-in harangue.

Everyone knew the occupants of the seven offices in the high offices located in Hell Hall.

No. 7 was King Leopold II of Belgium, guilty of instigating the deaths of 20 million natives during his plunder of the Congo. He headed the Office of Land & Development.

No. 6: Amelia Dyer, guilty of the murder of more than 400 babies from 1850 through 1890. Dubbed the "Ogress of

Reading," Dyer was a Victorian "baby farmer." She took money to raise unwanted babies, but instead put the babies in sacks and threw them into the River Thames. She ran Satan's Office of Games and Recreations.

No. 5: Satan knew putting two autocrats together in the same office would drive them both crazy. So that's just what he did with Mao Zedong and Joseph Stalin. Responsible for the combined deaths of more than 55 million of their respective countrymen through famine, mismanagement and homicide, the pair were co-heads of Hell's Office of Nutrition and Sustainable Farming.

No. 4: Mary I of England. Few things warmed Satan's minuscule heart like internecine wars between religious factions purported to worship the same God. That's why he loved "Bloody Mary" for her role in the wanton burning at the stake of Protestants, all in the name of God. Just the thought of it always cracked him up.

No. 3: Lucius Clay, the marketing advocate behind the New Coke who so upset Evan. He was director of the Office of Public Works. Nobody believed the force behind a soft drink misstep was evil enough to warrant such prominence. Most suspected Clay was simply a docile space holder 'til Putin got there.

Office No. 1 belonged to Satan himself. Like most of the best mortal bosses, he had an open door policy. But even the toughest men and women in Hell avoided running into Satan. He was too mercurial, too ill-tempered, too demanding and because he was too casual about oral hygiene his breath smelled like the bottom of a farmer's barn boot.

Satan was depressed by his persistent unpopularity. He'd have been lying if he'd said being the Great Deceiver didn't sometimes get to him, but lying was just what great deceivers did so the point was moot. Being Lucifer didn't make him immune to the same insecurities bedeviling 7th grade girls as they meekly walked past the lunch table where the popular kids ate. Was he cute enough? Did his clothes enjoy a stylish cut? He needed a fresh look. He needed a new public persona. He needed the PR genius who had boosted the popularity of the only man in history who he regarded as his equal in evil.

That man, no slouch himself when it came to evil geniuses, was waiting right then for Evan behind door No. 2.

He was Joseph Goebbels, the Nazi propagandist credited with the deification of Adolph Hitler.

Satan and Hitler had an odd relationship. Satan was sure Hitler was after his job and was eminently qualified to seize it. God knows Satan was ready to take a break from being the perennial bad guy. He was eager for people to see he had a playful side.

That's why Evan was there. Goebbels had suggested Evan profile Satan, a sort of "Did you know The Prince of Darkness has a Lighter Side?" puff piece.

Evan gave three quick raps loud enough to startle some coffee out of the mug Goebbels was in the middle of raising to his lips. The drops splashed up on the family picture of the six children he murdered in Hitler's bunker when he realized all was lost. He'd never see the children again and was vaguely aware he was more upset over the desecration of the picture than he'd ever been over the lethal kind he inflicted on the actual flesh and blood children.

"Go away!" he shouted in German.

"It's Evan Lee, sir."

"Then come in," Goebbels said, this time in English. "You're 25 minutes late. That's the problem with you Americans. You have disregard for appointments."

Evan briefly considered telling Goebbels about his grandfather, Paul Russell Lee, and the wristwatch he wore on D-Day, and how Americans had been most punctual on that historic day, but thought better of it.

"Traffic's a bitch, sir," he said.

"Excuses ... excuses ... reminds me of that corpulent little slug, whiny Winston."

Evan wondered if it'd be wise to present the Nazi a history lesson involving the victors of World War II and how Churchill was enjoying eternity in Heaven while thee two of them were at odds over things like hellacious traffic jams. Unwise, he concluded.

He'd been mostly bored when Goebbels posed a question so unnerving Evan wondered if Goebbels' dense statements had been part of a ruse to soften him up.

"I hear you have a girlfriend, a Jew," he said. "Is this true?"

If it wasn't true — and it wasn't — then why was Evan straining so hard to keep from proudly affirming it was? Was it revulsion over the veiled threat or being presented with the opportunity to shake the shackles of secrecy to which he'd been so long bound? He couldn't right then divine an answer, but he knew this much: admitting to any illicit love to Joseph Goebbels could expose his soul to torments as yet unimagined.

"Not me," he said. "I've sworn off women."

"Come now," Goebbels said. "You must be doing something useful with all that time we know you've been spending on the computer. A secret lover, perhaps, yes?"

"Nope."

"What are you doing on the computer all the time?"

"I spend my every waking moment trying to give the people in Hell the most entertaining blog that Hell permits."

"But why? Is it just for the distraction? Are you just killing time?"

"Maybe," Evan said. "Maybe Thoreau was correct when he asked, 'Is it possible to kill time without injuring eternity?' Maybe if I can injure eternity, we can all get through this and, you know, see what's next."

"We've known each other two minutes and already you've quoted to me Willie Nelson and Henry Thoreau. Who's next, Kermit the Frog?"

"How about a little Winston Churchill," Evan said. "'When going through Hell, go faster.'"

"I'd heard you were intellectually limber, it seems factual," Goebbels said. "You might be just the right man for the job."

"And what job would that be?"

"We want you to use your blog to foment an insurrection. We believe Satan's gone soft," he said as he reached into a desk drawer. He removed a poster of his Fuhrer giving the Nazi salute to throngs of goose-stepping admirers. Across the top it said, "Hell Needs Hitler!" On the bottom in smaller type, it read, "Hitler Gave 'em all Hell. Let's Give Hell Back to Hitler!"

∼

EVAN LOOKED OVER HIS SHOULDER. Was it a test? A trap? Could it be that mere steps from Satan's office, one of Hitler's henchmen was plotting his overthrow? Goebbels sensed the skepticism and hastened to alleviate it.

"We have the people behind us," he said. "They see the rats, the roaches, the decay, the appalling lack of discipline. They know Hell is going to hell, so to speak. And how bad must it be if me and you are plotting his overthrow in an office right next to his?"

"What possible benefit could you derive from deposing Satan," Evan asked.

"Conquest, for starters. The Fuhrer envisions an army that can mobilize and take over a toe-hold on Earth and use that as a base for operations and recruitment. The moral realm is ripe for takeover. Certainly, you remember the rampant evils. The hatred, injustice, bigotry, cruelty just for the sake of cruelty — just the thought of it makes me misty."

The thought of it made Evan misty, too, but for altogether different reasons. It made him sad. He thought of Elle and all she'd done to counter the darkness in which the old propagandist was reveling. It wasn't the Earth Evan remembered. He remembered laughter with loved ones, ice-cold beers around the campfires. He remembered holding his week-old nephew in his arms and thinking, yeah, hurricanes and earthquakes weren't the only acts of God.

He vowed right then he wouldn't rest until he got a chance to build a life like that with Elle.

Goebbels continued, "It's becoming clear the Devil is no longer demonic enough. We want you to write a blog suggesting that and make up some quotes suggesting it's time for him to step down. Then include some fabricated speculation saying how Hitler is rested and ready."

"What you're advocating is what we used to call fake news," Evan said.

"Around here we call them 'Alternative Facts.'"

"I think I've heard that someplace before. What evidence do you have that people want Hitler?"

"Didn't you see the inauguration? This was the largest audience to ever witness an inauguration. Period."

Evan said he thought The Nazi Megaphone was confusing his historical events.

"We believe the benefits far outweigh the risks," Goebbels continued, undeterred. "We're talking about the only prize greater than World Domination. That's Afterworld Domination."

He spent the next five hours talking religion, strategy, history — all viewed through the lens of vile hate. He spoke as if he were addressing unseen multitudes programmed to adore. During that entire oration only twice did he step down from the figurative podium from behind which he harangued. Each time was to ask Evan a question. The first: "When you killed your mother and father, did you feel any remorse?"

Evan explained that it had been a mercy killing that had gone terribly wrong, and the death of his father had been a bit of a whoopsie-daisy. He said, too, that he and his father were actually getting along marginally better since they became cellmates.'

Goebbels said, "I only wish I had the opportunity to kill my parents. And my Uncle Ernst. Father Wilhelm. And Helga, the shopkeeper's daughter who mocked my penis. Churchill, of course …

Although he'd never dare to ask to see the proof, Goebbels' list of people he wished he'd killed was clearly longer than his penis.

"And my mother-in-law Gertrude, my neighbor Gregor — the one with the mean poodle…"

"You were saying?" Evan interrupted.

Goebbels looked like his brain had turned into a cloud. He shook his head and his whole persona became mischievous. "Yes, and the nuns. Did you teach those bitches a real lesson?"

"No, it was an accident. I felt very bad about it. The whole day was an escalating string of bad timing and bad luck merging to tragic results. If any number of factors had shifted by even microscopic measures, then I wouldn't be here talking to you. Heck, I'll bet even the stupid cat would still be alive."

The dream-like look in Goebbels' eyes was instantly replaced by one of cold revulsion. "You killed a cat? What kind of monster kills a defenseless house pet?"

Evan sensed the unrepentant Nazi was looking at him with new eyes, eyes that now regarded him as a true menace. Evan on the spur of the moment decided to lie. "That cat had it coming. It was evil. It was possessed by Satan. I had to kill it. I'm confiding in you, you understand, because I sense we're brothers. But if I find out you're telling Satan, it's curtains for you, you short-peckered little flack, you."

He made an ear-to-ear slashing motion across his throat.

And with seeming approval, Goebbels resumed his tirade, this time in a manner that verged on frothing, as if the talk of murdered nuns, uncles and the owners of poorly trained poodles had lit a blow torch in the black void where humans have hearts.

By the time Goebbels finally wound down, Evan was exhausted by the bitter bile of unfathomable hatreds deep enough to elude all reason.

Evan judged him one of the most inhumane, cruelly racist, anti-Semitic, misanthropic bullies he'd ever known. And when he was done and had finished taking his bows for being the recipient of so much imaginary adulation, Evan threw a chummy arm around him and said, "Brilliant, minister! I've never heard these universal problems addressed with such visionary detachment. I'm sold. Just tell me how I can help."

He would have preferred the exchange had happened between him and, say, Gandhi, but he had no say in who called Hell home.

He was damned if he did and damned if he didn't. Damn it, he was going to take a chance.

37

ELLE'S PHONE CALL

Paige was pretty much convinced Elle was the victim of a phony phone call. The facts as related by Elle left him incredulous. "This doesn't sound like the Father Almighty," he said. "It sounds like Burt the dispatcher down at the old bus depot. And that's another thing: Who even knew Heaven had public transportation?"

But Elle was adamant. The caller on Adam's God phone knew all about her and Evan, and said He was eager to help. But He was too busy.

"Busy doing what?" Paige asked. "He hasn't been seen in Heaven, in like, forever."

"He said He was going through the Heavenly suggestion boxes. He said there were a lot of good ideas in there and for me to thank everyone for their thoughtfulness."

"Did He say anything about the conditional resumption of sexual relations between consenting adults?" Lyberty asked hopefully.

Elle said the subject hadn't come up.

"He said Paige and I could pick up the 33ZS from Dormont, then to just sit back and enjoy the ride."

Paige was startled. God had mentioned him? He was one of those Christians who believed in God, but had trouble believing God could ever believe in him. His head began to swell with pride. And, endearingly, he began to blush. He didn't want it clouding his thinking, so he tucked the nugget away for future examination.

"Where do you take the bus? Is there a purpose or is it just a joyride," he asked, forgetting the fact that every ride in Heaven was some sort of joyride.

"He said to put all my trust in the driver. The driver knows the route, the stops, fares. All that stuff. He said the driver is the perennial employee of the month. Guy really knows his stuff. Name is Starlit. Zeke Starlit."

Paige asked if there was anything she was holding back. Was the bus some sort of allegory or metaphor? But Elle said, no, it's an actual bus.

"He even said I should bring along a sweater. He said, 'You know those buses can get pretty cold, and they take forever to warm up this time of year.' It reminded me of my Mom telling me to be sure to bring along my toothbrush if I was going to visit Aunt Lil for an overnighter."

Paige said, "It just doesn't sound like God to me."

"Whose God do you mean exactly?" Lyberty said. "Maybe He's different things to different people. With me, maybe He's an old storyteller like my grandfather. Maybe with you He's a wise dapper gent to whom you used to serve his daily Pimm's Cup. Maybe with Pat He's a soulful pop balladeer."

"Or maybe He's some kindly old dude who schedules bus rides around Heaven and makes helpful apparel suggestions about keeping snug," Elle said. "Or maybe we'll just never know. All I know is the being whom I believe to be God appears to have a plan for me. After what happened to me at the bridge I am compelled to faithfulness."

Paige pondered. He asked once again if she was forgetting anything.

"Oh, yeah! Almost forgot. He said we'll need to get in touch with Arthur Thou IV. He said he'll be useful in what we're trying to do."

"And how does getting in touch with Art Thou help us get you together with Evan Lee?" Paige asked.

"He said the ..."

"... bus driver will know. This must be some amazing bus driver," Paige observed. "Well, let's get busy first thing next week planning this. We need to be prepared. We don't know what to expect so we must plan and pack for every contingency. We'll need to set up a communications network, pack provisions —"

Elle made a sound that was midway between a snort and a sneeze. "Oh, Paige, my dear, you don't understand. We don't have time to strategize. We leave in 10 minutes."

" ... What! ... But ... Can't ... There's no way ..." Paige was speaking the inarticulate language of the dumbfounded. Rescuing a soul from behind the Gates of Hell was an undertaking without precedent. Paige was reveling in the thought of day-long strategy sessions with security experts, hostage negotiators, extrapolators. There'd be reconnaissance, topo maps, supply chains — every contingency would need urgent addressing.

"It can't be done," he said. "Simply can't be done. Ten minutes isn't even enough time to assemble a decent playlist."

"Way ahead of you, boss," Elle said, pulling out her smart phone and showing him a playlist that included Meatloaf's "Bat Outta Hell," "The Devil Inside," by INXS,

"Magic Bus" by The Who, and "Won't Back Down" by Tom Petty.

"Well, can anyone explain to me the rush?" he said. "We have literally eternity. Why can't we at least have the weekend to get geared up and ready to run?"

"God — or whoever rang the phone at Adam's Apples — said He was enchanted by our story. Said it was the best love story He'd seen since Romeo and Juliet, and that ours was superior because it had the virtuous benefit of being true. There are some people who'll move Heaven and Earth to nurture young love."

Paige wondered to himself how the Almighty could claim to be such a romantic when His principal creation was in such an unsupervised shambles. So, he asked, we're on a mission to relieve from Hell a man responsible for the deaths of 37 humans and yes, yes, a cat, and we're expected to do it basically blind?

Lyberty said, "Something tells me you're gonna be in pretty good hands."

"And what of the fair Evan? Is he playing a passive role or is he an active participant?"

"That's where Art Thou comes in," Elle said, "and it'll be up to the —"

"I don't know why I even bothered," Paige said, "it'll be up to *THE BUS DRIVER* to blah, blah, blah … All I know is this guy must be some sort of a tactical genius."

"It's true," Lyberty said, "The Lord does work in mysterious ways."

"Yeah," Paige said, "who knew his mysterious work ways so relied on mass transportation."

The bus pulled up right on time. The door opened. Elle gave Lyberty a kiss that was all at once hopeful, buoyant and confident. Lyberty kissed her on the forehead and promised she'd pray. Next to Lyberty stood Lola. She gave her a long loving hug. There were tears in her eyes. So much of what would become of her future, not to mention her son's, was boarding that bus. Elle gave a reassuring smile turned and bounded up the stairs.

Then came Paige, who was distracted and, said farewell with far less ceremony. He was thinking of all the things he'd meant to tell Aziz, all the bar instructions and he was wondering why on Earth they needed to hurry along like they were responding to a fire alarm.

He was so distracted he nearly forgot what he considered his best decision when he learned they had just 10 minutes to prioritize his thinking. From his perch on the lower step of the touring bus he turned and over the loud, low drone of the idling bus shouted to Pat Finder, "You comin'?"

Pat took her hands out of her pockets and raised two fists into the perfect heavenly sky.

"Oh, you betcha!" She ran with such exuberance she nearly knocked poor Paige out of the bus.

It didn't say so on the generic destination placard on the front, but all three of them knew the ultimate destination.

That bus was going straight to Hell.

Albeit with a few scheduled stops along the way.

38

ON BOARD

The bus was bigger inside than it appeared on the outside. Comfy without being pretentious, it had plush chairs with seating for 42, tinted windows, and a spacious aisle. To Paige it looked perfectly suited for interstate cruising. It had a throw-back vibe, like it was designed specifically to be the setting for a thousand songs by rambling troubadours impatient to become prairie prophets. What kind of song this trip might inspire, Paige had no idea.

Finally, he turned his attention to the storied bus driver. His instant appraisal? They'd sent the wrong guy. This driver appeared to be far too young — unseasoned — to entrust with a mission of such primal import.

They were told the bus driver was wise. He was experienced. Savvy. Intuitive. Hand's on. Competent. A man who foresaw problems and deftly applied his exalted faculties to solve them. A real Mr. Fix-it.

Paige looked on in dismay as Mr. Fix-it was struggling to work the pre-set buttons on the dashboard radio.

"Jesus H. Christ! Isn't there anything on this bus that doesn't date back to the 1950s?" Mr. Fix-It growled.

"Are you somebody's last-minute replacement?" Paige asked in a voice that barely masked his exasperation.

"Nope, I'm your guy. Orders from on high," he said. "Name's Zeke. Zeke Starlit."

"How long have you been driving?"

"Oh, it's been 45 minutes."

"No," Paige said. "You misunderstood. I didn't ask how long it took for you to get here. I asked how long you've been a licensed driver."

"I heard ya, dude. It's 45 minutes or the amount of time it takes to drive the bus from the depot to here — that is if you factor in the extra 30 or so minutes it takes to exchange insurance information with one very pissed-off homeowner who just had his mailbox plowed over by a momentarily out-of-control converted school bus. "As far as a license goes, let's just say we're going to try like heck to avoid getting pulled over."

He reached into the ashtray and pulled out an ornate ceramic pipe like one Paige recalled seeing on the cover of an old Grateful Dead bootleg. He packed it tight and fired it up. The bus began to fill with hallucinogenic smoke.

Paige had been surprised by the size of the bus. He'd assumed they'd be deploying in a more nimble conveyance. He asked Zeke the purpose of the big bus when he assumed it'd be just the three of them.

"Change of plans, man," he said. "Orders from on high. Our little mission troop has expanded to 40!"

"Forty! What the hell! We'd discussed this as a stealth mission. How will we be able to maintain any element of surprise?"

Zeke laughed and said the bus was bound to be a dead

giveaway. "Besides, I have it on the highest authority that these are some very cool individuals. Speaking of very cool individuals isn't it time for some introductions?"

He turned to Elle and extended his hand. "Juliet, I believe?"

Elle blushed. "Oh, please! I understand the analogy, but I am fearful it trivializes all my boyfriend is going through. Turns out just being Elle is no day at the beach, you know. Pleased to meet you, Zeke. That is your name, isn't it?"

"That's what they call me all right, but I'll answer to just about anything. Oh, and let me congratulate you on bringing so many issues to the fore. Now," he said, turning to Pat, "just who is this young lady who's on the verge of being the recipient of the 'Most Enthusiastic Bus Rider of the Day Award?'"

"You're Jesus, aren't you!" she said. Paige had never seen her so excited and he understood why. The kid did look like an idealized Hollywood version of The Savior. Long dark hair, unpretentious beard, a face that was both kind and forgiving. Had he showed up on the back of a donkey, even Paige might have been confused. As it was, he assumed Zeke was just an amiable slacker, more charismatic than most, but far more likely to ride a surfboard rather than walk on water.

"I get that a lot," he said with a self-effacing chuckle. "We're going to have plenty of time to learn about one another. For now, please take your seats. Our adventure is about to begin. Any questions?"

Paige cleared his throat. "Uh, Zeke, how many times have you driven *any* motor vehicle?"

"This is the first," he said. He put the bus in gear — the wrong gear. As he was looking eyes wide open straight out the expansive front windshield, the bus lurched straight back into two parked cars.

"Ohh, not again," he moaned.

He handed Pat two cards with his contact info on the front. On the back, a perfunctory and generic apology for wrecking their cars.

Paige noted Zeke had a stack of them that looked several hundred deep. Pat dashed out and tucked the cards beneath the respective windshields, hopped back on board and took a seat in the row behind Elle.

Zeke put the bus in gear — the correct gear — and pulled out of the complex, twice grazing the curb and nearly hitting head-on a florist delivery van.

And off they went.

39

PASSENGERS

Elle began to sense the passenger manifest for their trip was unlike any other when Zeke pulled over, swung open the door and up the steps came Ronald Reagan, Amelia Earhart, Clara Barton, Tim Welty and Fred Rogers. Each took a moment to warmly acknowledge the bus driver while he reciprocated the hearty salutations.

They each nodded cheerful hellos to Paige, Elle and Pat before heading to the back of the bus to resume a conversation it looked like they'd been having for about a thousand years. Only Pat felt bold enough to encroach.

To Paige, watching it was a thing of beauty. She stood on the periphery until Mister Rogers acknowledged her and motioned her to join the circle. And in 10 minutes the historic fivesome were treating the 15-year-old as if she were their equal.

And in Heaven, that's exactly what she was.

"What on earth could those five have to do with helping Evan Lee escape from Hell?" Paige asked.

"Nothing," Zeke said. "There's a multi-tasking element to this voyage."

The lush country side rolled past at a lazy pace. Traffic was heavy but never burdensome. A long Sunday drive in Heaven never lost its appeal. Just like back home, packing up the family, cranking up the tunes and heading out to destinations unknown was a joyful pastime. And most of the souls in Heaven still referred to Earth as home, a place of ancestral yearnings deep in the corporeal places where bones used to be.

Elle was dozing when she felt the bus slam to a disconcerting stop outside a Nashville temple she recognized as the Grand Old Opry. Zeke muttered a terse complaint about brake malfunctions and pulled open the door.

One-by-one, in they walked: Johnny Cash, Minnie Pearl, Sojourner Truth, Tom Petty, John Lennon and Confucius.

They greeted Zeke the way loving cousins do at overdue family reunions, with affection and anticipation of joyful togetherness. Paige and Elle observed the interactions with bewildered amusement. Zeke and his bus seemed to be on a mission to gather many of the most consequential men and women in history.

The ones that Pat didn't recognize, she'd bluntly ask, "Who are you and what did you do?"

Paige was then tickled to hear the famed French chemist/physicist say, "My name is Marie Curie. I did studies in radioactivity and was the first woman to win the Nobel Prize, and the only one to win it twice. Now, your turn: Who are you and what did you do?"

When the bus pulled up to The Field of Dreams baseball diamond outside Dyersville, Iowa, on board climbed Roberto Clemente, Katharine Hepburn, Denny Clawson, Lou Gehrig, Jackie Robinson, Hank Aaron and Mother

Theresa. They'd just finished a pick-up game and were all still in their game duds. The euphoric group greeted Zeke like they'd just won a championship and were about to dump a big vat of Gatorade over his head.

Winston Churchill, Arnold Palmer, John McCain, Florence Nightingale, Chuck Berry, Albert Einstein, Georgia O'Keefe, Babe Didrikson Zaharias, Jimmy Stewart, Chuck Yeager, Jeff Page, Lester and Karen Sutton — they kept coming. William Shakespeare boarded and with a mischievous smile went straight for Elle. "So this is the fair lass who renders one of my best tales as positively pedestrian. Bravo! I surrender to your circumstance!"

Just as Paige was wondering how the roster could get any better, it suddenly did. Up the steps in order came Billy Graham, Nelson Mandela, Abraham Lincoln, Martin Luther King Jr. and Muhammad Ali. A huge cheer arose.

Zeke let it play out then announced, "Okay, we have just one more stop. Just one."

The bus made a sudden left and Paige recognized they were on Beale Street in Memphis. Another abrupt turn and they were cruising past Ebenezer Baptist Church on their way to the Edmond Pettis Bridge in Selma. Then, just like that, they were in Montgomery. Before it could dawn on anyone what was happening, the door was opening on Court Square in Montgomery.

And onto the bus walked Miss Rosa Parks.

The luminaries rose as one and burst into applause.

That's when it started. Johnny Cash said, "Miss Parks, I'd be honored if you'd take my seat." The statement was word-for-word repeated by Georgia O'Keefe and Lou Gehrig. Then Petty said she could have his spot the same time Minnie Pearl was offering hers.

Within seconds everyone on the bus was respectfully

and graciously offering the Civil Rights icon their seat. Clearly pleased by the spontaneous gesture, she laughed heartily. "You humble me with your sincerity and grace. I wish I could accept all your offers, but since I can only accept one, I say thank you President Reagan. I'll gladly take your seat."

Was she making a statement by opting to return to the back of the bus?

"Not at all," she said. "But if I accept the President's offer, I get to sit next to Fred!"

Everyone roared with laughter. Who wouldn't want to share a cross-country bus ride with Fred Rogers?

Paige had never enjoyed an Afterlife day more than he did that day. He had bar stories from his observations that would last him 25,000 years. Still, he couldn't figure for the afterlife of himself what role these giants would play in unifying Evan and Elle.

He asked Zeke.

"Oh, they have nothing to do with you guys. They're on a completely separate mission. Although in a way, it was all inspired by our Elle."

"And just what is their mission?"

"Conquer Hell."

∽

As a Wise Man, Paige knew enough to know he did not know everything. But the revelation that many of history's brightest lights were going to march on Hell left him bewildered. He looked at Zeke with new eyes. Clearly, he was no lightweight. Anyone who could organize and motivate Heaven's A-list to undertake such a fraught mission was upper echelon.

He wasn't ready to declare him The Savior, but he must have run in the same circles.

He spent his time doing things more important than mass transit, too (good on that, Paige said to himself). His mind raced through the gamut of logistical needs necessary to equip, transport and sustain an Army far behind enemy lines on unfamiliar terrain. He needed to know if unconventional weaponry would be brought to bear.

"What can you tell me, Zeke," Paige said. "What kind of artillery are they packin'? Do they have sidearms? Chemical weapons? What kind of heat are they bringin'?"

"They ain't packin' no weaponry."

"What are they bringing to battle?"

"Baked goods, for one. Tom Petty brought some brownies and I think Minnie Pearl made a sheet cake."

Incredulous, Paige said, "You mean you're going into battle with the forces of evil under the leadership of, oh, Gen. Betty Crocker?"

Zeke snorted. "Good one, Paige! Gen. Betty Crocker ... Maybe 'conquer' isn't the right word. It's more like infiltration. These passengers are willfully going to Hell to take up residence. They're moving in. It's where they believe they can do the most good."

They've already done their part, Paige countered. They'd already contributed so much to humanity in their respective realms. It was because of them that enduring advances in justice, science, the arts, humanity flourished still. What was there left for them to do?

"The pursuit for the common good shall not cease until even the uncommon bad is vanquished forever more. It's been agreed upon that all afterlife suffering should cease. How can we in Heaven truly enjoy Heaven when there's so much afterlife suffering among our brothers and sisters?"

"But they could all get killed."

"Then they all shall revive."

"They'll be mocked, shunned and ridiculed."

"They shall persevere."

"They will face challenges unprecedented in history."

"They shall adapt."

"It's gonna take forever."

"Then the only possible chance it has of failure will come if forever ever ends."

"They'll live lives of suffering, cruelty and disappointment, lives where setbacks are rife, progress elusive or unattainable. Their faith will be daily tested. There will be days when they're unsure if they can go on another day. It will be Hell."

"How soon they forget," Zeke said patiently. "They were once all human beings. Soul-testing torments? Been there. Done that."

"And now they're, what?" Paige asked. "Spiritual dare devils?"

"I think we'd prefer spiritual dare angels, but you're getting the gist."

∽

NONE OF THIS SURPRISED ELLE. It was all happening exactly as the voice on the God phone said it would. Did she think it was God? He didn't say He was God. He didn't behave the way she'd been raised to believe God behaves.

But He had told her the way things were going to happen and conveyed a serene assurance it would all work out just so, like He'd been privy to a God-like master plan. He told her what was going to happen in the same even assurance the local TV meteorologist brings to the five-day forecast, itself a very God-like prognostication.

Infiltrating Hell had been her idea. She'd said she'd willingly sacrifice her soul to spend eternity with the man with whom she'd fallen in love. The God-phone voice said maybe it was time to "go big." If sending one really good person to Hell might make a difference, why not send 5? Or 10? Or 50?

Besides, why punish her for following her heart, even if her heart was Hellbound. Soon her hopes would transfer from a voice on Adam's God phone to a murderous mystery man named Arthur Thou IV.

She looked out the window. She looked at her watch. Out the window, she saw off in the distance what looked like a ribbon of the Rockies. Why the ride was taking so long no one knew. But instead of serving to ratchet up the tension, a sense of peace settled on the bus. It was a supreme confidence, like the outcome was pre-ordained.

It was a confidence she did not share. She'd resigned herself to eternity in Hell. She didn't admit this to the God-phone voice. It just seemed like the most plausible result. She'd deal with it. She worried how the scenario might hurt her friends and those who believed in her. She worried what it might do to Pat. Without thinking, she looked mindlessly at her watch. The minute hand had barely budged.

"Elle, you sleepin'?"

It was Zeke. She shook her head and crossed the aisle and leaned up over the driver's shoulder. Both were facing straight ahead as the bus rolled along the straight desolate highway. It was a good thing there were no other cars on the road. In addition to being straight, the road was also exceedingly narrow.

"What's up?" she said.

"You nervous?" he asked.

"I wouldn't call it nervous. Just fretful, really. Anxious that things won't go as planned. That something bad will happen. Apprehensive. Fidgety. Restless ... But nervous? No! Not me."

They both laughed at her semantic surrender.

She felt a sublime peace in his presence, as if nothing bad could happen as long as he were around. Pat swore Zeke was Jesus. Paige didn't think so. Neither did Elle. She just thought he was the most charismatic, handsome, understanding and beautiful soul she'd ever imagined. She didn't think he could turn water into wine, but she imagined he'd be mighty good company after the cork was yanked.

She had to ask.

"Pat swears you're Jesus. Are you?"

"Will you believe me if I swear I'm not?"

"I will."

"I'm not Jesus. But a long time ago I made up my mind to behave in ways that would lead people like, for instance, you and Pat, to think I was."

Elle asked what motivated him to do that.

"I couldn't think of a single better soul to emulate. I used to be one of people who believed in God, but had trouble believing God could ever believe in me. I'd go to church on Sundays and pray for God to change the world. Then I'd spend the rest of the entire week ignoring all the God-given abilities I had to change the world."

He said he'd vowed to live a Christ-like life. And, by God, it was looking like he was going to have a real run at it. He'd ministered to the poor, fed the hungry, protested injustice.

"It was so fulfilling," he said. "I was making a real difference. I could tell it even on minor sidewalk encounters. I'd begun to practice what they now call 'Defiant Kindness.' I was going to be kind, helpful and complimentary to people whether they liked it or not. People said being really, really nice was really, really weird. I was on a mission to make being really, really nice, really, really normal."

In the end, he said, that's what got him killed.

He heard through subsequent testimony during her trial that the woman, Karen Holsopple, had tensed up when Zeke smiled and made eye contact — very suspicious behavior — as he fell in line with her as they'd strolled across the supermarket parking lot.

She testified he appeared to be holding in his right hand a weapon and reeked of marijuana smoke.

"Then he started with the dirty talk," she testified. "Oh, I must say, ma'am, you have a lovely pair of melons.' Said my cans were real works of art, and that my caboose looked so playful it made him wish he could take his boots off and climb on inside.

"So I shot the creep."

As evidence, prosecutors introduced the shopping receipt that included purchase of two cantaloupes, four cans of Campbell's Tomato Soup — the kind celebrated by pop artist Andy Warhol — and a novelty train collectible she'd purchased for her grandson's birthday.

Oh, and what she suspected was a lethal weapon was a box of Skittles.

The jury deliberated for 45 minutes before handing down a verdict of "Not Guilty."

"The pity — and I mean besides me getting lethally ventilated for bein' sweet — was I really thought 'Defiant Kindness' was just about to take off and make a real difference in peoples' attitudes. I guess it just wasn't meant to be."

"How many years," Elle asked, "had you been promoting it?"

"Years?" he asked. "It just came to me as I was crossing

the parking lot and spotted that babe and those great melons."

"And how long before that had you been emulating Jesus?"

"About the same time. I was heading into the store to get some Pepto Bismol. I had a hangover that I thought was going to kill me. Ironic, wasn't it? I go to the store to get some hangover medicine and wind up getting murdered by some trigger-happy Karen."

"What kind of life were you leading before that?"

"Oh, I was Hell-bound, for sure. Boozin, whorin', drugs, robbed a few banks —you could say my soul was saved just in the nick of time."

He said he was so surprised to wind up in Heaven he began devouring the Bible, studying the Savior. There's nothing supernatural about the way He lived and the rewards of such a life, no matter whether if it's here or Earth, are bountiful.

"It all boils down to The Golden Rule, which I've modified for my special circumstances," he said. "Do Unto Others And You'd Have Them Do Unto You (and remark upon the cans, cantaloupes and cabooses of your fellow shopper at your own peril!)"

The revelation left Elle bewildered, hurt even. She thought Zeke was Evan's sort of afterlife doppelgänger. One had been mostly good, but with one bad day; while it seemed Jesus/not Jesus deserved Hell, but wound up being some sort paradisiacal concierge.

She asked if it was his ambition to understudy for Jesus to maybe step in for the Real Thing when the time for the Second Coming arrived. It was widely speculated that, logistically at least, the Second Coming had better happen soon — at least before AI deemed humans too flawed to exist and systematically began to wipe out the species.

He shook his head.

Then what? The Third Coming?

"Nah, in fact, my ambition might surprise you. My goal is to come back as The King. Not The King of Kings. I'm talking TCB as E.P. I'd like to come back as Elvis. I've checked with him. He's cool with it."

"So you'd return to Earth as Elvis and do what?"

"The talk is Elvis will be the new John The Baptist, although 'the Baptist' part might be too narrow for him. Remember, Elvis famously used to wear an Egyptian ankh, a star of David, and a crucifix around his neck. And when people would say 'Are you confused?' he would say, 'No, not at all. I just don't want to miss Heaven on a technicality.'"

"I can see you pulling that off."

"Thank you. Thank you, very much."

With what appeared to be The Rocky Mountain Range looming in the distance, Elle changed the subject.

"So was it worth it? All those outlaw years. All that *sssssinnn* ...." she said with a reptilian hiss.

"Speaking from the plus-side of eternity and in hindsight, ah, yes! Yes! You can't sin in Heaven, so you might as well get your fill in, say, Philly. I enjoyed human beings, and I enjoyed being human. I knew early on I'd only get one shot at being human."

The bus seemed to be accelerating through the pre-dawn gloom. The highway stretched on toward the impregnable-looking Rockies. Zeke said it was now her turn to answer some questions.

"Shoot!"

"What is this lust to sin? You're already beloved. You could lose everything. Even your soul."

"I've told you. I feel like I got cheated out of my humanity. I went straight from being Daddy's little angel to being an actual angel. I'm convinced every full life must have at least a little folly and a little failure. Heaven's great, but I know way too many people fail to appreciate it while they're back home."

"Your fella, are you sure he's worth it?"

"Absolutely. We're going to get married and our love will last forever. Forever and ever. Amen. 'Til death us do part"

"Lastly, is your seatbelt fastened? While you and I have been talking, the bus has accelerated to 675 mph. See that ramp up ahead? We need to hit 750 to reach launch altitude or else we'll tumble into the abyss. It's a maneuver I've never even tried, not even once in the three days I've been driving this bus. Technically we're still in Heaven so nothing bad can happen to us. Oh, and you have 30 seconds to make your call to your Hellion."

She gulped. This was really happening. She was playing a central role in breaking people out of Hell, and weirdly, breaking some in. She fumbled with her phone. She hit his number.

Straight to voicemail.

She said, "You're going to meet a man named Arthur Thou, Art Thou —" then the phone went dead.

The ramp was rapidly approaching. The bus had accelerated to 701 mph. It was going to be close.

Her fellow passengers began to rouse. They saw the bus was operating on an unnatural level. They looked out the front windshield and saw the road terminating on a ramp that looked insufficient for the rigors of the apparent task.

"We're all gonna die!" Paige said, before realizing the mortal impossibility of his dire warning.

When the wheels of the bus left the ramp, it was traveling 741 mph. It surged toward the brilliant light of the distant sun. Elle thought it was going to be all right. Then it was like somebody'd pulled the plug on a very long extension cord. The bus lost all power and the upward arc the bus had been etching against the sky began to falter. In seconds, gravity began to assert itself and the bus was in what crash investigators call a catastrophic spiral.

Elle grabbed Zeke by the arm and held on for dear life. He gave her a squeeze that let her know she might find a something a little more carnal than comfort in his arms. She thought of the irony that they were beginning their quest to save the unforgiven soul of a man who was in Hell, in part, because of a tragic bus wreck with all the earmarks of a tragic bus wreck.

If anyone else on the bus felt was fearing for their lives, they didn't let on.

They were all too busy going *"Wheeeeeeeee!!!"*

40

EVAN SCHEMING IN HELL

There are some people who maintain a gruff facade to conceal a softer side that exposing might put them at a disadvantage. Appearing cutthroat evil to them is a social strategy. But even in Hell, the cracks would sometimes emerge. Evan never forgot the guy who was in Hell for massacring 40 men, women and children in one of the pointless Middle East My-God-Is-Better-Than-Your-God wars. He was a remorseless, cold-blooded killer, but when in a quiet moment he revealed to Evan that, gee, he sometimes teared up when watching "Little House on the Prairie" reruns, he never forgot it.

It reminded him that even the most heinous monsters sometimes had flickers of humanity. They could be reasoned with, cajoled, brought to sensible compromise.

It didn't take him long to realize Joseph Goebbels was not among them. He was pure evil. His inhumanity was all-consuming. There was no other side to him. If, by chance, he'd happen upon a "Little House on the Prairie" rerun, he'd instinctively root for the venomous Nellie Oleson to poison, torture and dismember sweet, innocent Laura

Ingalls and feed the body parts to the pigs. And then if it didn't happen, he'd shoot the TV.

Evan felt the man overseeing the "Satan's Gone Soft" campaign was driven by an appetite for hate that could not be quenched. He scared Evan in ways even the Devil didn't.

Satan stole souls; J.G. devoured them

It's why he let Elle's call go straight to voicemail. But he had no intention of possibly revealing any of his plans to anyone but Judas and his dad, the only two men in Hell he felt he could trust.

But how much did he trust them?

Enough to tell them that Elle used the precious few seconds of a clearly urgent call to twice mention the name Arthur Thou IV? Not yet.

From what Judas had told him, Thou was the only man to ever escape from Hell. Elle predicted he was going to meet him. But where? In Hell? On Earth? A neutral territory?

He was not yet ready to share the cryptic news.

He was instead focused on keeping Goebbels happy. He wrote copy that said Satan wore a dress, was busted being nice and had become a DINO (Devil In Name Only). Judas felt sure Goebbels could never be happy.

"Satan's not unreasonable," Judas said. "And he's not going soft, certainly. He's just fed-up with being so wrong for so long. For years, he was going around saying, 'The arc of the moral universe is long, but it bends toward evil.' Well, we know that didn't turn out to be true. It's embarrassing.

"He says he doesn't care about things like that or being so unpopular but, believe me, he surely does. He's very competitive. We used to joke that when the Devil really gave someone Hell it used to mean a pitiless torment of the soul. More and more, when the Devil gives someone Hell it's a standard real estate transaction. And he's thrilled that Halloween has become so popular."

Evan asked how Judas thought the Devil was going to respond to the news that the Germans were mounting an insurrection, that he was a pussy.

"How do I think he's going to take it? I think he'll methodically go after each of the ringleaders and lock them away in Hell's Hell until the end of time. He may be the Devil, but give him his due. He's proud of what he's built here. He doesn't view us as subjects. It's like he's the warden and we're his inmates. We're his dudes — and the 15 percent or so females here are his skanks, ho's, etc. He's still very misogynistic, you know.

"But these 4th Reich guys are maniacs. There was a time when even the worst people in Hell understood the benefit of working together. And there was never any question of who was in charge."

When Judas asked how he planned to foment a rebellion, while simultaneously plotting to become only the second being to escape Hell, Evan figured it was time to talk. He asked if he was planning on coming with him.

Judas looked at him with eyes that had seen millenniums of misery. His friend looked exhausted. "Change is so hard, especially in my case. I can't say I like it here, but it is home. But Hell's changing in ways I never imagined it would. It's dirtier and more dangerous than I ever imagined it would be. And the scum they let in here ... man Hell used to have standards that —"

"I'm sorry to interrupt, but this whole thing could be coming to a head," Evan said, "and I get the feeling it could all pivot around Mr. Arthur Thou IV."

Judas nodded. "I figured it would. He'll be humping you

somewhere, I guess. He's experienced. Knows his way around. I'm not sure I'd trust the guy."

"Don't worry," Evan said. "Even my backup plans have backup plans."

Eager for details, Judas asked him to expound, "'cause I have some really big ideas. Stuff you may not have dreamed of."

"Shoot," Evan said. "I'd love to hear your ideas, but I gotta warn you, I think I'm set. I tell you, friend, what I have in mind is going to really raise Hell."

"Well, how about this?" he said. "Tinker with the environment to change the very climate in Hell. In the summer you'll have scorching heat, drought and violent storms. But in the winter, there will be freakish snowstorms, floods and temperatures that confuse people over whether it's getting too hot or too cold. Pretty soon there will be deep divisions between different interests and nothing will get done and people will stand in one place and argue while the world around them is destroyed."

Not wanting to appear rude, Evan broke it to him gently that the plan would require millions of tons of chlorofluorocarbons, immense herds of burping and farting bovines and that most of the people in Hell were already familiar with climate change.

"Okay, how about this: we have a free and fair election where 49.95 percent of the electorate votes for one candidate who is revered by that half and despised by the other. And one half claim it says in the Constitution in the event of a tie vote 'the winner shall be determined by a Tic-Tac-Toe playing rooster from the nearest county fair.'"

"Seems too ripe for fraud," Evan said. "The word 'preposterous' comes to mind."

"Okay, how about we start a pandemic where our best

experts advise wearing masks, but then they're demonized for —"

"Just when did you stop watching the news?"

"Oh, I think it was the night of the Tet Offensive. Can I give you just one more?"

"Oh, all right, one more. Go ahead."

"Show people this picture," Judas held out a photo of a common dress, "and ask them if the dress is blue-and-black striped or white-and-gold striped,"

"What's divisive about that," Evan asked. "Anyone can see the dress is white and gold."

"No, it isn't. It's blue and black. Watch this …"

The first guy to walk by was Attila The Hun. Judas called him over — "Hey, Hunny" — and asked his opinion: "Is the dress white and gold or blue and black?"

"Blue and black obviously. And don't call me 'Hunny.' I'm aware of your mockery and will kill you for it."

Evan said, "I see! It has the potential to be very divisive. Not sure I'm gonna use it, but let me have the picture. I still plan on going with Plan A."

And what, Judas asked, is Plan A?

"I'm going to really, really raise Hell."

41

MEANWHILE, BACK IN HEAVEN

The restaurants had begun seeing a surge in something unexpected and for which the staff were wholly unprepared. It was snark. Sarcasm. Mockery. It was Heaven, but parts of it were starting to sound like Brooklyn.

Angels were bustin' balls.

Lyberty pointed it out to Lola while they were enjoying lunch at The Dog. The pair had made it their HQ during the time when Aziz Ahl's drone was droning on-and-on like so much visual static. Viewers had seen the bus sail off into the void, but did not know of it landed safely or had been obliterated.

As many of the passengers were listed among the most popular in history and Heaven, people were hoping it was the former. And they suspected it was because that would be the happy ending to which the Heavenly were accustomed. But the introduction of outside elements meant that success, or winning, and the customary happy ending were no longer guaranteed.

And people were diggin' it!

As Lyberty explained, people can take only so much winning — so much Heavenly perfection. A reminder that there were still underdogs in the world added a welcome speed bump to the heavenly highway's spiritual complacency.

"Elle and your son have given us a refreshing reminder of how sweet things can be when the outcome is in doubt," she said. "It's given folks a chance to recall what it was like on Earth when walking out the door every single day meant there lurked the unbidden opportunity for either euphoria or disaster. It made life that much sweeter."

Lola asked what that had to do with the rise in restaurant service complaints.

"Our friend Paige has a saying, 'The only time bitch, bitch, bitch turns into anything positive is when you're running a thriving dog grooming business,'" she said. "But complaints also have a way of boosting the self-esteem of the complainer. Sending the wine back always makes one feel superior."

"I wouldn't know," Lola said. "I've never sent back a bottle of wine."

"And seeing Elle," Lyberty said, "this poised, charismatic and beguiling young girl arrive in Heaven and begin throwing her weight around, not taking no for an answer, it's had a real effect."

People were becoming more assertive, more caustic, less likely to settle for something merely because it was perfect. Who could blame them?

They were only human.

Aziz poked his head through the doorway and stared at Lyberty until he'd secured her attention. A slight nod of his head, and Lyberty was up and heading his way. Lola finished her wine in two big slugs and was right behind her.

In the meeting room, the big screen was on pause. Aziz pushed play and the mass of gray resumed its swirl.

Then the drone camera zoomed in and out with a dizzy abandon. Back and forth. Back and forth. Four or five times. It then settled on the bus, intact, upright and seemingly none the worse for wear. It appeared to be on the bank of a great gray moat, churning and writhing with what seemed impenetrable ferocity. The drone lowered to just above the waters, low enough to discover the waters weren't water.

They were the souls of those deemed not good enough for Heaven, not bad enough for Hell.

It was a pedestrian voyage of the danged.

The drone maintained its low-altitude reconnaissance, the gray ones never bothering to look up. It zoomed and scooted, zoomed and scooted until it got to the other side where it followed the terrain of the bank and up to what looked like a small desolate encampment.

To Lyberty and Lola's amazement, a man in a preposterous red hat popped out of the tent. He was dressed like a psychedelic court jester. And he smiled like one, too!

He waved at the drone camera like he was bidding a pal across the street to meet him for a drink. And the drone obeyed. It came right up near his face like a trained humming bird. He blew the camera a little kiss then reached out and with a deft hand plucked it from the sky.

Still smiling, he mouthed a two-word compound profanity to the lens, set the drone upside down on the stony bank and brought his boot crashing down on it.

The picture went black.

42

AMONG THE ROAMERS

When the bus finally, mercifully settled to a stop, Paige dashed out the doors and did something he'd not done for more than 130 years. He dropped to his knees and blew chow.

He heaved. Chunked. Barfed. Aired the technicolor yawn. Spoke the visual burp. Hurled. Tossed his cookies. Delivered some sidewalk pizza.

He upchucked.

He wasn't necessarily surprised at the physical reaction. The bus had done so many somersaults, loopity-loops and reversals that he was surprised they weren't all what his Aussie pub pals called chundering.

What did surprise him was the sensation was not wholly unpleasant. He'd momentarily experienced a corporal act. He'd felt human. It felt good.

Clara Barton resumed her role as Angel of Mercy and in an instant Paige was feeling like his new old self again. He wiped his face on his sleeve, popped in a breath mint he had no recollection of buying, and took a look around. His first impression? He couldn't have picked a better place to vomit. It was so starkly desolate it made stark desolation appear lush.

The bus had landed in some kind of loamy, egg shell white substance with which Paige'd had no experience. It reminded him of about an acre of marshmallow fluff spilled and left exposed for too long in the elements. The bus was in it up to its axles. Stuck, Paige thought.

The vehicle landed on the only piece of terrain that would not have resulted in their being smashed to smithereens. Pure luck, he figured. The landscape was bathed in a gloomy twilight illumination from a source that could not be spied. A huge rock pit of varying elevations, it looked to Paige like a vast, indoor slag heap.

Pat ambled up looking like Gen. Patton used to when he was set to storm a beach.

"You all better, chief?" she said.

"Fit as a fiddle," he said, not wanting to acknowledge a flaw to a youth whom he more and more was beginning to consider flawless, a born leader. Together they surveilled the bleak landscape. The most prominent feature was the filthy, gray river that seemed composed entirely of dingy washing machine detergent run-off. It ran along at a sluggish pace.

Its inhabitants reminded Pat of her nerdy cousin Barry's ant farm. The giant mass of insects seemed uniformly incapable of mustering the moxie to step outside the grooved channel. But Pat and Paige knew better.

They knew the rivers were Roamers.

It wasn't difficult to recollect the identities Roamers had back in mortality, they were the bad cholesterol in the arteries of life. It was Roamers who added mundane drudgery to every Earth task. Lumbering along, never in a straight line, oblivious to the timely needs of others. Earthbound Roamers were the ones who made rush-hour traffic such a bear, and the ones who added hours to what should be a routine visit to the local DMV. And somewhere out there, a speck among them, roaming at will, was the mass murderer whom they'd chosen to help them break into Hell, kidnap a demonic resident, and get back out.

The task seemed increasingly preposterous. Thus, it tickled Paige's whimsy, thinking maybe he could with his oratory spark some signs of life.

"Friends, Roamers, countrymen …," he said. "Lend me your ears! We're here to save you from involuntary conscription in the godforsaken Roamin' Empire."

Not one faced turn. The mass continued to move like massive amoebas being wrung through sausage casings at the corner deli.

He tried one more direct appeal: ""Roameos! Roameos! Where is IV Art Thou?" Roameos! Roameos!"

The river fascinated Paige, so many souls defective in their mortal pursuits. He felt sad for them and, yeah, a little smug that despite never having made any real money, he'd lived an Earth life as rich and rewarding as any king or sultan. And it was all thanks to his native interest in his fellow man.

Truly, he'd loved being human, and he'd loved human beings.

The river dialogue failed to hold Pat Finder's interest. She nodded so long to Paige and walked up the gentle slope back to the bus with Elle . She was just in time to hear Maya Angelou recite the poem she'd been cajoled into writing about the journey so far. She was sure Paige was fine amusing himself with other plays on Roamers and other topics. It dawned on her how she was feeling a surreal sense of righteous calm for someone who within the next day or so was bound to do any number of things destined to secure her name on Satan's shit list.

Now, Paige felt he was all alone. He didn't think the Roamers counted. And he was mostly right, as he was about to empathically find out. His stomach now fully settled, he began to sense a summons from another internal organ.

Paige had to piss. The closer he got to Hell, the more his being began to reanimate with odd biological imperatives. He looked left, right, and behind. No one was looking. He began to undo his fly and liberate his pecker as he absent-mindedly stumbled toward the river to do his business. That's when he heard the "river" speak.

"You better not be thinking of peeing on me!"

He looked up. His jaw went slack. His face lost all expression. It was a good thing his penis was attached because if it wasn't, he'd have dropped it.

∽

"I SAID, 'You better not be thinking of peeing on me!'"

Her name was Bea. He would have known this if he'd have bothered to look at the name tag she wore. It read "Hello! My name is BEA." She didn't think his urinating on her would have been intentional, and she was very forgiving.

Plus, she thought the dude was kind of cute.

Paige, gobsmacked, managed to blurt out, "You can talk!"

She jumped up like a cheerleader and threw her arms around his neck and said, "I can kiss, too!" And she did. It was a deep, surprisingly soulful kiss.

It happened just like that. Love at first site. He was happy someone or something had slipped the breath mints in his pocket. Paige was metaphysically as close to Hell as he'd ever been, but the kiss made him feel like he'd died and gone to Heaven. It's like he'd completely forgotten what it was like to have a sensual body. Hot damn, it felt good.

They'd been briefed that the Roamers were incapable of thought, speech or independent action. They were useless vessels, couch potatoes in a fruitless search for couches. Not dead, not alive. Not good, not bad. They were humanity's past-their-expiration-date leftovers mindlessly trudging through eternity like old jalopies stuck on auto-pilot. They just cruised along on the same mindless path. It was oddly compelling, like the lava in the lava light.

Apparently, the intel was tellingly bad.

Both Zeke and Pat had seen the romantic interlude and had come running. They wanted to hear her story and a moment later she confirmed what her name tag stipulated.

Her explanations came spilling out in a giddy rush. Her name was Bea Long. She'd been dead five years, a victim of smoke inhalation. She'd been binge-watching "The Sopranos."

"I was settled in to watch the finale," she said. "I was so engrossed I became oblivious that the house was on fire. I died of smoke inhalation. I died before I got to see what happened in the end. I'm dying to find out. Can you tell me?"

"I can't," Paige said.

"Can't or won't?"

"Both."

Alas, the divisiveness of "The Sopranos" finale carried over into eternity.

She was convinced her Roamer designation had been one big mistake, and she was positive she'd one day be delivered to heavenly glory. "And here you are! My A-Team! And you're my Mr. T!"

She said she used to watch a lot of television, staring at it for hours and hours. She thought it factored into her not being deemed good enough for Heaven, but too tame for Hell.

"Most everyone here spent their entire lives slack-jawed and staring at the TV. There was no way to grade us. We'd left no mark, nothing upon which we could be judged. So, on our Judgment Days, it was as if our trials were continued. It was as if we'd never been born. They just stuck us all here."

"But I never hurt a soul, and I did my best to encourage the people in my life. And my regulars all loved me."

"Regulars?" Paige asked.

"Yeah, I was a breakfast waitress at this divey little joint near Youngstown," she said. "It had great regulars. The coffee was the best, and people would come from all over to get the apple pie-stuffed French Toast. The place was called the Youngstown Grille."

Paige was beaming. Breakfast waitress!

He told her she was not the object of their mission, but he could, ahem, add her to their priorities, he boasted with flirtatious authority.

He told her about Evan and Elle and the story of their undying love. He told of their clandestine communications, their devotions, their pledges of faithfulness against fleshy temptations. And how this mission came about.

They walked back to the bus where Ben Franklin and Maria E. Beasley had built a campfire from scrub brush and were roasting hunks of the marshmallow-like crash cushion that had saved the bus upon landing. Beasley, in the early

1880s, had invented a life raft that was a vast improvement over previous versions. Franklin was crushing on her.

Bea said, "Boy, that sounds like it would make a great mini-series. You could get Reese to play Elle and maybe Joseph Gordon-Levitt to play Evan. Then you cast Morgan Freeman to play ..."

With the enthusiastic expertise of an A-list aficionado, she rattled off the names of a dozen other actors Paige had never heard of and suggested locations for filming pertinent scenes. She had an animated way of talking about turning their story into a film that led him to believe she was once in the business.

Pat asked how many out of the numberless multitudes were as articulate and with it as she was.

"Maybe, to a lesser degree, a couple hundred. I think so many of us being here is really some kind of clerical error. That's what Artie thinks, at least."

Zeke and Paige piped up in near-perfect unison, like a barbershop duet, "Artie? You know Arthur Thou IV?"

"Oh, yeah, we're buds. He's the greatest."

Paige asked if he was near. Bea said she had no way of knowing. The bartender stood up facing the river. He cupped his hands around his mouth and shouted, "Roameos! Roameos! Where is IV Art Thou? Roameos! Pray tell, where is IV Art Thou?"

From behind them, they heard a rustle of scrub brush. A man in a big, red, floppy hat emerged and said, "No need to shout! I art here!"

"So you're the killer we're hoping will unite me with the man I love?"

It was Elle. She said speaking in a manner that was more observational than accusatory. He was not offended. He knew it was true. He'd thought about it. He'd thought a lot about it. He'd thought about everything. It was all he did.

His was a free-range mind.

He'd been standing there the whole time. He'd camouflaged himself in tedium and apathy. Forget the racial stereotypes, the people who look most alike are the ones who've stopped caring. But he cared, and cared deeply. A murderer of eight, he was a firm believer in universal redemption.

Just not his. Not yet.

His face broke into a grin as he extended his open hand. "Arthur Thou the Fourth, scoundrel at your service."

Both Paige and Pat were unprepared to be charmed, but the scoundrel had a way about him. He was dashing in an understated way that both found very appealing. Elle understood why Bea had begun to glow when she'd been talking about him.

And they began to talk. He explained how escaping from Hell had been an achievement, but a Pyrrhic one. Like the dog on the chase, Thou had no plan for when he metaphorically caught the car.

"I didn't think it through," he lamented. "I'd escaped from some jails during my mortality and, man, what a rush. Nothing beats the feeling of being free and out on the prowl after you've been locked up. You'd think escaping from Hell would be the bigger deal. Huh-uh. Nobody even comes after you. You're just stuck out here in this crazy purgatory. It'll drive you nuts.

"What turned it around for me? Meeting Bea and realizing the potential of even the most stoic Roamer. There've been others, but she was the first one to really click."

So, Pat asked, you're like some kind of teacher?

"I guess in a way that's all I ever wanted to be. It's just my methods have changed."

"I'll say," Paige said. "You've gone from mass murder to motivation. That's some giant leap on the instructional scale."

"I know the thought of the credo doesn't play well for those who consider anything that doesn't begin with, 'In the beginning ...' but I'm with Charles Darwin. We're all capable of evolving."

It became for Paige one of the oddest philosophical encounters he'd ever had in his 157 years — and he'd once spent a day at the ballpark deciphering the diamond wisdoms of Yogi Berra.

He told Thou about how the plan to unite Evan and Elle was all everyone in Heaven was talking about. The chatter was all-consuming.

And by the end of the day, both Paige and Pat considered the killer to be a friend and believed him when he said he wanted to help. On one condition:

"I want unsupervised guest privileges in Heaven one weekend a month," he said.

He said he had no plans to abandon the Roamers. It was his ministry, he said. He believed that although many had lived and died in persistent vegetative states, he believed he could get these former couch potatoes to bear fruit. But he wanted the heavenly hall pass to incentivize the Roamers.

And, lastly, he wanted the fair Bea to get another crack at Heaven.

"She never had a chance, and look how she's blossomed. She'd be a great addition."

Paige had no authority to make any of that happen, but it was his intention to recommend they accede to his wishes. He'd already grown to admire Art's character, his pluck, his chutzpah. Thou was putting his neck on the line. If he got caught, Paige could only imagine what they'd do to make an example out of him.

If he succeeded, he'd be the only man in history to go through Hell ('n' back) (twice) to get to Heaven.

As for Bea, all he really knew of her was the girl sure knew how to kiss.

43

ROAMER-VIEW PICNIC

There were no apostles, no foreboding and, despite what some passengers believed about Zeke, no Messiah. There were no quarrels about betrayals. No fears the bill distribution would be inequitable or that the waitress would get stiffed.

This was no Last Supper.

Rather, there were mimosas and French breads and cheeses, so in some ways it was more like a Last Brunch. They were enjoying a picnic feast featuring Jamison lamb prepared by Julia Child. Chuck Yeager had extricated the bus from the muck and nearly broke the sound barrier doing recon near Hell. Watching the Roamers felt less dreadful after meeting Bea and Arthur and hearing their arguments that they deserved salvation.

The setting was desolate, but they'd fostered a sense of camaraderie, a unity of purpose that seemed to lighten the landscape. There was nothing final about what they were feeling. The conversations were hopeful. They knew they were united and believed the odds of succeeding were in their favor. Still, they were talking about swarming Hell, breaking down infernal barriers, stickin' it to the man.

The only difference was in this case "the man" was Satan.

"How bad is it?" Elle asked Arthur. "I mean living in Hell."

"I call it tolerable misery," he said. "There is no such thing as a good day — at least there wasn't the nearly 20 years I was there. You can't trust anyone. Nothing functions. It stinks.

"You know how it used to suck when you were having 'one of those days' in the mortal world? In Hell, every day is one of those days. Nothing good ever happens — to anyone. So you can't enjoy a vicarious thrill if, say, Burt bowls a perfect game. All the bowling balls have a flat side guaranteeing no one ever gets a true roll."

Even the most downtrodden Earthling can find even a slim reason to nurture daily hope, he said. They dream of hitting the lottery, spending time with the grandkids or cheering on the local ball team during the pennant race, he said.

"I was friends with a guy who was so broke his idea of a really good day was one that involved him finding a quarter. Another story, same guy. He said he always felt like a big shot whenever he could order a pizza with pepperoni *and* sausage. A two-item pizza was his idea of a real splurge. And this guy never had a bad day. He was hopeful that every day things would get better. I don't think they ever did, but the hope that they would carried him through to the day he died when I have to assume everything got much, much, better. It being Heaven and all."

The worst part of Hell, he said, was knowing Hell had a Hell. As bad as things were, rest assured, they could always get worse. Hell's Hell was Old Testament. It was Lakes of Fire, festering wounds and worms that eat your eyeballs.

"If they catch me, that's where I'm going," he said, for the first time no longer jovial. "But I won't get caught. There's no way. I'll kill every goddamned one of 'em before that happens."

A respectful silence pressed in on the picnickers. Being good — being right — had a way of boosting one's confidence. At least until it turned out you were all wrong.

Artie pulled a shiny machete, about 18 inches long, from a hidden sleeve in his boot. He held it up for others to admire the way a father admires a son who just struck out the kid the guys on the other team nicknamed "Slugger."

"Do you have any idea how difficult it is to get away with making and concealing deadly contraband in Hell?" he asked, turning the blade over and over like he was charging it with an ambient electricity visible only to himself. "Well, I managed to fashion this little crippler over five years while in metal shop. They thought I was making fireplace tools."

Being evil and being intelligent rarely went hand-in-hand, he said.

"The thing is, I never got to use it. And the blade is thirsty for blood."

Elle thought she was watching him transform before her eyes from a decent guy into a homicidal maniac. She was surprised to realize the transformation felt reassuring. She didn't think sending a diplomat to Hell to help her boyfriend escape would cut it. But a guy with a thirsty machete, man, he was all about cutting.

"It surprises me even now how easy it was to bust out. They had a new girl working the gate. She had a fearsome rep and I'd heard she'd even been wed to Satan.

"I tell you what, to me she was a real pushover. I thought

if I was going to have to kill anyone it would have been her. But I found out she has a secret weakness: fashion. She's dress-crazy. I started showing her some samples, and she got all distracted. She turned her back on me, and I was gonzo."

Paige said he found it hard to believe escaping from Hell was that easy.

"She was the new girl and might have been in over her head," he said. "But part of what made it so easy was the inherent incompetence of Hell. Once I got on the other side of the door, it was like she'd become a partner in crime. She had nothing to gain by reporting that I'd walked out on her watch. I knew this instinctively."

Elle asked if he'd kill her if he had to.

"Yeah, but just once."

That singular designation confused everyone.

He explained that unlike in Heaven where even goldfish can live forever, it's possible to in Hell kill anything multiple times.

"Our greatest fear is the fear of dying," he said. "In Hell, you can die at least once a day. But if you kill somebody in Hell, the house rule is you have to assist with the revival and clean up the mess. There are so many killers there that it's just understood that any killing involves a lot of mess and a lot of paperwork. It's hardly worth it."

"So," Paige said, "if you stab someone in the heart with your blade and it kills them, the rule is you have to bring them back to life. What if you refuse? Do they stay dead?"

"Legend has it they slowly regenerate. I never saw it and I'm not sure I believe it, but that's the word. But if I have the time, I'd cut the bastards into so many tiny pieces it'd take them years to put their evil Humpty Dumptys back together again. When it comes to killin' something purely evil, I have zero squeamishness."

The thought of such bloody overkill was sobering to Paige, who just moments ago had felt the promising hints of a budding wine buzz. Art's dissertation had sobered him up.

"I guess there are some evils you just can't kill."

He had another question, one so simple he wondered if he should even ask it: How was he going to break *in* to Hell?

The crimson glow had begun to leave Thou's face. The bloodlust was being replaced by a sort of game face. He was getting ready for business.

"You don't break into Hell," he said, a knowing smile beginning to crease his cheeks. "You just walk in through the front door. There's even a welcome mat. There's a line, sure, but no one minds if you cut. It is my intention to walk right in and start my howdy-doos."

44

EVAN, RUSTY & JUDAS

Evan had always said the greatest faith wasn't the belief in God. The greatest faith was when Curly was in some bone-headed predicament and yelled, "Hey, Moe! Hey, Larry! I need help! Come quick!" And honestly believed the situation would improve.

He looked across the table at his scheming mates and wondered if he wasn't misplacing his trust.

He studied Judas. He was only the most famous turncoat in history. But Judas was his friend. He felt he could trust Judas. Judas valued his friendship. Judas couldn't be bought. He thought that and realized, hey, Jesus felt the exact same way. And look how that turned out!

Certainly Judas, having had ample time to think about his folly, had realized the error of his ways.

Surely.

After all, how many times had he heard him say, "You can trust me, friend, or my name ain't Judas Iscariot!"

It was funny the first dozen or so times he said it, but lately it had become sort of macabre. Was he mocking Jesus? Himself? Evan?

Rusty was a whole other matter entirely. He'd started out bellicose, but had morphed to maudlin. Evan thought he was crackin' up, that Hell was getting to him. He could've sworn he'd been trying to express feelings of fatherly affection.

Sure, he'd been angry that his own son had murdered him, but that was sorta an accident. That he wound up in Hell had surprised Rusty because he never believed himself to be the bad guy. He'd been the victim of an abusive father and a neglectful mother. He'd been the one with the artistic side who never had the chance to see it flourish. And it was him, Rusty Lee, who wound up in Hell. It didn't seem right.

It didn't seem right to Evan, either. That's why he fully intended to break out with Judas and Rusty in tow. What they intended to accomplish was nothing less than the resolution of the very definition of right and wrong.

Evan believed the rosters in Hell were full of "sinners" who barely deserved to be in Heck, let alone Hell. It was his hope that Arthur Thou would help usher in a new realm of more generous forgiveness, one that would let men like him, his father and Judas ("You can trust me or my name ain't") Iscariot a running shot at real providential redemption.

Evan believed it would be a boon to almost everyone in Hell. Everyone but the worst of the worst.

Everyone but the likes of Josef Goebbels.

The propagandist had been up Evan's ass for two weeks now demanding he implement the putsch that would elevate Hitler over Satan, who would assume a more ceremonial role — just like Paul von Hindenburg back in the old Weimar Republic glory days.

If Satan was aware of the treachery, he hadn't let on. There'd been no security crackdowns, no interrogations, no waterboarding of innocents. The lack of interest seemed to embolden the old Nazi.

"You know if this works out, you'll probably get to meet the old man," he told Evan. "I've told him of the importance of your role and the skill you're applying to get it done. He could make your time here so much better."

It was in every way disconcerting to be seduced by Hitler's wingman. He knew Goebbels used to set Hitler up on blind dates. He wondered if this was the same sort of banter he used in those situations.

He fancifully imagined the pitches went something like: Oh, I think you two really have a lot in common. Do you like kids? Yes, he, too, likes kids. Well, most kids. The right kind of kids. You do instinctively hate millions of people for just being born different from you, yes? No queasiness about genocide, I hope. That's good. He's just a bit of control freak, and he can be a bit moody. I hope that's not a deal-breaker. And he's what they're calling a reluctant heterosexual, so bring your adult pleasure toy.

He'd been showing Goebbels dispatches that berated the devil for being insufficiently demonic, arguing, in essence, that Hell should be more hellish. As a rosy platform for support, Evan didn't know just how this would appeal to the rank and file. It was useful to Evan, though, because it had the prospect of riling them up, and he assumed chaos would be beneficial to his escape plans.

The urgency of Elle's last call convinced him that Arthur Thou IV was on his way. He was going to shepherd him and his fellow schemers out the door. How Art Thou planned to achieve this was a mystery. Was he an explosives expert? A con artist? A negotiator? A mix of those talents? Evan had no idea.

As he'd been prone to wondering lately if he was going

through all this for Elle or for his own selfish ass. He understood none of this would have happened without Elle's drive and talents. It had been her initiative. She was the one who'd gotten Heavenly higher ups — and they don't come any higher than that — to pay attention and to act.

Had he done his part? No, but he was, being in Hell, laboring under more institutional duress and with threats of severe repercussions if he'd gotten caught. And he wondered what the future held if they got away with it.

Would Heaven consider him damaged goods? Was there a prison in Heaven for guys sort of like him, guys who broke the laws, but were good dudes at heart? Maybe he could go on work release or wear an ankle monitor. Or maybe there was a third place he could go, one where he could redeem himself.

And, yeah, he worried about the lifelong commitment he'd be making to Elle. He'd owe her big time. He suspected he'd at the very least he'd have to be faithful to her, something he'd never been.

He'd struggled with the stifling idea of monogamy and often would observe how monogamy and monotony were just a few careless key strokes away from being the very same thing. Same goes for back in his earth days when he'd advise young newlyweds against marriage on the grounds that "if marriage were so good for a man how come there's no Mrs. God?" Heck, there wasn't even a Mrs. Jeter for a long time, he'd say, referring to the long-time happy Yankee bachelor short stop Derek Jeter.

All he really knew was that tomorrow he was going to raise Hell. Raise it and hope that Elle had found a way to lower Heaven.

He tried not to think of the repercussions if he failed, so dire they promised to be.

He'd long ago concluded he couldn't pray to God to spare him Hell. God wasn't listening.

He thought he could ask Larry and Moe for an assist, but was doubtful their participation would lead to an improved situation.

45

ART THOU IV GOES BACK TO HELL

The bus full of historical A-listers was idling just over the horizon from the Gates of Hell, which weren't nearly as foreboding as the literary legends implied. Having big, impregnable gates implied a certain exclusivity, like they were trying to keep out the riffraff. Nothing could have been further from the truth. Riff raff in Hell?

Come on down!

So getting into Hell was like applying for club membership at some of the cheaper gated communities down along Florida's Space Coast. You didn't need much in the way of credentials or referrals. You didn't have to prove you were a baby rapist, a wife beater or random serial killer to earn admission. They'd take your word for it.

The entrance looked more like the facade of one of those old columned city banks that sometimes get turned into pricey restaurants. There was a sign that listed "Today's Activities" and included times and places for shuffleboard, karaoke and Early-Bird dinner specials. The sign, thoughtfully, didn't have a date, which might have confused those standing before it.

Of course, no one ever saw the sign twice. They'd see it once and think, "Hmmm, maybe this won't be so bad."

About this they were wrong because on the other side of the doors, it was Hell.

There's even a "WELCOME" mat.

The line to get in moved at a fairly brisk clip. Still, Thou had no trouble getting in front of other men and women, some of whom had been waiting in line for years. No one complained. They were in no rush.

The pervading sense of hopelessness kept the line intact. Even the most villainous sinner felt an heirloom deference when he or she was bound for some face time with Satan.

Thou pushed open the door and stepped inside. He'd imagined this scenario many times, knowing as he did the reality would never match the imagination. It was way worse.

To him it was like the scene where Willy Wonka pushes open the door to expose the Golden Ticket winners and their designates to the wonders of Wonka's world. There are bonbon lollipop bumbershoots, and the chocolate river that's soon to be desecrated by Augustus, the gluttonous Gloop kid.

It's a scene of idyllic, almost pastoral rapacity for those prone to tooth decay.

So it's the exact opposite of what you experience when you set foot in Hell.

To the left, a pack of white supremacists was gang-raping an elderly disabled pedophile. The cock gobblers and turd burglars waited nearby. Close enough to hear the anguished moans knelt a once-prim young lady, who'd murdered, through deliberate neglect, 14 senior citizens under her care; she was digging her eyes out with a fork to no real result. They always grew back.

And just a little past her a clutch of women — they met for coffee once a week — stood a social group of women who'd killed their children. They surrounded a large man who in mortal times had been described by the media, not without admiration, as a "Caribbean strong man." He stood naked, his feet immersed in buckets of dry cement up past his ankles. Thus exposed, *El Presidente* , sobbed as he awaited his daily punishment. The women each gripped whips they'd made on craft night.

Into this milieu of misery Art Thou strode boldly right up to the registration table and confronted Jill Keyes eyeball to eyeball.

"Remember me? Sure you do. I'm the guy who escaped from Hell on your watch. And I'm the guy who can make the afterlife miserable for you if you don't do what I say."

The woman who was known for her all-consuming eyes suddenly became all ears. He began to tell her how he was determined to retrieve a mistake, and if she didn't step aside she'd wind up in Time Out — no matter what happened to him.

"Now, you just keep quiet and stand out of the way when you see me and my companion coming."

Evan ID'd him right away. He was attuned enough to a variation of routine to detect the anomaly of someone confronting Keyes. He turned to Judas and said, "Art Thou just walked back into Hell. C'mon."

Judas seemed hesitant.

"Well, c'mon," Evan prompted.

They met Thou on the outskirts of the rec yard. There was no handshake, no salute, no man hug, no outward signs of brotherhood, just a mutual admiration between kindred spirits. Men like Evan and Art may not have believed in love at first sight, but they could instantaneously detect a future drinking buddy.

Evan had waited until Thou had exited the main floor and was in the hallway. Art wasn't prepared for a plus one, especially one as notorious as Judas. Still, he didn't care. The actions resulting from those decisions were no concern of his. But he became a bit more emphatic when Evan said, "Hold on. I have to run and get my Rusty."

He conveyed with firm insistence that, although they were dealing with eternal elements, time was not on their side. Every second counts, he said, and every second we spend on this side of the door is a second that means we may never ever get back to the other side. And that would break Elle's heart.

"Yes, I understand, but he's my, er, Rusty," he said, before adding more forcefully, "He's my father."

"Didn't you kill your father?"

"Yes, I did, but it was kind of an accident, and we've patched things up, being roommates in Hell and all."

Art gave a "whatever" sort of shrug and followed Evan down past the cafeteria, past the laundry, the business center and still deeper and deeper into Hell. Rusty was sitting on the edge of his cot like he'd been awaiting their appearance. If he didn't know better, Evan would have sworn his father had been engaged in prayer.

No time for introductions, they turned around and retraced their route past the business center, past the laundry, past the cafeteria and up to the edge of the rec yard.

"I wasn't planning on having to get three of you plus myself out, and it's going to be tricky. I think each of us can play a role and it's important that —

"Ah, sorry," Evan said, "but there's one last thing I've

committed to doing before we can vamoose. I probably should have mentioned it sooner. Really, it's not that big a deal. Should only take a sec."

Art at first thought he was goofing around. He said nothing could be more important than them having a functional escape plan. To have frittered away as much as 30 minutes may already have been a crucial mistake. Those minutes could make all the difference. In the balance hung everlasting eternity.

"So what is it now?" Art said. "What do you have to do that could possibly lead us to delay leaving Hell for even another minute? What?"

"I have to start a war."

∽

THE SHORTEST WAR in recorded history is judged to be the Anglo-Zanzibar War fought August 27, 1896. It was a dispute over the succession of the reigning sultanate.

The "war" lasted 48 minutes, or about the time it takes to watch an episode of "Survivor" when you can zip through the commercials. In the end, over 500 Zanzibarians were killed or wounded to one British sailor who suffered a broken toe when he accidentally dropped a cannonball on his foot.

So the shortest war in unrecorded history was what came to be known as The Afterworld War for Evil Supremacy. It lasted about 22 minutes or about the time it took to watch a syndicated episode of "Friends," sans commercials.

Here's what happened:

Evan had done just as he was told. He printed and posted a list of grievances against Satan. He'd written that

Satan had gone soft. That Hell had become more like Heck. He said Hell was becoming too comfortable and that some discipline needed to be restored. He said Satan had been spotted wearing a frilly dress and sipping poolside daiquiris near the Lake of Fire. He said he'd lost touch with the common man. Called him a pussy.

And he signed it Joseph Goebbels.

Then he rewrote the note, but the only thing he changed was wherever he'd referred to Satan he changed the name to Hitler.

Signed that one Goebbels, too.

He blasted out copies to each of their followers under shock headlines about illegal aliens coming to take over Hell; that taxes would skyrocket under one or the other; and that nepotism and foreign trade were stealing jobs from workers.

Each missive declared an insurrection was in the works and that combatants should prepare to go wild in the rec yard at high noon on January 666. Sure, the 666 was a sloppy typo, but Evan was too pressed for time to engage a proper editor.

He knew, too, that the very presence of a letter challenging Lucifer would cause partisans to mass in the rec yard. He was surprisingly popular among residents. And, truly, the thought of anyone else — especially Hitler — running Hell scared the crap out of people. They knew what to expect from Satan, but Hitler was a real wild card.

It was a literal case of the devil they knew being better than the devil they didn't.

So that started the melee. People with so much in common, with shared interests and a mutual understanding that only through united efforts could positive results be achieved, began to bash each other's brains in.

As distractions go, this one was a doozy. A bloody one. There was hair-pulling, eye gouging, shiv thrusting, treachery.

It just wasn't enough.

Jill Keyes threw herself in front of the only door in or out of Hell. She was wearing a sleeveless Nicole Miller flower print that on any other women in any other setting would have been considered fetching. Her guards had disappeared. It was just her and that one door.

Evan looked to his right and there was Rusty, wearing a look he'd never seen before. It was resolution. His father had undergone a miraculous transformation. He'd gone from juvenile antagonist to a strong ally, a role model. In that moment, Evan imagined a future with the father he'd never knew. In a flash, he saw them playing catch on the sandlot where he'd taught himself to ride a bike. He foresaw them going fishing, working on cars and, late at night out on the porch, the two of them sipping beers late into the night and conspiratorially talking — say, *psst* — remember that night we busted out of Hell with that crazy gang of sinners.

Rusty was before his very eyes redeeming himself. Evan felt a poignant twinge that gave him an odd confidence that it was all going to work out.

That confidence began to wobble when he looked behind him and Judas was nowhere to be seen. He'd said, "Don't worry, man, I've got your back ... or my name ain't Judas Iscariot!" Now, his back was exposed. He was fully vulnerable.

Evan looked at Art and understood he was being led by a natural-born killer. Evan's Earth kill total tripled his, but he felt each of his should have an explanatory asterisk. Not so for the 10 Thou had on his rap sheet. Those murders were precise, operatic, purposeful. He had killer eyes and those eyes were now drilling in on Keyes.

Art drew his thirsty blade from its boot sheath and raised it above his head. Evan braced himself for a quenching spray of cranial blood before crossing the threshold. But the blade's drought would endure just a bit longer.

"That's them! They're the two that started all this! They're the ones you want ... or my name ain't Judas Iscariot!"

They were suddenly surrounded by Goebbels and half-a-dozen stormtroopers. They'd been betrayed by Judas Iscariot. He'd been keeping authorities apprised the whole time. Evan felt like a fool. At least they were now in all-time good company. Evan began feeling a corpuscular cocktail of rage and stupidity. He saw the apparent boss of the corps hand Judas a jingly purple Crown Royal bag.

"Your 30 pieces of silver, no doubt," Evan said bitingly.

"Casino chips. Don't take it too hard, Evan. Your friendship means the whole world to me. I couldn't let you just walk away."

"But you could have thrown in with us," Evan said. "You could have taken your chances with the better angels. You could have turned over a new leaf!"

"You never had a chance, Evan," Judas said. "Even your own father agrees with me. He said so. And where is he now? Nowhere to be seen."

It was heartbreakingly true, Evan thought. Rusty had split. So much for redemption. He'd need to find a different role model. It was nice while it lasted.

A gnawing disappointment began to ramble through his empty stomach. He knew the risks, but how could it have all gone so wrong. After all, they had God on their side.

"My God, my God, why hast thou forsaken me?"

Judas overheard him and said, "I can name that tune in three notes …"

Goebbels' cool veneer was shedding. He was becoming more and more agitated. He knew his patriarch would be enraged, a case of inFUHRERation, more acute than infuriation.

As the jiffy little war was escalating all around him, he began to dial up his wrath against Evan. He was in his mind picturing electrodes attached to nipples and the penis.

"And we're talking hundreds of years. Hundreds! We can be patient as we want. Torture will be the day-to-miserable-day sum of your entire existence. Even on the remote chance that we get bored with the, ah, 'examinations,' we can impose the work on your friend here.

"It's very satisfying to sit back and watch compadres deliver pain to their friends, pain so elemental you'll pray to a God that no longer listens how you wish you'd never been born," Goebbels hissed.

Evan was determined not to flinch. He wouldn't give the propagandist the satisfaction. He looked at Art Thou IV. The Killing Machine looked like he was starting to rev his engines. He felt if he could just find an opening, a momentary gap in their concentration, then he and Thou could go deep. If only …

"I tell ya, the dress is blue with black stripes," Keyes said. "Any idiot can see that."

"I disagree. I swear the dress is white with gold stripes."

It was Rusty. He hadn't chickened out at all. He'd been his very own Plan B. He was distracting Keyes from both the door and the escape attempt. She was adamant that the dress was surely blue with black stripes.

A squad of guards goose-stepped up and awaited orders. "Take a look at this," she said to the nearest guard. "This idiot says this dress is white with gold stripes when any fool can see it's a blue dress with black stripes."

The guard was non-committal, but two others were adamant, no question. It was white with gold stripes.

Annoyed, Goebbels petulantly insisted he be given the photo. "This juvenile lack of discipline must stop. And, besides, anyone can plainly see the dress is …"

A flicker of understanding was all it took for Evan and Art to begin a synchronized mayhem.

The world's shortest war was about to conclude. Rec floor combatants were already slowing down, tending to their wounded and beginning to formulate stories of their heroic contributions to the Shortest War in History. So no one was prepared for the brutal spasm of crimson violence that erupted within splatter distance from the Gates of Hell.

They'd made a tactical mistake when they decided their priority was to determine the color of the dress. They did this without ever realizing that shadows over-represent blue light and that, further, by mentally subtracting short wavelength light from an image tends to make it appear yellowish. And natural light works a similar magic by tricking viewers into thinking a natural light would shift the color actualization.

And, of course, anyone with eyes and a brain could plainly see the dress was white with gold stripes.

In hindsight they realized, they probably should have instead taken the thirsty machete from Art Thou. Because it drank heavily from the guards. Before Evan had even had time to assume his vaunted karate pose, Thou's desiccated blade had severed three of the arms of his foes. It could take months for the arms to be reattached.

Thou's prowess with the machete softened the spines of the other guards who fled the battle site. Less fleet of foot was Goebbels, who began to beg to be spared. His pleas were, however, in vain and Thou spent his fury at evil on the murder-minded Big Lie propagandist who, in the end became the only fatality in the Afterworld's Shortest War.

Thou hacked him into a thousand tiny pieces. And all the King's horses and all the King's men ... He'd been hacked so thoroughly that first responders were at a loss as to how to begin re-animation techniques. So, what the hell, they just scooped up the bits and shoveled them into the incinerator.

Farewell to a man too evil for Hell.

The slaughter was so complete Hell went momentarily silent, a quiet that was only broken by Judas who at last stood between Evan, Art, Rusty, and the gate.

"Sorry, fellas, but you're going to have to go through me if you wanna get to Heaven." He pointed a gun at Art and instructed him to drop the blade.

Evan cursed and said, "Man, when you're a company man you're full on board aren't you?"

"I can't deny who I am. Plus, I like my chances here better than outside of here. It's the Devil you know, you know?"

"Now the two of you are coming with me, and we're going to show you what a hell Hell can be."

Evan saw him creeping along out of the corner of his eye. He never knew his father had the stealth. Or the balls. He was small, but he was wiry. He was within 2 feet of Judas before the turncoat finally saw him. Too late. Nimble as a monkey and ferocious as a hyena, he was on him in an instant. His arms wrapped around his shoulders, his teeth sunk into his left ear.

Judas howled in pain and confusion. He never suspected Rusty had the grit to act on his own, or to risk the enduring pain Rusty could only fathom. So as Rusty began gouging out his eyeballs with his thumbs, Judas had to give him some grudging credit.

Evan was almost too stunned to react. His father was sacrificing his very soul to save his son. It was redemptive beyond measure.

"Save yourselves!" Rusty exclaimed. "Run! I love you, son!"

"Daddy! I love you, too!"

On the loud speaker playing for the 139th consecutive time was "The Worst," a plodding, faintly country 1994 song by the Rolling Stones. Evan did not know if naming a song "The Worst" in the prophetic understanding it was bound to one day be considered by fans as *the* worst Stones song ever was an inside joke or a self-deprecating warning to listeners.

"The Worst" was the only Stones song Evan would ever hear in Hell, surprising to Evan considering their best song was the demonic Valentine "Sympathy for The Devil." Made him wonder if Satan deep down had a humble streak.

"C'mon!" Thou yelled. "They'll be swarming this place any second!" He practically shoved Evan out the door. Evan turned in time to see security ripping his father apart. He couldn't be sure if he really saw it or if it was a trick of the brain, but he could have sworn he saw his father wink and flash the thumb's up sign. Then the door slammed shut.

It was the last of Hell Evan would ever see.

46

OUTSIDE HELL

Once they got clear of the gates, Evan took off. He ran as fast and as far as he could, faster and farther than he'd ever been. He ran out of fear he was being chased. When he finally turned to gauge the proximity of his pursuers, he was surprised to see Thou just a short stroll from the gates lighting a cigar.

So Evan sat down and waited. He looked back at where he'd been. Hell looked like a strip mall, so ordinary, so banal. He wondered about the condemned souls waiting in line. Would any of them try to escape? Would security be ramped up after the war and the escape of two hombres? He doubted it. Evil was very bureaucratic. Security measures would probably die in committee.

It took Art about 20 minutes to catch up. "Man, you got some pistons on you. I'm glad they won't be chasing us. They'd snag me and let you go."

"You know, I think that's the first time I ever called him 'Daddy,'" Evan said.

"He knew he wouldn't be escaping with us," Art said. "He knew he'd be dragged away to a Hell exponentially worse than the one you and I experienced. I'd guess that was the bravest thing I ever saw. You killed him?"

"I say it was accidental, but the man I killed was not the man we saw sacrificing his life so we'd get a second chance. I saw him changing, but I would never have predicted he'd have done something like that."

"I'd say he made the most of his second chance. But just look where it got him."

Evan was thoughtfully silent for a moment. "Just brainstorming here. What do you think the chances are that they'll send in a SEAL Team 6 to save some souls?"

"Near zero," Art said, his eyes scanning the horizon. "As heroic as your father was, I doubt they'd construct a mission around one man. No, it is my understanding the powers that be have something more dramatic in mind. A real game changer."

He stood up and pointed to a barely visible line snaking across the desolation. It was heading their way. "And unless I'm mistaken the game changer is heading this way."

~

MANY OF THE most consequential men and women in history, fervent believers that if given enough time they were capable of improving any situation, no matter how vexing, were at that very moment marching on Hell. And leading the way was a 15-year-,old girl who just 18 months earlier had spent a good deal of her time planning to prematurely end her mortal life.

"Why am I not surprised you're first in line?" Art asked Pat Finder. "And just whose idea was this?"

"It was mine," she said, sheepishly grinning.

"And just what do you hope to accomplish?"

"Comfort and convert," she said. "It's the same thing they've been doing for sinners back home. Pray the Hell out of them. Or in this case, pray them out of Hell. We won't quit until we convert Satan."

She and her fellow Christian soldiers believed it was high time to stomp out evil. They intended to make the deaf hear the word, the blind see the light and the mute sing the praises.

"My, that could take forever."

"We all have forever."

"Who talked you into this?"

"Mark Twain," she said. "He said no one ever prays for Satan, the one who needs prayers the most."

Evan piped up. ""The exact quote, if I may, is, 'Who prays for Satan? Who in 18 centuries has had the common humanity to pray for the one sinner that needs it most, our one fellow and brother who most needed a friend, yet had not a single one, the one sinner among us all who had the highest and clearest right to every Christian's daily and nightly prayers for the plain and unassailable reason that his was the first and greatest need.'

"Or something like that …"

Pat turned to him with an endearingly goofy look on her face. "Well done. And you must be Evan." She sized him up and admiringly said she could see what Elle sees in him. She held out her hand and he shook it.

He asked her what she was going to miss about Heaven. She said the opportunity to travel anywhere in the universe, to the past and the future, Starbucks, and going on movie dates with guys like James Dean and River Phoenix.

"And I think I'll miss flowers. Heaven is just full of flower arrangements. You see them everywhere and there's a florist on every block. Right next to the Starbucks! I'm going to miss vinyl records, shopping for shoes and the butterflies that used to land on my nose when I was reading Harry Potter in the hammock down at the beach. But there'll be time for that. Right now, we have work to do."

She asked if there was anything he'd miss about Hell.

"The liver and onions," Evan said. "It was lunch every Thursday. It just really hit the spot. So I'll miss that. That and the opportunity to get closer to my Dad. But that's another story."

Art put an arm on his shoulder and gave him a reassuring squeeze. He was reminded, not for the last time of the Churchill quote: "When going through Hell, go faster."

The conversation resumed a carefree turn, but they soon realized they could have stood there and talked forever — and that's always an afterlife option — but they each had places to be.

"I'm glad we got to talk," Evan said to Pat. "I'm sure Elle will tell me all about you. I admire what you're doing. It's not going to be easy."

"It should have been done years ago — and who doesn't love a challenge? I wish you the best of everything. I don't know what they have planned for you, but I'm sure it'll all be for the best. Elle's a dynamo. She makes everywhere she goes better. Even Heaven. I don't know what they have planned for you guys."

"Me either," he said. "I'm just grateful for all that's been done for me. I just thank God."

"'Thank you.' That's the best prayer there is."

They hugged and said goodbye, neither sure when they'd meet again, both super-sure they would. One day. Neither of them had anyway of knowing it'd be an eternity before they'd see each other again.

47

EVAN & ELLE

There is no video record of what happened when Evan from Hell met Elle from Heaven. There would be a cottage industry of re-creators and deep fakers interpreting from the shallow pool of facts of what exactly happened. Some were more realistic than others, some were artsy and some were as close to rawdog pornography as it was in good taste to get in Heaven.

The only eye-witness account comes from Paige, who admitted to having been wine drunk from a picnic with Bea Long, with whom he was wholly smitten. She was boisterous, ribald, spontaneous and so full of life Paige had to remind himself she was dead. Well, her soul wasn't. They'd spent nearly every moment of the previous week together. Love was in the air.

And now it was in the back of the bus, too. That's where Evan and Elle went to make out after their initial embrace, as euphoric a coupling as one could imagine in a realm that looked like an old steel mill slag heap.

Paige later told viewers her first words to Evan were, "I thought you'd be taller," to which he replied, "And I wasn't expecting after all this for you to be hung up on superficialities."

As Zeke began to introduce himself, a smile of recognition animated Evan's face. "Hey! Aren't you ..."

"I get that a lot," he said. "I'm Zeke, and I'm so happy to meet you." There'd be time to talk later, Zeke understood. He wanted to give the most highly scrutinized couple in history since Adam and Eve time to acquaint.

It wasn't just love at first sight. It was a love that activated all the senses. They felt lust, security, promise, hopefulness, comfort, but most of all they felt relief, a relief so substantial it could have floated the two of them on a raft past all the swooning doubts they'd harbored.

Because their love was no sure thing. In essence, their entire courtship had been one really long blind date. It had been chaste, long-distance and strewn with relevant trust issues that had to be overcome. For instance, when he told her that one of his most trusted pals in Hell was Judas, she told him she didn't think he was trustworthy, which when he spilled the details of the Shortest War in History, it led to the first really big, "I-told-ya-so's!" in their relationship.

Evan and Elle needed to click and clicking is more important than love in most long-term relationships. Love is sex and admiration and looking nice together at dinner parties.

But clicking is the mortar that holds the whole shebang together. Clickers finish each other's sentences. The click between lovers is what gets you through the rough patches. Rough patches like being steadfast when one of you is going through pure hell.

Evan and Elle right away clicked. And the couples that click are the couples that stick. This became important when Elle revealed she was sacrificing something tangible, something precious, to cement her love to Evan.

She was giving up Heaven. In fact, getting back into Heaven would have been extremely difficult under any circumstances.

Because of all the departure commotion, Elle'd forgotten to get her hand stamped.

And as she'd been told on the God phone, if and when Evan was liberated and they insisted on being together, he couldn't come to Heaven. The decision was irrevocable. You can't remove someone from Hell and just say, whoops, clerical error. C'mon down. Or up, as it were. It was determined that Evan would need a new life sample before it was decided where his soul belonged for the duration of all eternity.

"Well," he said, "if I can't get into Heaven and I can't go back to Hell, what's left?"

∽

THE WEDDING PARTY posed under the "Welcome to Fabulous Las Vegas Nevada" sign for almost 30 minutes. They laughed, mugged and guzzled champagne. Then it was back into the limo and off to the next stop. They were alternately respectful, sometimes rude and rowdy, but they made no apologies.

They were only human.

And they were having the time of their lives, lives that in spite of their best planning were guaranteed to be riven with disappointment, heartbreak, physical pain and mental anguish. There would be loss, betrayal, skinned knees, embarrassments and the eventual understanding that each would only be as happy as their least happy child.

That was just in their own lives. As empathetic human beings, they would shed tears over gun violence, pandemic loss, catastrophic climate change. They would lament the collapse of bee colonies, melting polar ice caps and once-verdant regions rendered uninhabitable by rising temperatures.

They would fret over weight gain and hair loss and try with every interaction to remember that the genius Albert Einstein had said the whole reason for living was to help one another.

Life had the odds-on potential to be a series of disappointments, each one greater than the last, leading inexorably to the grave. And when it was all over and their souls would come into play for eternal disposition, they would say puny human prayers that they'd be judged worthy of a better place, a place where joy and justice prevailed.

But with the stakes so high, nothing was guaranteed.

It's what made Evan so full of life and imbued his effervescent personality with an appreciation so vivid he practically glowed in the dark. He turned down a job as a corporate event planner to work as a community organizer with the Big Brothers and Sisters, where he daily inspired young men and women with his infectious zest for humanity.

Elle started off as recreation and leisure director at a local senior citizens' home. She loved her senior saints and they loved her. But she also loved that her bosses gave her free rein to work on projects that benefitted all of mankind.

Yes, she was pleased to be able to brighten the lives of 100 elderly sweethearts, but she wouldn't be content until she could help brighten the whole world.

Their long marriage would be challenged by infidelities, addictions, secrets and a chronic lack of income. These blemishes would be offset by shared commitments, mutual admiration and the steadfast determination to persevere through the hard times they both from experience knew were bound to arise.

And in the end, they'd always have Elvis.

Their children would mock them mercilessly at every anniversary because, while they were on their Vegas frolic, they'd gotten married by Elvis Presley at the Elvis Chapel.

It'd started as a lark, but became serious when they both noticed something about Elvis that made them think of what they jokingly referred to as their "first date."

Evan was the first to notice. "Say," he said, "aren't you …?"

"Man, I get that all the time," Elvis said with a wink and a grin.

The secular ceremony would always seem in hindsight precious, sacred even. It seemed to summon the good faith, ecumenical angels and unite in them a blessing that would endure throughout time

And when Elvis, impossibly handsome with those perpetually kind eyes, got to the part about "till death us do part," the trio shared a knowing laugh.

They all knew better.

48

HEAVEN'S SUGGESTION BOX

It was becoming one of Paige's favorite parts of the week. It was every Tuesday after everyone had finally left and it was just him alone in the quiet pub. Another day of making everyone in Heaven feel right at home was in the books (the library was closed, too).

Since meeting Bea and getting the ad hoc advisory board to approve her relocation, Heaven for him had been getting better and better. The lonely parts of his soul had found their soulmate. He had Zeke to thank for the relative ease in her transfer from what he called Roam to Heaven, and he knew Zeke would demur if thanked.

Zeke was very humble. He didn't seek credit, but there'd be no denying none of it would have happened without him. The dude had connections. He was gracious, patient, cheerful, generous and cool in any circumstance. Time and again, no matter the difficulty, he'd proved himself to be a real savior.

It wasn't just with Bea. Paige also believed it was Zeke pulling the strings that secured for Lyberty, a black woman, the lead in Gene Kelly's "Singin' in the Rain." The role traditionally went to a white man like, well, Gene Kelly. But it became a huge hit with Lyberty in the lead.

The non-traditional casting would have had some stodgy mortals in a petty snit, but not in Heaven, where things that used to ignite controversy were no big deal.

He figured it was Zeke, again, who'd been the promotional force behind the early success of the "Gettin' Dirty with Lola Lee" show. As the devoted mother of Evan, interest in Lola surged and she proved to be a natural on camera talking about gardening, wine, parenting and raunchy recollections of mortal lovemaking. The Evan & Elle saga had kicked off a renewed curiosity of all things Earthy, and Lola was at the forefront of it all.

But Paige reserved his most divine gratitude for what Zeke had done for him and Bea. He got her case reviewed and, just like that, his Heaven-sent dream girl was sent to Heaven.

This was all on his mind as he put a dollar in the jukebox and played the Kinks' "Misfits" in its entirety. It was Heaven, sure, but it was agreed upon that bars were better when you actually had to plug the jukebox and hunt down the songs. It was a small victory of quaint over smartphone efficiency, but it was one that Paige savored.

Only then would he fix himself a Wild Turkey Old Fashioned and retrieve from his office the package the courier had dropped off the day before. And only then would he exercise the privilege of sorting and categorizing the contents of that week's Heavenly Suggestion Box.

He'd clear space on the bar for two folders. Into the one he'd labeled "OTHER" he put the offbeat suggestions about things like the one that suggested God host an ice skating party for some kid's birthday "to make it extra special for our Billy."

It's also the basket where he'd put the ones about turning up the ambient temperature so the old ladies wouldn't need sweaters, and that God would sit down for an interview with Larry King. The former CNN host was a popular pick for the interviewer because many suspected King and God were contemporaries.

Beside it was the folder with a more substantial pile. In it went the majority of the notes from that week's Suggestion Box. The notes ranged from silly to heartbreakingly poignant.

"In Heaven, we should have one day each week where there's really terrible weather. Like 4 feet of snow. Snow that nobody saw coming. Snow so bad no one can leave the house and everything is closed. That way we'd all have to stay in and spend the time together making soup and watching 'Chitty Chitty Bang Bang' and 'Wizard of Oz.'"

Many suggestions dealt with allowing more adversity in Heaven. Typical was the letter from a woman who'd died of ovarian cancer in 2015. She wanted to talk about the emotional lift she'd reveled in during the 12 years she'd spent having *beaten* cancer.

"The worst year of my life was the year I found out I had breast cancer. But fighting cancer — beating cancer — gave me the best years of my life. I'd been an aerobics instructor before cancer. But fighting and beating cancer for so many years gave me an opportunity to be something I never dreamed I could ever be. I became an inspiration."

Many lamented being denied a second chance at the one job they really screwed up: parenting. More than a few of them were like the one from the Illinois mother, 72, who died of COVID-19 in 2020. She wrote: "I understand it would be a terrible inconvenience to the families, not to mention the children themselves, but it would be great if we could go back and start all over. I know I was a terrible mother, but if given a second chance I could do a much, much better job. I learned so much in my life, and this time I'd be much more patient."

A New Jersey bully suggested men like him should, in effect, be able to turn back time and be a mentor rather than a menace to his victims. Suggestions like these always filled Paige with sweet pity. So sad. Jesus had forgiven these men and women, but they'd spend eternity being unable to forgive themselves.

And there were lots and lots of suggestions about sex with the vast majority of people solidly in favor of letting people have it. But opinions began to fray over who could have it and with whom.

Some wanted to have sex with just one person for all eternity. Some wanted to have sex for all eternity with just about anybody they could get their hands on.

But many people missed having sex in Heaven and resented being told to, in effect — fuhgeddabowttit — that sexual relations led to too many unanticipated consequences: jealousy, possessiveness, performance anxiety and little blue pills down at the corner pharmacy.

As always, he was a bit chagrined to see he was down to just a couple notes. The first one suggested it would be beneficial to morale and set a good example if folks could see God riding His bike around once in a while.

He stuck the note in the "OTHER" stack.

Then he picked up the very last note. In flawless penmanship, it said, "Thank you in advance for considering my ideas on how to make our Heavenly experience better for all time.

"I suggest the idea of eternal life be scrapped in favor of the very real possibility that each day could be our last. This should reinforce the idea that every moment is precious and ripe for creative advancement.

"Allow us to have regular bodies because, although they are prone to underperform and malfunction, they are the one keepsake most of us would like to bring with us from our mortality. Even when they start to expire, they serve the purpose of bringing people together to say nice things and let us know we're loved.

"Give us the chance to co-exist with the people with whom we disagree. Let there be consequences to our actions. And about this eternity thing, how about giving us an option so eternity doesn't wind up taking forever. Let us love, be profound, be vulgar. Let us soar, and let us flail. Give us all the opportunities we had on Earth.

"If we're going to live forever, by God, let us forever truly live."

The note reminded him of Elle and Evan, and Hell and Heaven, and he felt joy at having been part of such an historic escapade. He thought of it often. He took the one about God becoming a more visible cyclist in the folder labeled "OTHER." He took the second letter and put it on the top in the folder he'd in big block letters labeled:

"MAKE HEAVEN MORE LIKE EARTH, BUT WITHOUT ALL THE HELL."

He put the folders in the pouch, sealed it up, and set it outside the door to the bar for the morning courier to retrieve. He gave one last look around The Dog, then turned out the lights. He walked out the door and headed home to be with the woman he swore he'd love forever.

He was in Heaven, and tomorrow was another day.

— 33 —

ABOUT THE AUTHOR

Chris Rodell is the author of 10 books, four of which he doesn't deem worthy of public acknowledgement. He was from 1992-2012 America's most swashbuckling feature writer. All for the sake of a story, Rodell wrestled alligators, raced Ferraris, leapt out of airplanes from 3,000 feet, flirted with death atop a bed of nails, and gained twenty pounds in one week eating like Elvis. His 2017 debut novel, *"The Last Baby Boomer: The Story of the Ultimate Ghoul Pool,"* is the winner of the 2018 TINARA Award for best satire. He is an in-demand motivational speaker whose talks sparkle with uproarious humor, indelible characters, and poignant appreciation for what it means to be a thoughtful Earthling in the 21st century.

He is at the moment living in Latrobe, Pa., with his wife Valerie, their two daughters, Josie and Lucy, and a small, loud dog named Snickers.

Book it right now: "Chris Rodell & His Rip-Roaring Stories & Life-Lessons on Arnold Palmer, Fred Rogers & Humans Being Human." Reach Chris: 724 961-2558; storyteller@chrisrodell.com

facebook.com/chris.rodell.1
twitter.com/8Days2Amish
instagram.com/chrisrodell